~~~~~~

Nick and Jane were glad that they had gone to see the end of the world, because it gave them something special to talk about at Mike and Ruby's party. One always likes to come armed with a little conversation. Nick and Jane waited until they thought enough people had arrived. Then Jane nudged Nick, and Nick said gaily, "You know what we did last week? Hey, we went to see the end of the world!"

"The end of the world?" Henry asked.

"You went to see it?" said Henry's wife, Cynthia.

"How did you manage that?" Paula wanted to know.

"It's been available since March," Stan told her. "I think a division of American Express runs it."

~~~~~~

The Late Great Future

edited by
Gregory Fitz Gerald
and John Dillon

A FAWCETT CREST BOOK

Fawcett Publications, Inc., Greenwich, Connecticut

THE LATE GREAT FUTURE

A Fawcett Crest Original

Copyright © 1976 by Fawcett Publications, Inc.

ISBN 0-449-23040-6

Library of Congess Catalog Card Number: 76-26804

Printed in the United States of America

10 9 8 7 6 5 4 3 2 1

The editors and publisher are grateful for permission to reprint the following:

"When We Went to See the End of the World" by Robert Silverberg. Reprinted by permission of the author and his agents, Scott Meredith Literary Agency Inc., 580 Fifth Avenue, New York, N.Y. 10036.

"A Thing of Custom." Copyright © 1956 by King-Size Publications, Inc.

"The Pedestrian" Copyright © 1952 by Ray Bradbury. Reprinted by permission of Harold Matson Company, Inc.

"William and Mary" Copyright © 1959 by Roald Dahl. Reprinted from *Kiss, Kiss,* by Roald Dahl, by permission of Alfred A. Knopf, Inc.

"Flowers For Algernon," by Daniel Keyes, published in *Fantasy and Science Fiction.* Copyright © 1959 by Mercury Press. Reprinted by permission of the author.

"The Country of the Kind" by Damon Knight, from *Science Fic-*

Contents

. . . [A] whirlwind came out of the north, a great cloud, and a fire infolding itself, and a brightness *was* about it, and out of midst thereof as the colour of amber . . . [and] of the fire . . . *came* . . . four living creatures . . . [,] and they had the likeness of a man. . . . [A]nd they sparkled like the colour of burnished brass.

Ezekiel I: 4–7

The
Late
Great
Future

Introduction

Death—the demise of our world as we know it, and, out of its corpse, the horrid growth of even nastier new worlds— that's what this book is all about. Many of the stories in this anthology could justify a slightly altered title: *THE LATE GREAT HUMAN RACE*. For an example, see Ray Bradbury's "The Pedestrian."

Science fiction is replete with admonitory, anti-utopias in which the tendencies of our own ambience are extended into a future they dominate. That's why science fiction is such an exciting literature: it prepares us psychologically for a future that is *different* from the present, though perhaps not for a future that will actually exist. That is, science fiction can help soften "future shock."

What future shock? Can we really pretend that science fiction predicts the future? There are a few recorded instances in which a scientific or technological development yet to occur was "predicted" in a science fiction story. Lester del Rey's "Nerves," for instance, written in the early 1940s, long before Hiroshima, depicted a nuclear eruption or accident. But the precision of such a prediction is not regularly to be expected. As Alvin Toffler suggests, thinking about the future, even a future that may never occur, is an important beginning.

The point is: if we survive at all, we'll be living in greatly differing circumstances even in the relatively near future. After Toffler and so many other futurists, we're convinced about change and the need to prepare for experiencing it. Ability to adapt to change is much more than just another individual survival technique—it probably is this species' defense against joining the pterodactyl, brontosaurus, and tyrannosaur. Therefore, a literature that depicts multifarious change is a practical one that will help us adjust to the coming rigors, the coming psychological traumas.

But of course most of us don't read science fiction to be educated for change. We read it just for the fun of it— what the highbrows are likely to call "escape." Yet the fun of science fiction is very apt to be in its intellectual provocativeness—as in Bradbury's story, which depicts a future most of us would love to avoid. As John Galsworthy aptly put it, "If you do not think about the future, you cannot have one."

Why are these portraits of the future so grim? If we are going to escape, why can't it be to limpid streams and fields of poppies instead of such horrid despairs? Do these negative futures put us more at ease in our less horrid, even if uncomfortable, present?

Thinking of the future as unpleasant is a consequence of historical process. During the previous century or two, many wanted to believe that technology was the savior which might so improve man's lot that he could be loosed from his slave chains and led out into the promised land. In the early glow of the Industrial Revolution there was fervent hope that science and technology would liberate humanity from want. Accordingly, writers devised utopias which, consistent with the etymology meaning "no place," were too optimistic. Gradually, though, science and technology began to be perceived as neutral, neither positive nor negative. Technology could be rather like a Saturday-night special handgun. If multitudes were murdered and maimed, it wasn't the gun's fault but rather the fault of that prehensile and wicked finger forever unable to resist tightening against the trigger.

The wave of optimism concerning man's apparently bright future at last broke against the shores of World War I, dashed itself to droplets on the rocks of Hitler's futuristic modes of warfare and methods of exterminating the unwanted and unpopular. That the technology of ovens might be extrapolated to the cooking of humans themselves, instead of the cooking of food *for* humans, gave us all pause as to our future. Were there other such crooked fingers on triggers? Having lost not only religion, but even God Himself, we could nevertheless still, with even greater poignancy, quite paradoxically appreciate the Biblical metaphor of Eden. After Dachau and Belsen, we could well understand why we were all booted out of paradise. We could, of course, blame it all on the other fellows, Hitler and the nasty Germans. But what about Hiroshima? The Nisei are by definition American nisei? My Lai? After the smoke of our various wartime propaganda settled, we found out a new unpleasantness: we had the technology and the power to carry out our fantasies. Ah, what innovations might Attila, Genghis Khan, Napoleon, or John Brown have achieved with modern science? Those who complain of science fiction's pessimism would do better to heed the warnings.

Most of the stories in this collection concern humanity's loss of Eden and its attempts to return. We want to make it back, but we've lost the map; and it's said the Mapmaker's dead and buried. It seems we're traveling along a crazy highway full of potholes, craters, fissures, and twists, with each wayfarer following different directions. We can't go back; the road closes behind us. Mist covers the road ahead, but we can see the way beginning to slope downward: a steep hill ahead, no doubt. Don't you wish the brakes were better, more reliable?

Let us experience some bitter futures in these science fiction stories. Perhaps these fictional glimpses into the mist will allow us to avoid such futures in reality.

Robert Silverberg

When We Went to See the End of the World

Nick and Jane were glad that they had gone to see the end of the world, because it gave them something special to talk about at Mike and Ruby's party. One always likes to come to a party armed with a little conversation. Mike and Ruby give marvelous parties. Their home is superb, one of the finest in the neighborhood. It is truly a home for all seasons, all moods. Their very special corner-of-the-world. With more space indoors and out . . . more wide-open freedom. The living room with its exposed ceiling beams is a natural focal point for entertaining. Custom-finished, with a conversation pit and fireplace. There's also a family

17

room with beamed ceiling and wood paneling . . . plus a
study. And a magnificent master suite with 12-foot dressing room and private bath. Solidly impressive exterior
design. Sheltered courtyard. Beautifully wooded 1/3-acre
grounds. Their parties are highlights of any month. Nick
and Jane waited until they thought enough people had
arrived. Then Jane nudged Nick and Nick said gaily,
"You know what we did last week? Hey, we went to see
the end of the world!"

"The end of the world?" Henry asked.

"You went to see it?" said Henry's wife Cynthia.

"How did you manage that?" Paula wanted to know.

"It's been available since March," Stan told her. "I
think a division of American Express runs it."

Nick was put out to discover that Stan already knew.
Quickly, before Stan could say anything more, Nick said,
"Yes, it's just started. Our travel agent found out for us.
What they do is they put you in this machine, it looks
like a tiny teeny submarine, you know, with dials and
levers up front behind a plastic wall to keep you from
touching anything, and they send you into the future.
You can charge it with any of the regular credit cards."

"It must be very expensive," Marcia said.

"They're bringing the costs down rapidly," Jane said.
"Last year only millionaires could afford it. Really,
haven't you heard about it before?"

"What did you see?" Henry asked.

"For a while, just grayness outside the porthole," said
Nick. "And a kind of flickering effect." Everybody was
looking at him. He enjoyed the attention. Jane wore a
rapt, loving expression. "Then the haze cleared and a
voice said over a loudspeaker that we had now reached
the very end of time, when life had become impossible
on Earth. Of course we were sealed into the submarine
thing. Only looking out. On this beach, this empty beach.
The water a funny gray color with a pink sheen. And

then the sun came up. It was red like it sometimes is at sunrise, only it stayed red as it got to the middle of the sky, and it looked lumpy and sagging at the edges. Like a few of us, hah hah. Lumpy and sagging at the edges. A cold wind blowing across the beach."

"If you were sealed in the submarine, how did you know there was a cold wind?" Cynthia asked.

Jane glared at her. Nick said, "We could see the sand blowing around. And it *looked* cold. The gray ocean. Like in winter."

"Tell them about the crab," said Jane.

"Yes, and the crab. The last life-form on Earth. It wasn't really a crab, of course, it was something about two feet wide and a foot high, with thick shiny green armor and maybe a dozen legs and some curving horns coming up, and it moved slowly from right to left in front of us. It took all day to cross the beach. And toward nightfall it died. Its horns went limp and it stopped moving. The tide came in and carried it away. The sun went down. There wasn't any moon. The stars didn't seem to be in the right places. The loudspeaker told us we had just seen the death of Earth's last living thing."

"How *eerie!*" cried Paula.

"Were you gone very long?" Ruby asked.

"Three hours," Jane said. "You can spend weeks or days at the end of the world, if you want to pay extra, but they always bring you back to a point three hours after you went. To hold down the baby-sitter expenses."

Mike offered Nick some pot. "That's really something," he said. "To have gone to the end of the world. Hey, Ruby, maybe we'll talk to the travel agent about it."

Nick took a deep drag and passed the joint to Jane. He felt pleased with himself about the way he had told the story. They had all been very impressed. That swollen red sun, that scuttling crab. The trip had cost more than a month in Japan, but it had been a good invest-

ment. He and Jane were the first in the neighborhood
who had gone. That was important. Paula was staring
at him in awe. Nick knew that she regarded him in a
completely different light now. Possibly she would meet
him at a motel on Tuesday at lunchtime. Last month she
had turned him down but now he had an extra attractive-
ness for her. Nick winked at her. Cynthia was holding
hands with Stan. Henry and Mike both were crouched
at Jane's feet. Mike and Ruby's 12-year-old son came into
the room and stood at the edge of the conversation pit.
He said, "There just was a bulletin on the news. Mutated
amoebas escaped from a government research station
and got into Lake Michigan. They're carrying a tissue-
dissolving virus and everybody in seven states is supposed
to boil his water until further notice." Mike scowled at
the boy and said, "It's after your bedtime, Timmy." The
boy went out. The doorbell rang. Ruby answered it and
returned with Eddie and Fran.

Paula said, "Nick and Jane went to see the end of the
world. They've just been telling us all about it."

"Gee," said Eddie, "we did that too, on Wednesday
night."

Nick was crestfallen. Jane bit her lip and asked Cynthia quietly why Fran always wore such flashy dresses.
Ruby said, "You saw the whole works, eh? The crab
and everything?"

"The crab?" Eddie said. "What crab? We didn't see
the crab."

"It must have died the time before," Paula said. "When
Nick and Jane were there."

Mike said, "A fresh shipment of Cuernavaca Lightning
is in. Here, have a toke."

"How long ago did you do it?" Eddie said to Nick.

"Sunday afternoon. I guess we were about the first."

"Great trip, isn't it?" Eddie said. "A little somber,
though. When the last hill crumbles into the sea."

"That's not what we saw," said Jane. "And you didn't see the crab? Maybe we were on different trips."

Mike said, "What was it like for you, Eddie?"

Eddie put his arms around Cynthia from behind. He said, "They put us into this little capsule, with a port-hole, you know, and a lot of instruments and—"

"We heard that part," said Paula. "What did you *see?*"

"The end of the world," Eddie said. "When water covers everything. The sun and the moon were in the sky at the same time—"

"We didn't see the moon at all," Jane remarked. "It just wasn't there."

"It was on one side and the sun was on the other," Eddie went on. "The moon was closer than it should have been. And a funny color, almost like bronze. And the ocean creeping up. We went halfway around the world and all we saw was ocean. Except in one place, there was this chunk of land sticking up, this hill, and the guide told us it was the top of Mount Everest." He waved to Fran. "That was groovy, huh, floating in our tin boat next to the top of Mount Everest. Maybe ten feet of it sticking up. And the water rising all the time. Up, up, up. Up and over the top. Glub. No land left. I have to admit it was a little disappointing, except of course the *idea* of the thing. That human ingenuity can design a machine that can send people billions of years forward in time and bring them back, wow! But there was just this ocean."

"How strange," said Jane. "We saw an ocean too, but there was a beach, a kind of nasty beach, and the crab-thing walking along it, and the sun—it was all red, was the sun red when you saw it?"

"A kind of pale green," Fran said.

"Are you people talking about the end of the world?" Tom asked. He and Harriet were standing by the door taking off their coats. Mike's son must have let them in.

Tom gave his coat to Ruby and said, "Man, what a spectacle!"

"So you did it too?" Jane asked, a little hollowly.

"Two weeks ago," said Tom. "The travel agent called and said, Guess what we're offering now, the end of the goddamned world! With all the extras it didn't really cost so much. So we went right down there to the office, Saturday, I think—was it a Friday?—the day of the big riot, anyway, when they burned St. Louis—"

"That was a Saturday," Cynthia said. "I remember I was coming back from the shopping center when the radio said they were using nuclears—"

"Saturday, yes," Tom said. "And we told them we were ready to go, and off they sent us."

"Did you see a beach with crabs," Stan demanded, "or was it a world full of water?"

"Neither one. It was like a big ice age. Glaciers covered everything. No oceans showing, no mountains. We flew clear around the world and it was all a huge snowball. They had floodlights on the vehicle because the sun had gone out."

"I was sure I could see the sun still hanging up there," Harriet put in. "Like a ball of cinders in the sky. But the guide said no, nobody could see it."

"How come everybody gets to visit a different kind of end of the world?" Henry asked. "You'd think there'd be only one kind of end of the world. I mean, it ends, and this is how it ends, and there can't be more than one way."

"Could it be a fake?" Stan asked. Everybody turned around and looked at him. Nick's face got very red. Fran looked so mean that Eddie let go of Cynthia and started to rub Fran's shoulders. Stan shrugged. "I'm not suggesting it is," he said defensively. "I was just wondering."

"Seemed pretty real to me," said Tom. "The sun burned out. A big ball of ice. The atmosphere, you know, frozen. The end of the goddamned world."

The telephone rang. Ruby went to answer it. Nick asked Paula about lunch on Tuesday. She said yes. "Let's meet at the motel," he said, and she grinned. Eddie was making out with Cynthia again. Henry looked very stoned and was having trouble staying awake. Phil and Isabel arrived. They heard Tom and Fran talking about their trips to the end of the world and Isabel said she and Phil had gone only the day before yesterday. "Goddamn," Tom said, "everybody's doing it! What was your trip like?"

Ruby came back into the room. "That was my sister calling from Fresno to say she's safe. Fresno wasn't hit by the earthquake at all."

"Earthquake?" Paula said.

"In California," Mike told her. "This afternoon. You didn't know? Wiped out most of Los Angeles and ran right up the coast practically to Monterey. They think it was on account of the underground bomb test in the Mohave Desert."

"California's always having such awful disasters," Marcia said.

"Good thing those amoebas got loose back east," said Nick. "Imagine how complicated it would be if they had them in L.A. now too."

"They will," Tom said. "Two to one they reproduce by airborne spores."

"Like the typhoid germs last November," Jane said.

"That was typhus," Nick corrected.

"Anyway," Phil said, "I was telling Tom and Fran about what we saw at the end of the world. It was the sun going nova. They showed it very cleverly, too. I mean, you can't actually sit around and *experience* it, on account of the heat and the hard radiation and all. But they give it to you in a peripheral way, very elegant in the McLuhanesque sense of the word. First they take you to a point about two hours before the blowup, right?

It's I don't know how many jillion years from now, but a long way, anyhow, because the trees are all different, they've got blue scales and ropy branches, and the animals are like things with one leg that jump on pogo sticks—"

"Oh, I don't *believe* that," Cynthia drawled.

Phil ignored her gracefully. "And we didn't see any sign of human beings, not a house, not a telephone pole, nothing, so I suppose we must have been extinct a long time before. Anyway, they let us look at that for a while. Not getting out of our time machine, naturally, because they said the atmosphere was wrong. Gradually the sun started to puff up. We were nervous—weren't we, Iz?— I mean, suppose they miscalculated things? This whole trip is a very new concept and things might go wrong. The sun was getting bigger and bigger, and then this thing like an arm seemed to pop out of its left side, a big fiery arm reaching out across space, getting closer and closer. We saw it through smoked glass, like you do an eclipse. They gave us about two minutes of the explosion, and we could feel it getting hot already. Then we jumped a couple of years forward in time. The sun was back to its regular shape, only it was smaller, sort of like a little white sun instead of a big yellow one. And on Earth everything was ashes."

"Ashes," Isabel said, with emphasis.

"It looked like Detroit after the union nuked Ford," Phil said. "Only much, much worse. Whole mountains were melted. The oceans were dried up. Everything was ashes." He shuddered and took a joint from Mike. "Isabel was crying."

"The things with one leg," Isabel said. "I mean, they must have all been wiped *out*." She began to sob. Stan comforted her. "I wonder why it's a different way for everyone who goes," he said. "Freezing. Or the oceans. Or the sun blowing up. Or the thing Nick and Jane saw."

"I'm convinced that each of us had a genuine experience

in the far future," said Nick. He felt he had to regain control of the group somehow. It had been so good when he was telling his story, before those others had come. "That is to say, the world suffers a variety of natural calamities, it doesn't just have *one* end of the world, and they keep mixing things up and sending people to different catastrophes. But never for a moment did I doubt that I was seeing an authentic event."

"We have to do it," Ruby said to Mike. "It's only three hours. What about calling them first thing Monday and making an appointment for Thursday night?"

"Monday's the President's funeral," Tom pointed out. "The travel agency will be closed."

"Have they caught the assassin yet?" Fran asked.

"They didn't mention it on the four o'clock news," said Stan. "I guess he'll get away like the last one."

"Beats me why anybody wants to be President," Phil said.

Mike put on some music. Nick danced with Paula. Eddie danced with Cynthia. Henry was asleep. Dave, Paula's husband, was on crutches because of his mugging, and he asked Isabel to sit and talk with him. Tom danced with Harriet even though he was married to her. She hadn't been out of the hospital more than a few months after the transplant and he treated her extremely tenderly. Mike danced with Fran. Phil danced with Jane. Stan danced with Marcia. Ruby cut in on Eddie and Cynthia. Afterward Tom danced with Jane and Phil danced with Paula. Mike and Ruby's little girl woke up and came out to say hello. Mike sent her back to bed. Far away there was the sound of an explosion. Nick danced with Paula again, but he didn't want her to get bored with him before Tuesday, so he excused himself and went to talk with Dave. Dave handled most of Nick's investments. Ruby said to Mike, "The day after the funeral, will you call the travel agent?" Mike said he would, but Tom said somebody would probably shoot the new President too and there'd be another funeral. These funerals were demolishing the gross national product, Stan observed, on account of how everything had to close all the time. Nick saw Cynthia wake Henry up and ask him sharply if he would take her on the end-of-the-world trip. Henry looked embarrassed. His factory had been blown up at Christmas in a peace demonstration and everybody knew he was in bad shape financially. "You can *charge* it," Cynthia said, her fierce voice carrying above the chitchat. "And it's so *beautiful,* Henry. The ice. Or the sun exploding. I want to go."

"Lou and Janet were going to be here tonight too," Ruby said to Paula. "But their younger boy came back from Texas with that new kind of cholera and they had to cancel."

Phil said, "I understand that one couple saw the moon come apart. It got too close to the Earth and split into chunks and the chunks fell like meteors. Smashing everything up, you know. One big piece nearly hit their time machine."

"I wouldn't have liked that at all," Marcia said.

"Our trip was very lovely," said Jane. "No violent things at all. Just the big red sun and the tide and that crab creeping along the beach. We were both deeply moved."

"It's amazing what science can accomplish nowadays," Fran said.

Mike and Ruby agreed they would try to arrange a trip to the end of the world as soon as the funeral was over. Cynthia drank too much and got sick. Phil, Tom and Dave discussed the stock market. Harriet told Nick about her operation. Isabel flirted with Mike, tugging her neckline lower. At midnight someone turned on the news. They had some shots of the earthquake and a warning about boiling your water if you lived in the affected states. The President's widow was shown visiting the last President's widow to get some pointers for the funeral. Then there was an interview with an executive of the time-trip company. "Business is phenomenal," he said. "Time-tripping will be the nation's number one growth industry next year." The reporter asked him if his company would soon be offering something besides the end-of-the-world trip. "Later on, we hope to," the executive said. "We plan to apply for Congressional approval soon. But meanwhile the demand for our present offering is running very high. You can't imagine. Of course, you have to expect apocalyptic stuff to attain immense popularity in times like these." The reporter said, "What do you mean, times like these?" but as the time-trip man started to reply, he was interrupted by the commercial. Mike shut off the set. Nick discovered that he was extremely depressed. He decided that it was because so many of his friends had made the journey, and he had thought he and Jane were the only ones who had. He found himself standing next to Marcia and tried to describe the way the crab had moved, but Marcia only shrugged. No one was talking about time-trips now. The party had moved beyond that point. Nick and Jane left quite early and went right to sleep, without making love. The next morning the Sunday paper wasn't delivered because of the Bridge Authority strike, and the radio said that the mutant amoebas were proving harder to eradicate than originally anticipated. They were spreading into Lake Superior and everyone in the region would have to boil all drinking water. Nick and Jane discussed where they would go for their next vacation. "What about going to see the end of the world all over again?" Jane suggested, and Nick laughed quite a good deal.

A Thing of Custom

Rajendra Jaipal, liaison officer of the Terran Delegation to the Associated Planets, said fluently but with a strong Hindustani accent: "Parson to parson, please . . . I wish to speak to Milan Reid, at Parthia 6-0711, Parthia, Pennsylvania . . . That is right."

While he waited, Jaipal looked at the telephone as if it were a noxious vine that had invaded his garden. An unreconstructed antimechanist, he regarded most features of the Western world with a dour, gloomy, and suspicious air.

"Here's your party," said the telephone.

28

Jaipal said: "Hello, Milan? This is R. J. How are you? . . . Oh, no worse than usual. Millions of calls to make and letters to write and hands to shake. Ugh! Now, listen. The railroad has given us two special sleepers and a baggage-car through from New Haven to Philadelphia. We shall put the delegates aboard Friday evening, and a train will pick these cars up and drop them off at Thirtieth Street at seven-thirty Saturday morning. Have you got that? Seven-thirty a.m., daylight saving. Write it down, please. You will have your people there to pick them up. The baggage-car will contain the Forellians, as they are too large for a sleeper. You will have a truck at the station for them. How are things doing at your end?"

A plaintive voice said: "Mrs. Kress got sick, so as vice-chairman of the Hospitality Committee I have to—to do all the work, rush around and check up and pump hands. I wish I'd known what I was getting into."

"If you think you have something to complain about, you should have my job. Have you got that letter with the list of delegates?"

"Yes . . . Um . . . Right here."

"Well, cross off the Moorians and the Koslovians, but add one more Oshidan."

"What's his name?"

"Zla-bzam Ksan-rdup."

"How do you spell it?"

Jaipal spelled. "Got it?"

"Uh-huh. You—you'll stay with us, of course?"

"Sorree, but I can't come."

"Oh, dear! Louise and I were counting on it." The voice was pained. Jaipal had met the Reids a year before when a similar week-end visit had been arranged with families of Ardmore. Jaipal and Reid were drawn together at once by a common dislike of the rest of the world.

"So was I," said Jaipal, "but a ship from Sirius is due

Saturday. Now, there is one couple I want you to assign to yourself."

"Who?"

"The Osmanians."

There was a rustle of paper as Reid consulted his list. "Mr. and Mrs. Sterga?"

"Yes, or Sterga and Thvi. No children."

"What are they like?"

"Something like octopi, or perhaps centipedes."

"Hm. They don't sound pretty. Do they talk?"

"Better than we do. They have a—what do you call it? —a knick-knack for languages."

"Why do you want me to take them?"

"Because," explained Jaipal, "their planet has natural transuranic elements in quantity, and we are negotiating a mining-lease. It's veree delicate, and it wouldn't do for the Stergas to pfall into the wrong hands. Like—who was that uncouth buffoon I met at the Kresses'?"

"Charlie Ziegler?"

"That's the one." Jaipal snorted at the memory of Ziegler's tying a napkin around his head and putting on a burlesque swami-act. As Jaipal had no sense of humor, the other guests' roars at Ziegler's antics rubbed salt in the wound. He continued: "Those people would not do for hosts at all. I know you are tactful, not one of these stupid ethnocentrics who would act horrified or superior. Now, have you got the diet-lists?"

Mumble, mumble. "Yes, here's the list of those who can eat any human food, and those who can eat some human food, and those who can't eat any."

"The special pfood for the last group will be sent along on the train. Be sure it's delivered to the right houses."

"I'll have a couple of trucks at the station. You be sure each crate is clearly marked. But say, how—how about these Osmanians? I mean, what are they like aside from their looks?"

"Oh, quite jolly and convivial. High-spirited. They eat anything. You won't have any trouble." Jaipal could have told more about the Osmanians but forbore for fear of scaring Reid off. "Now, be sure not to send the Chavantians to anybody with a phobia about snakes. Remember that the Steinians eat in seclusion and consider any mention of food obscene. Be sure the Forellians go where there's an empty barn or garage to sleep in . . ."

"Louise!" called Milan Reid. "That was R. J. Can you help me with the lists now?"

Reid was a slight man who combined a weakness for aggressively stylish clothes with a shy, preoccupied, nervous, hurried air, all of which made him a natural target for the jeers of any gang of street-corner slopeheads. He was an engineer for the Hunter Bioresonator Corporation. He was a natural choice to manage the visiting extraterrestrials, being one who found foreigners easier to deal with than his own countrymen.

His wife entered, a slender woman of much his own type. They got to work on the list of delegates to the Associated Planets who were going to visit Parthia, and the lists of local families who would act as hosts. This was the third year of giving A. P. personnel an informal weekend in Terran homes. These three visits had all been to American homes because the A. P. headquarters was in New Haven. The success of the project, however, had made other nations demand that they, too, be allowed to show what nice people they were. Hence Athens, Greece, was the tentative choice for next year.

Milan Reid said: ". . . the Robertsonians have no sense of time, so we'd better give them to the Hobarts. They haven't any either."

"Then none of them will arrive for anything," said Louise.

"So what? How about the Mendezians? Jaipal's note

says they can't bear to be touched."

"Rajendra can't either, though he tries to be polite about it. Some Hindu tabu."

"Uh-huh. Let's see, aren't Goldthorpes fanatics on sanitation?"

"Just the people! They wouldn't want to touch the Mendezians either. Their children have to wash their hands every time they handle money, and Beatrice Goldthorpe puts on rubber gloves to read a book from the public library for fear of germs."

"How about the Oshidans?" he asked.

"What are they like, darling?"

"R. J. says they're the most formal race in the Galaxy, with the most elaborate etiquette. As he puts it here, 'they are what you call puffed shirts, only they don't wear shirts.' "

"I didn't know Rajendra could make much of a joke," said Louise Reid. "How about Dr. McClintock? He's another puffed shirt."

"Darling, you're wonderful. The Reverend John R. McClintock shall have them."

"How about the Zieglers? Connie Ziegler called to remind us they'd applied well in advance."

Reid scowled. "I'm going to juggle this list to put the Zieglers too far down to get any e.t.'s."

"Please don't do that, sweetheart. I know you don't like them, but living next door we have to get along."

"But R. J. said he didn't want the Zieglers as hosts."

"Oh, dear! If they ever find out we cheated them out of their guests . . ."

"Can't be helped. R. J.'s right, too. They're—they're typical ethnocentrics. I've squirmed in embarrassment while Charlie told bad jokes about our own minority groups here, feeling I ought to stop him but not knowing how. Can't you just see Charlie calling some sensitive extraterrestrial a bug in that loud Chicago bray of his?"

"But they did go out of their way to get on the list . . ."

"It's not that they like e.t.'s; they just can't bear to be left out."

"Oh, well, if we must . . . Who's next?" she asked.

"That's all, unless R. J. calls up again. Now, what shall we do with Sterga and Thvi?"

"I suppose we can put them in George's room. What do they enjoy?"

"It says here they like parties, sight-seeing, and swimming."

"We can take them to the pool."

"Sure. And since they're arriving early, we could drive 'em home for breakfast and then out to Gettysburg for a picnic."

During the next few days, Parthia was convulsed by preparations for the exotic visitors. Merchants filled their windows with interplanetary exhibits: artwork from Robertsonia, a stuffed fhe:gb from Schlemmeria, a photomontage of scenes on Flahertia.

At the Lower Siddim High School, performers at the forthcoming celebration rehearsed on the stage while volunteers readied the basement for the strawberry festival. Mrs. Carmichael, chairman of the Steering Committee, swept about supervising:

". . . Where's that wretched man who was going to fix the public address system? . . . No, the color-guard mustn't carry rifles. We're trying to show these creatures how peaceful we are . . ."

The Quaker rolled into Thirtieth Street. The hosts from Parthia clustered about the three rearmost cars at the north end of the platform. While the trainmen uncoupled these cars, the doors opened and out came a couple of earthmen. After them came the extraterrestrials.

Milan Reid strode forward to greet the taller earth-man. "I'm Reid."

"How d'you do; I'm Grove-Sparrow and this is Ming. We're from the Secretariat. Are your people ready?"

"Here they are."

"Hm." Grove-Sparrow looked at the milling mass of hosts, mostly suburban housewives. At that instant the Chavantians slithered off the train. Mrs. Ross gave a thin scream and fainted. Mr. Nagle caught her in time to keep her from cracking her skull on the concrete.

"Pay no attention," said Reid, wishing that Mrs. Ross had fallen on the tracks and been run over. "Which of our guests is which?"

"Those are the Oshidans, the ones with faces like camels."

"Dr. McClintock!" called Reid. "Here's your party."

"You take it, Ming," said Grove-Sparrow. Ming began a long winded formal introduction, during which the Oshidans and the Reverend McClintock kept up a series of low bows as if they were worked out by strings. Grove-Sparrow indicated three large things getting off the baggage-car. They were something like walruses and something like caterpillars, but two were as big as small elephants. The third was smaller. "The Forellians."

"Mrs. Meyer!" shouted Reid. "Is the truck ready?"

"The Robertsonians." Grove-Sparrow referred to four badger-like creatures with respirators on their long noses.

Reid raised his voice: "Hobart! No, their hosts aren't here yet."

"Let them sit on their kit; they won't mind," said Grove-Sparrow. "Here come the Osmanians."

"They-uh-they're mine," said Reid, his voice raising to a squeak of dismay. A group of gawkers had collected farther south on the platform to stare at the extraterrestrials. None came close.

The Osmanians (so called because their planet was

discovered by a Dr. Mahmud Osman) were built something on the lines of saw-horses. Instead of four legs, they had twelve rubbery tentacles, six in a row on each side, on which they scuttled briskly along. They were much alike fore and aft, but one could tell their front end by the two large froglike eyes on top and the mouth-opening between the foremost pair of tentacles.

"You are our host?" said the leading Osmanian in a blubbery voice. "Ah, such a pleasure, good dear Mr. Reid!"

The Osmanian flung itself upon Reid, rearing up on its six after tentacles to enfold him in its six forward ones. It pressed a damp kiss on his cheek. Before he could free himself from this gruesome embrace, the second Osmanian swarmed up on him and kissed his other cheek. As the creatures weighed over two hundred pounds apiece, Reid staggered and sank to the concrete, enveloped in tentacles.

The Osmanians released their host. Grove-Sparrow helped Reid to his feet, saying in a low voice:

"Don't look so bloody horrified, old boy. They're only trying to be friendly."

"I forget," blubbered the larger Osmanian. "Your method of greeting here is to shake the anterior limb, is it not?" It extended a tentacle.

Reid gingerly put out a hand. The Osmanian caught the hand with three tentacles and pumped Reid's arm so vigorously that he was nearly jerked off his feet.

"Let's dance!" cried the Osmanian, slithering around in a circle and swinging Reid opposite him. "Guk-guk-guk!" This last was a horrid coughing, cackling sound that served the Osmanians for laughter.

"No, no, Sterga!" said Grove-Sparrow. "Let him go! He has to sort out the delegations."

"Oh, all right," said Sterga. "Maybe somebody would like to wrestle. You, madam?" The Osmanian addressed

Mrs. Meyer, who was fat and of mature years.

"No, please," said Mrs. Meyer, paling and dodging behind Grove-Sparrow. "I—I have to see to the Forellians."

"Quiet down, you two," said Grove-Sparrow. "You'll get exercise later."

"I hope so," said Sterga. "Perhaps Mr. Reid will wrestle with us at his home, guk-guk. It is the main sport of Nohp." This was the name of Osmania in Sterga's language. The Osmanian spoke to his mate in this tongue while Reid frantically paired off guests and hosts. The rest of the Quaker rumbled off.

When each set of guests had been sent off with its host, and the Forellians had crawled up on to their truck-trailer, the four little Robertsonians were left sitting on the platform. There was still no sign of the Hobarts. The employees of the railroad wheeled crates out of the baggage-car, marked FOOD FOR FORELLIANS, FOOD FOR STEINIANS, and so forth. Reid said to Grove-Sparrow:

"Look, I—I've got to find my truck-drivers and give them these addresses. Will you keep an eye on the Osmanians and Robertsonians till I get back?"

"Righto."

Reid dashed off, followed by two porters pushing a hand-truck piled with crates. When he returned, the Robertsonians were still sitting in a disconsolate circle. There was no sign of Grove-Sparrow, Ming, the Hobarts, or the Osmanians. There was broken glass on the concrete, a smear of liquid, and an alcoholic smell.

As he stared about wildly, Reid felt a tug at his trouser-leg. A Robertsonian said: "Please, is dere any sign of our host?"

"No, but he'll be along. What's happened to the others?"

"Oh, dat. Dey were lying on de platform, waiting,

when an eart'man came along, walking dis way and dat
as if he were sick. He saw Mr. Ming and said somet'ing
about dirty foreigners. Mr. Ming pretended he didn't
hear, and de man said he could lick anybody in de place.
I suppose he meant dat custom you call kissing, dough
he didn't look as if he loved anybody."

"What *happened?*"

"Oh, de Osmanians got up, and Sterga said: 'Dis nice
fellow wants to wrestle. Come on, Thvi.'

"He started for de man, who saw him for de first time.
De man took a bottle out of his pocket and trew it at
Sterga, saying: 'Go back to hell where you belong!' De
bottle broke. De man ran. Sterga and Thvi ran after him,
calling to him to stop and wrestle. Mr. Grove-Sparrow
and Mr. Ming ran after. Dat's all. Now please, can you
find de people who are going to take us?"

Reid sighed. "I'll have to find the others first. Wait
here . . ."

He met the missing members of the expedition returning
to the platform. "The drunk is on his way to the police-
station," said Grove-Sparrow. "Still no sign of your
Hobarts?"

"Not yet, but that's not unusual."

"Why don't you take the Robertsonians to the Hobart
place?"

"We'd probably pass the Hobarts on their way here.
Tell you, though; I'll 'phone to see if they've left."

The Hobart telephone answered. Clara Hobart said:
"Oh, Milan! We were just ready to go. I'm sorry we're
late, but you know how it is."

Reid, resisting an impulse to grind his teeth, did indeed
know how it was with the Hobarts. They had a way of
arriving at parties just as everybody else was leaving.
"Stay where you are and I'll deliver your guests in about
an hour."

He went back and bid good-bye to Grove-Sparrow and

Ming, who were returning to New Haven. Then he herded his two groups of extraterrestrials up the ramps to his car.

To a man who hated to be made conspicuous, the drive to Parthia left much to be desired. The Robertsonians curled up in one large furry ball on the front seat and slept, but the Osmanians bounced around in back, excited and garrulous, pointing with their tentacles and sticking them out the windows to wave at passers-by. Most people had read about extraterrestrials and seen them on television enough not to be unduly surprised, but an octopoid tentacle thrust in the window of your car while you are waiting for a light can still be startling.

After the Osmanians had almost caused a collision, Reid ordered them sternly to keep their tentacles inside the car. He envied Nagle and Kress, who had flown their guests home from the roof of the Post Office Building in their private helicopters.

West of the Susquehanna, the Piedmont Expressway turns south towards Westminster, to swoop past Baltimore and Washington. Milan Reid turned off and continued west. In response to his pleas, the Osmanians had been fairly quiet.

Near York he found himself stuck behind an Amishman's buggy, which the heavy eastbound traffic kept him from passing.

"What is that?" asked Thvi.

"A buggy," said Louise Reid.

"Which, the thing with the wheels or the animal pulling it?"

"The thing with the wheels. The animal is called a horse."

"Isn't that a primitive form of transportation here?" said Sterga.

"Yes," said Louise. "The man uses it because of his religion."

"Is that why he wears that round black hat?"

"Yes."

"I want that hat," said Sterga. "I think I should look pretty in it, guk-guk-guk."

Reid glanced around. "If you want a Terran hat you'll have to buy one. That hat belongs to the man."

"I still want it. If Terra is going to get this mining-lease, it can afford me that one little hat."

The eastbound traffic ceased for a moment. Reid passed the buggy. As the automobile came abreast, Sterga thrust his front end out the quadrant-window. A tentacle whisked the black hat from the head of the Amishman.

The sectarian's broad ruddy chin-whiskered face turned towards the car. His blue eyes popped with horror. He gave a hoarse scream, leaped from the buggy, vaulted a split-rail fence, and ran off across a field. As the car drew ahead of the buggy, the horse had a view of Sterga too. The horse shrieked and ran off in the other direction, the buggy bouncing wildly behind it.

Reid braked to a stop. "Damn it!" he yelled.

In the back seat, Sterga was trying to balance the Amishman's hat on his head, if he could be said to have a head. Reid snatched the hat. "What kind of trouble are you trying to make?"

"No trouble; just a little joke," bubbled Sterga.

Reid snorted and got out. The Amishman had disappeared. His horse was in sight across a plowed field, eating grass. It was still attached to the buggy. Reid crossed the road, holding the hat, and started across the field. His feet sank into the soft earth, and the soil entered his shoes. The horse heard him coming, looked around, and trotted off.

After several tries, Reid plodded back to his automobile, hung the hat on a fence-post, shook the dirt out of his shoes, and drove off. Fuming, he promised Rajendra Jaipal some hard words.

The Osmanians were subdued for a while. At Gettysburg they went into the exhibition-building. From the gallery they looked down upon a relief-map of the Gettysburg region covered with colored electric lights. A phonograph-record gave an account of the battle while a young man worked a set of keys that lit the lights to show the positions of the Federal and Confederate troops at various times:

"Now, at the beginning of the second day, Longstreet spent the morning ranging his artillery around the salient where the Third Corps occupied the peach orchard." (Lights blinked on.) "At noon the Confederates began a bombardment, and McLaws' Division advanced . . ."

There was a stir among the spectators as the Osmanians wormed their way into the front row and hung their tentacles over the rail. The young man working the lights lost track of his keys and sat gaping while the recording ground on. Then he tried to catch up, became confused, and for a time had Meade's Federals in full retreat.

Reid led his guests outside. They climbed the observation-tower, from which they saw the Round Tops and the Eisenhower Memorial rising from the farm which that President had owned. When Reid and his wife started down, Sterga blubbered something at Thvi. The next thing, the Osmanians were scrambling down the outside of the steelwork.

"Come back! You'll be killed!" yelled Reid, who hated high places.

"No danger," called back Sterga. "This is more fun."

The Reids clattered down the stairs. Reid expected to hear the plop of an Osmanian striking the concrete. He got to the bottom just ahead of the Osmanians, who slid from girder to girder with the greatest ease.

Milan Reid sat down on the bottom step and pressed

his fists against his head. Then he said in a hollow voice: "Let's eat lunch."

At the Rose Hill Swimming Pool, Wallace Richards, the lifeguard, was showing off his dives. He was a young man of vast thews and vaster vanity. Girls sat around the pool watching, while other young men, all looking either skinny or potbellied by contrast, gloomed in the background. The Forellians had swum in the morning but now had gone away. While they were there, there had been no room for anybody else in the pool. Now there were no extraterrestrials until Milan and Louise came out in bathing-suits, followed by Sterga and Thvi. Reid spread a blanket and prepared to settle down to a sun-bath.

The Osmanians aroused the usual stir. Wallace Richards never noticed. He stood tautly, tapering from shoulders to ankles like an inverted isosceles triangle, while he gathered his forces for a triple flip.

Thvi slipped into the pool and shot across it with a swirl of tentacles. Richards bounded off the board, clasped his knees, turned over three times, and straightened out. He came down on top of Thvi.

Sterga shouted in his own language, but too late. Then he too entered the water. The watchers cried out.

The surface of the pool was beaten by thrashing limbs and tentacles. Richards' head appeared, shouting:

"Damn it, give me back my trunks!"

The Osmanians whipped across the pool and shot out. Thvi waved Richards' trunks (little more than a G-string) in one tentacle and called: "You will jump on top of me, will you?"

"I didn't do it on purpose!" screamed Richards. The audience began to laugh.

"Knocked all the breath out of me, guk-guk-guk," bubbled Thvi, trying to work a couple of her tentacles through the leg holes.

Sterga scrambled up the ladder to the high-diving board. "Earthman!" he called down. "How did you do that jump?"

"Give me back my trunks!"

"Like this?" Sterga leaped off the board.

However, instead of diving, he spread all twelve tentacles and came down on Richards like a pouncing spider. Richards ducked before the hideous apparition descended on him and began to swim away. But his speed in the water was as nought compared to the Osmanian's. Sterga caught him and began tickling him.

Reid said to Thvi: "For God's sake, make that mate of yours let the man go. He'll drown him."

"Oh, all right. You Earthmen never want any fun." Thvi swam over to where the pair were struggling.

A limp Richards was hauled out and laid on the concrete. Somebody pumped his lungs for ten minutes until he came around and sat up, coughing and gasping. When he pulled himself together he glared about and wheezed: "Where are those God-damned octopussies? I'll . . ."

But Reid and his charges had left.

For cocktails, the Reids had an older couple in: Professor and Mrs. Hamilton Beach, of Bryn Mawr College. Beach, a sociologist, wanted to talk about such serious matters as interspecies relations, but Sterga and Thvi had other ideas. They swallowed their cocktails so fast that Reid could do little but mix new ones. They made horrible noises which, they explained, were an Osmanian song.

Reid worried lest they get drunk and become even more obstreperous, but Sterga reassured him: "These are nothing to what we drink on Nohp. There anything less than four-fifths alcohol is a—how would you say it—a light-wines-and-beer."

The Reids eased the Beaches out at seven so as to have time to eat and get to the strawberry festival. Reid went back into the livingroom to find Sterga and Thvi drinking alternately out of the shaker. Sterga said:

"Mr. Reid, I understand you people have the same reproductive methods we have."

"Uh—well—that depends on your method," said Reid, appalled by the turn of the conversation.

"You do reproduce bisexually, don't you? The male carries . . ."

"Yes, yes, yes."

"Why haven't you and Mrs. Reid done so?"

Reid bit his lip. "We have. Our son is away at camp, as a counsellor."

"Ah, that is fine. Then you can comply with the custom of the Hliht."

"What custom?"

"We always trade mates with our guests. It is inhospitable not to."

"What?"

Sterga repeated.

Reid goggled. "You—you're not serious?"

"Certainly. It will be—"

"But that's physically impossible, even if our customs allowed it."

"No, we are not so different as you might think. I have investigated the matter. Anyway, we can have a lot of fun experimenting, guk-guk."

"Out of the question!" snapped Reid. "Our customs forbid it."

"You Earthmen want that mining-lease, don't you?"

"Excuse me," said Reid, and went into the kitchen. There Louise was helping the temporary maid to put the final touches on the dinner. He drew her aside and explained the latest demand of their guests.

Louise Reid goggled in her turn. She opened the door to get a glimpse of Sterga in the living-room. Sterga caught her eye and winked. This was an unnerving spectacle, as the Osmanians blinked their eyes by withdrawing them into their heads and popping them up again.

She turned away and pressed her hands over her face. "What shall we *do*?"

"Well, I—I can tell you one thing. I'm going to get rid of these so-called guests. If I ever catch R. J. . . ."

"But what about the mining-concession?"

"To hell with the mining-concession. I don't care if it causes an interplanetary war; I won't put up with these rubber jokers any longer. I hate the sight of them."

"But how? You can't just push them out the front door to wander the streets!"

"Let me think." Reid glanced out the window to make sure the Zieglers' lights were on. "I know; we'll give them to the Zieglers! It'll serve both of them right."

"Oh, darling, do you think we ought? After all . . ."

"I don't care if we ought or not. First you'll get a wire that your mother is sick and you have to pack and leave for Washington tonight . . . Start serving; I'll set the wheels in motion."

Reid went to the telephone and called his friend Joe Farris. "Joe?" he said in a low voice. "Will you ring me back in fifteen minutes? Then don't pay any attention to what I say; it's to get me out of a jam."

Fifteen minutes later, the telephone rang. Reid answered it and pretended to repeat a telegraphic message. Then he came into the dining room and said sadly:

"Bad news, sweetheart. Your mother is sick again, and you'll have to go to Washington tonight." He turned to Sterga. "I'm sorry, but Mrs. Reid has to leave."

"Oh!" said Thvi. "We were so looking forward—"

"Now, I can't be properly hospitable by myself," continued Reid. "But I'll find you another host."

"But you are such a fine host—" protested Sterga.

"Thanks, I really can't. Everything will be all right,

though. Finish your dinner while I make arrangements. Then we'll go to the festival together."

He slipped out and walked to the Zieglers' house next door. Charles Ziegler, wiping his mouth, answered the bell. He was stout and balding, with thick hairy forearms. He wrung Reid's hand in a crushing grip and bellowed: "Hey there, Milan old boy! Whatcha doing these days? We ought to get together more often, hey? Come on in."

Reid forced a smile. "Well, Charlie, it's like this. I—I'm in a predicament, but with a little help from you we can fix it up to please everybody. You wanted A. P. guests on this visit, didn't you?"

Ziegler shrugged. "Connie felt she had to get into the act, and I guess I could have put up with a houseful of lizard-men to please her. Why, whatcha got in mind?"

Reid told of his mother-in-law's illness as if it were real. "So I thought you could come to the celebration and pick up my Osmanians . . ."

Ziegler slapped Reid on the back. "Sure, Milan old boy, I'll take care of your double-ended squids. I'll fill 'em full of G-bombs." This was a lethal gin-drink of Ziegler's own concoction. "Hey, Connie!"

At the strawberry-festival, people and extraterrestrials stood in a line that wound past a counter. There they were served strawberry ice-cream, cake, and coffee, cafeteria-style. Strips of colored paper festooned the ceiling; planetary flags draped the walls. Some guests, either because they could not eat Terran food or because they were not built for standing in line with trays, made other arrangements. The Forellians occupied one whole corner of the basement while their hosts fed them special provender with shovels.

The extraterrestrials were identified by tags pinned to the clothes of those species who wore them, or hung around their necks otherwise. As the Osmanians had neither clothes nor necks, the tags were fastened to straps, tied around their middles, with the tags uppermost like the brass plates on dog-collars.

Reid found himself opposite a Chavantian coiled up on a chair. The Chavantian reared up the front yard of its body and daintily manipulated its food with the four appendages that grew from the sides of its neck.

"I," squeaked the Chavantian, "am fascinated by the works of your Shakespeare. Such insight! Such feeling! I taught Terran literature, you know, before I entered the diplomatic service."

"So?" said Reid. "I used to teach, too." He had become a high-school mathematics-teacher under the mistaken belief that teaching was an occupation for timid, ineffectual people who feared to face the world. He soon learned that it called for brawn and brutality far beyond anything demanded by the business world. "Have you been well treated so far?"

"Oh, we are sometimes made aware of our unfortunate resemblance to an order of Terran life towards whom most of you do not feel very friendly." (Reid knew the Chavantian meant snakes.) "But we make allowances."

"How about the other guests?" Reid craned his neck to see who was present. The Hobarts and their Robertsonians had not arrived.

"All fine. The Steinians are of course not here, as this would be a revolting spectacle to them. 'Just a thing of custom: 'tis no other; only it spoils the pleasure of time.' "

The Reids and their guests finished eating and went up to the auditorium, which was already half full. The young of several species had rubber balloons, each balloon straining gently upward on its string. They made so thick a cloud that those in the rear found their view of the stage obscured.

The program opened with a concert by the high-school band. Then the local Boy Scout troop presented colors.

The Reverend McClintock officially welcomed the guests and introduced them, one by one. As they were introduced, those who could, stood up and were applauded.

Then followed songs by a local choral society; dances by a square-dancing club; more songs; American Indian dances by a cubscout pack; awards of prizes to Associated Planets essay-contest winners . . .

The trouble with amateur shows of this sort is not that the acts are bad. Sometimes they are quite good. The real difficulty is that each performer wants to give his all. This means he wants to put on all the pieces in his repertory. As a result, each act is twice as long as it should be. And, because the contributors are unpaid volunteers, the manager can't insist on drastic cuts. If he does, they get hurt and pull out altogether.

The show was still grinding on at ten-thirty. Balloons, escaped from their owners, swayed gently against the ceiling. The young Forellian snored like a distant thunderstorm at the back of the hall. The young of several other species, including *Homo sapiens,* got out of hand and had to be taken away. The Osmanians fidgeted on seats never designed for their kind and twiddled their tentacles.

Milan Reid ostentatiously looked at his watch and whispered to Sterga: "I have to take my wife to the train. Good-night. Good-night, Thvi."

He shook their tentacles, led Louise out, and drove off. He did not, however, drive to the railroad station or the airport. He did not think that the situation called for Louise's actually going to Washington. Instead, he left her at the apartment of one of her girl-friends in Merion. Then he went home.

First he went up to the Zieglers' front door. He put out his thumb to ring, to make sure his plans had gone through. Then he drew back. From within came screams of laughter: Connie's shrill peals, Charlie's belly-roars, and the Osmanians' hideous cackle.

His guests had obviously made contact with their new hosts. There was no need for him to go in. If he did, Charlie would insist on his joining the party, and he loathed raucous parties.

Reid went to his own house and got ready for bed. Though not much of a late-evening drinker, he mixed himself a strong rye-and-soda, turned on the radio to a good-music station, lit his pipe, and relaxed. From next door, outbursts of crazy laughter rose up from time to time, with odd thumping sounds and once the crash of breaking glass. Reid smiled quietly.

The telephone rang. Reid frowned and lifted the handset.

"New Haven calling," said the operator. Then came the nasal tones of Rajendra Jaipal: "Hello, Milan? This is R. J. I didn't know if you would be home yet from the celebration. How are your guests?"

"I got rid of them," said Reid.

"You *what?*"

"Got rid of them. Gave them away. I couldn't stand them."

"Where are they now?" Jaipal's voice rose tautly.

"Next door, at the Zieglers'. They seem—"

"Oh, you did *not!*"

"Damn right I did. They seem to be having a high old time."

"*Ai Ram Ram!* I thought I could trust you! You have upset interplanetary relations for centuries! My God, why did you do that? And why the Zieglers, of all people?"

"Because the Zieglers were handy, and because these squids are a pair of spoiled brats; impulsive, irresponsible children, with no manners, no morals, no sense, no nothing. If—"

"That does not matter. You have your dutee to humanity."

"My duty doesn't include trading wives with a space-octopus—"

"Oh, you could have found a way around that—"

"And why—why didn't you warn me of their cute little ways? My day has been pure hell."

Jaipal's voice rose to a scream. "You selfish, perpidious materialist—"

"Oh, go jump in the lake! You're the perfidious one, palming these interstellar zanies off on me. I suppose you neglected to tell me what I was getting into for fear I'd back out, huh? Well, didn't you? Didn't you?"

The telephone was silent. Then Jaipal said in a lower voice: "My dear friend, I admit that I too am a sinful, imparfect mortal. Please forgive my hasty remarks. But now let us see if we can repair the damage. This is most serious. The economic future of our planet depends on this mining-lease. I shall ply down at once."

"It won't do you any good to get here before seven. I'm going to bed, and I won't even answer the doorbell till then."

"Then I shall be on your doorstep at seven. Good-bye."

When Reid looked out next morning, there was Rajendra Jaipal in a gray-flannel suit sitting on his doorstep. As the door opened, Jaipal's gaunt, somber figure arose. "Well, are you readee to show me the wreckage of mankind's hopes?"

Reid looked across at the Zieglers' house, where all was silent. "I think they're still asleep. Uh—have you had breakfast?"

"No, but—"

"Then come in and have some."

They ate in gloomy silence. Since awakening, Reid had begun to worry. In morning's cold light, his bold stroke of last night no longer seemed so dashing. In fact it might prove a colossal blunder. Of course one couldn't submit one's wife to an extraterrestrial's amatory experiments. (Or could one, for the sake of one's planet?) In any case, he could surely have gotten around that. He could have sent Louise away but himself put up with the Osmanians for a few more hours. It was his cursed lack of social skill again. Why did the fate of planets depend on a wretched caricature of a man like him?

It was after nine of a bright sunshiny day when Reid and Jaipal approached the Ziegler house. Reid rang. After a while the door opened. There stood Charles Ziegler, wearing a pair of purple-and-white checkered shorts. For an instant he glowered through bloodshot eyes. Then he grinned.

"Hel-lo there!" he cried. "Come on in!"

Reid introduced Jaipal and went in. The living room was a shambles. Here lay an overthrown floor-lamp; there a card-table with a broken leg teetered drunkenly. Cards and poker-chips bespangled the floor.

From the kitchen came sounds of breakfast-making. Sterga slithered in, balancing an ice-bag on his head with two tentacles, and said, "Such a night! My dear Mr. Reid, how can I thank you enough for finding such a congenial host? I did not think any being in the Galaxy could drink me down, guk-guk!"

Reid looked questioningly at Ziegler, who said: "Yeah, we sure hung one on."

"It meant we could not carry out the experiment as I hoped," said Sterga. "But that is all right. Next year, even if the rest go to Athens, Thvi and I will come here to the Zieglers'." The Osmanian reared up and clutched Ziegler's neck, while Ziegler patted the rubbery hide. "We love them. He is a good wrestler, too. And don't worry about your mining-lease, R. J. There will be no difficulty."

Reid and Jaipal excused themselves. Outside, they looked at each other. Each made the same gesture, raising his shoulder while spreading his hands with the palms up.

Then they saluted each other with a wave of the hand, while their faces expressed despairing incomprehension. Reid turned back to his house, and Jaipal walked swiftly away.

The Pedestrian

To enter out into that silence that was the city at eight o'clock of a misty evening in November, to put your feet upon that buckling concrete walk, to step over grassy seams and make your way, hands in pockets, through the silences, that was what Mr. Leonard Mead most dearly loved to do. He would stand upon the corner of an intersection and peer down long moonlit avenues of sidewalk in four directions, deciding which way to go, but it really made no difference; he was alone in this world of 2053 A.D., or as good as alone, and with a final decision made, a path selected, he would stride off, sending patterns of frosty air before him like the smoke of a cigar.

Sometimes he would walk for hours and miles and return only at midnight to his house. And on his way he would see the cottages and homes with their dark windows, and it was not unequal to walking through a graveyard where only the faintest glimmers of firefly light appeared in flickers behind the windows. Sudden gray phantoms seemed to manifest upon inner room walls where a curtain was still undrawn against the night, or there were whisperings and murmurs where a window in a tomb-like building was still open.

Mr. Leonard Mead would pause, cock his head, listen, look, and march on, his feet making no noise on the lumpy walk. For long ago he had wisely changed to sneakers when strolling at night, because the dogs in intermittent squads would parallel his journey with barkings if he wore hard heels, and lights might click on and faces appear and an entire street be startled by the passing of a lone figure, himself, in the early November evening.

On this particular evening he began his journey in a westerly direction, toward the hidden sea. There was a good crystal frost in the air; it cut the nose and made the lungs blaze like a Christmas tree inside; you could feel the cold light going on and off, all the branches filled with invisible snow. He listened to the faint push of his soft shoes through autumn leaves with satisfaction, and whistled a cold quiet whistle between his teeth, occasionally picking up a leaf as he passed, examining its skeletal pattern in the infrequent lamplights as he went on, smelling its rusty smell.

"Hello, in there," he whispered to every house on every side as he moved. "What's up tonight on Channel 4, Channel 7, Channel 9? Where are the cowboys rushing, and do I see the United States Cavalry over the next hill to the rescue?"

The street was silent and long and empty, with only his

shadow moving like the shadow of a hawk in mid-country. If he closed his eyes and stood very still, frozen, he could imagine himself upon the center of a plain, a wintry, windless Arizona desert with no house in a thousand miles, and only dry river beds, the streets, for company.

"What is it now?" he asked the houses, noticing his wrist watch. "Eight-thirty P.M.? Time for a dozen assorted murders? A quiz? A revue? A comedian falling off the stage?"

Was that a murmur of laughter from within a moon-white house? He hesitated, but went on when nothing more happened. He stumbled over a particularly uneven section of sidewalk. The cement was vanishing under flowers and grass. In ten years of walking by night or day, for thousands of miles, he had never met another person walking, not one in all that time.

He came to a cloverleaf intersection which stood silent where two main highways crossed the town. During the day it was a thunderous surge of cars, the gas stations open, a great insect rustling and a ceaseless jockeying for position as the scarab-beetles, a faint incense puttering from their exhausts, skimmed homeward to the far directions. But now these highways, too, were like streams in a dry season, all stone and bed and moon radiance.

He turned back on a side street, circling around toward his home. He was within a block of his destination when the lone car turned a corner quite suddenly and flashed a fierce white cone of light upon him. He stood entranced, not unlike a night moth, stunned by the illumination, and then drawn toward it.

A metallic voice called to him:

"Stand still. Stay where you are! Don't move!"

He halted.

"Put up your hands!"

"But——" he said.

"Your hands up! Or we'll shoot!"

The police, of course, but what a rare, incredible thing; in a city of three million, there was only *one* police car left, wasn't that correct? Ever since a year ago, 2052, the election year, the force had been cut down from three cars to one. Crime was ebbing; there was no need now for the police, save for this one lone car wandering and wandering the empty streets.

"Your name?" said the police car in a metallic whisper. He couldn't see the men in it for the bright light in his eyes.

"Leonard Mead," he said.

"Speak up!"

"Leonard Mead!"

"Business or profession?"

"I guess you'd call me a writer."

"No profession," said the police car, as if talking to itself. The light held him fixed, like a museum specimen, needle thrust through chest.

"You might say that," said Mr. Mead. He hadn't written in years. Magazines and books didn't sell any more. Everything went on in the tomb-like houses at night now, he thought, continuing his fancy. The tombs, ill-lit by television light, where the people sat like the dead, the gray or multi-colored lights touching their faces, but never really touching them.

"No profession," said the phonograph voice, hissing. "What are you doing out?"

"Walking," said Leonard Mead.

"Walking!"

"Just walking," he said simply, but his face felt cold.

"Walking, just walking, walking?"

"Yes, sir."

"Walking where? For what?"

"Walking for air. Walking to *see*."

"Your address!"

"Eleven South Saint James Street."

"And there is air *in* your house, you have an air *conditioner,* Mr. Mead?"

"Yes."

"And you have a viewing screen in your house to see with?"

"No."

"No?" There was a crackling quiet that in itself was an accusation.

"Are you married, Mr. Mead?"

"No."

"Not married," said the police voice behind the fiery beam. The moon was high and clear among the stars and the houses were gray and silent.

"Nobody wanted me," said Leonard Mead with a smile.

"Don't speak unless you're spoken to!"

Leonard Mead waited in the cold night.

"Just *walking,* Mr. Mead?"

"Yes."

"But you haven't explained for what purpose."

"I explained; for air, and to see, and just to walk."

"Have you done this often?"

"Every night for years."

The police car sat in the center of the street with its radio throat faintly humming.

"Well, Mr. Mead," it said.

"Is that all?" he asked politely.

"Yes," said the voice. "Here." There was a sigh, a pop. The back door of the police car sprang wide. "Get in."

"Wait a minute, I haven't done anything!"

"Get in."

"I protest!"

"Mr. Mead."

He walked like a man suddenly drunk. As he passed the front window of the car he looked in. As he had expected, there was no one in the front seat, no one in the car at all.

"Get in."

He put his hand to the door and peered into the back seat, which was a little cell, a little black jail with bars. It smelled of riveted steel. It smelled of harsh antiseptic; it smelled too clean and hard and metallic. There was nothing soft there.

"Now if you had a wife to give you an alibi," said the iron voice. "But——"

"Where are you taking me?"

The car hesitated, or rather gave a faint whirring click, as if information, somewhere, was dropping card by punch-slotted card under electric eyes. "To the Psychiatric Center for Research on Regressive Tendencies."

He got in. The door shut with a soft thud. The police car rolled through the night avenues, flashing its dim lights ahead.

They passed one house on one street a moment later, one house in an entire city of houses that were dark, but this one particular house had all of its electric lights brightly lit, every window a loud yellow illumination, square and warm in the cool darkness.

"That's *my* house," said Leonard Mead.

No one answered him.

The car moved down the empty river-bed streets and off away, leaving the empty streets with the empty sidewalks, and no sound and no motion all the rest of the chill November night.

~~~~~~

William and Mary

William Pearl did not leave a great deal of money when he died, and his will was a simple one. With the exception of a few small bequests to relatives, he left all his property to his wife.

The solicitor and Mrs. Pearl went over it together in the solicitor's office, and when the business was completed, the widow got up to leave. At that point, the solicitor took a sealed envelope from the folder on his desk and held it out to his client.

"I have been instructed to give you this," he said. "Your husband sent it to us shortly before he passed away."

The solicitor was pale and prim, and out of respect for a widow he kept his head on one side as he spoke, looking downward. "It appears that it might be something personal, Mrs. Pearl. No doubt you'd like to take it home with you and read it in privacy."

Mrs. Pearl accepted the envelope and went out into the street. She paused on the pavement, feeling the thing with her fingers. A letter of farewell from William? Probably, yes. A formal letter. It was bound to be formal—stiff and formal. The man was incapable of acting otherwise. He had never done anything informal in his life.

My dear Mary, I trust that you will not permit my departure from this world to upset you too much, but that you will continue to observe those precepts which have guided you so well during our partnership together. Be diligent and dignified in all things. Be thrifty with your money. Be very careful that you do not . . . et cetera, et cetera.

A typical William letter.

Or was it possible that he might have broken down at the last moment and written her something beautiful? Maybe this was a beautiful tender message, a sort of love letter, a lovely warm note of thanks to her for giving him thirty years of her life and for ironing a million shirts and cooking a million meals and making a million beds, something that she could read over and over again, once a day at least, and she would keep it for ever in the box on her dressing-table together with her brooches.

There is no knowing what people will do when they are about to die, Mrs. Pearl told herself, and she tucked the envelope under her arm and hurried home.

She let herself in the front door and went straight to the living-room and sat down on the sofa without removing her hat or coat. Then she opened the envelope and drew out the contents. These consisted, she saw, of some fifteen or twenty sheets of lined white paper, folded over once and held together at the top left-hand corner by a clip. Each sheet was covered with the small, neat, forward-sloping writing that she knew so well, but when she noticed how much of it there was, and in what a neat businesslike manner it was written, and how the first page didn't even begin in the nice way a letter should, she began to get suspicious.

She looked away. She lit herself a cigarette. She took one puff and laid the cigarette in the ashtray.

If this is about what I am beginning to suspect it is about, she told herself, then I don't want to read it.

Can one refuse to read a letter from the dead?

Yes.

Well . . .

She glanced over at William's empty chair on the other side of the fireplace. It was a big brown leather armchair, and there was a depression on the seat of it, made by his buttocks over the years. Higher up, on the backrest, there was a dark oval stain on the leather where his head had rested. He used to sit reading in that chair and she would be opposite him on the sofa, sewing on buttons or mending socks or putting a patch on the elbow of one of his jackets, and every now and then a pair of eyes would glance up from the book and settle on her, watchful, but strangely impersonal, as if calculating something. She had never liked those eyes. They were ice blue, cold, small, and rather close together, with two deep vertical lines of disapproval dividing them. All her life they had been watching her. And even now, after a week alone in the house, she sometimes had an uneasy feeling that they were still there, following her around, staring at her from doorways, from empty chairs, through a window at night.

Slowly she reached into her handbag and took out her spectacles and put them on. Then, holding the pages up high in front of her so that they caught the late afternoon light from the window behind, she started to read:

This note, *my dear Mary,* is entirely for you, and will be given you shortly after I am gone.

Do not be alarmed by the sight of all this writing. It is nothing but an attempt on my part to explain to you precisely what Landy is going to do to me, and why I have agreed that he should do it, and what are his theories and his hopes. You are my wife and you have a right to know these things. In fact you *must* know them. During the past few days I have tried very hard to speak with you about Landy, but you have steadfastly refused to give me a hearing. This, as I have already told you, is a very foolish attitude to take, and I find it not entirely an unselfish one either. It stems mostly from ignorance, and I am absolutely convinced that if only you were made aware of all the facts, you would immediately change your view. That is why I am hoping that when I am no longer with you, and your mind is less distracted, you will consent to listen to me more carefully through these pages. I swear to you that when you have read my story, your sense of antipathy will vanish, and enthusiasm will take its place. I even dare to hope that you will become a little proud of what I have done.

As you read on, you must forgive me, if you will, for the coolness of my style, but this is the only way I know of getting my message over to you clearly. You see, as my time draws near, it is natural that I begin to brim with every kind of sentimentality under the sun. Each day I grow more extravagantly wistful, especially in the evenings, and unless I watch myself closely my emotions will be overflowing onto these pages.

I have a wish, for example, to write something about you and what a satisfactory wife you have been to me through the years, and I am promising myself that if there is time, and I still have the strength, I shall do that next.

I have a yearning also to speak about this Oxford of mine where I have been living and teaching for the past seventeen years, to tell something about the glory of the place and to explain, if I can, a little of what it has meant to have been allowed to work in its midst. All the things and places that I loved so well keep crowding in on me now in this gloomy bedroom. They are bright and beautiful as they always were, and today, for some reason, I can see them more clearly than ever. The path around the lake in the gardens of Worcester College, where Lovelace used to walk. The gateway at Pembroke. The view westward over the town from Magdalen Tower. The great hall at Christchurch. The little rockery at St. Johns where I have counted more than a dozen varieties of campanula, including the rare and dainty C. Waldsteiniana. But there, you see! I haven't even begun and already I'm falling into the trap. So let me get started now; and let you read it slowly, my dear, without any of that sense of sorrow or disapproval that might otherwise embarrass your understanding. Promise me now that you will read it slowly, and that you will put yourself in a cool and patient frame of mind before you begin.

The details of the illness that struck me down so suddenly in my middle life are known to you. I need not waste time upon them—except to admit at once how foolish I was not to have gone earlier to my doctor. Cancer is one of the few remaining diseases that these modern drugs cannot cure. A surgeon can operate if it has not spread too far; but with me, not only did I leave it too late, but the thing had the effrontery to attack me in the pancreas, making both surgery and survival equally impossible.

So here I was with somewhere between one and six months left to live, growing more melancholy every hour —and then, all of a sudden, in comes Landy.

That was six weeks ago, on a Tuesday morning, very early, long before your visiting time, and the moment he entered I knew there was some sort of madness in the wind. He didn't creep in on his toes, sheepish and embarrassed, not knowing what to say, like all my other visitors. He came in strong and smiling, and he strode up to the bed and stood there looking down at me with a wild bright glimmer in his eyes, and he said, "William, my boy, this is perfect. You're just the one I want!"

Perhaps I should explain to you here that although John Landy has never been to our house, and you have seldom if ever met him, I myself have been friendly with him for at least nine years. I am, of course, primarily a teacher of philosophy, but as you know I've lately been dabbling a good deal in psychology as well. Landy's interests and mine have therefore slightly overlapped. He is a magnificent neurosurgeon, one of the finest, and recently he has been kind enough to let me study the results of some of his work, especially the varying effects of prefrontal lobotomies upon different types of psychopaths. So you can see that when he suddenly burst in on me Tuesday morning, we were by no means strangers to one another.

"Look," he said, pulling up a chair beside the bed. "In a few weeks you're going to be dead. Correct?"

Coming from Landy, the question didn't seem especially unkind. In a way it was refreshing to have a visitor brave enough to touch upon the forbidden subject.

"You're going to expire right here in this room, and then they'll take you out and cremate you."

"Bury me," I said.

"That's even worse. And then what? Do you believe you'll go to heaven?"

"I doubt it," I said, "though it would be comforting to think so."

"Or hell, perhaps?"

"I don't really see why they should send me there."

"You never know, my dear William."

"What's all this about?" I asked.

"Well," he said, and I could see him watching me carefully, "personally, I don't believe that after you're dead you'll ever hear of yourself again—unless . . ." and here he paused and smiled and leaned closer ". . . unless, of course, you have the sense to put yourself into my hands. Would you care to consider a proposition?"

The way he was staring at me, and studying me, and appraising me with a queer kind of hungriness, I might have been a piece of prime beef on the counter and he had bought it and was waiting for them to wrap it up.

"I'm really serious about it, William. Would you care to consider a proposition?"

"I don't know what you're talking about."

"Then listen and I'll tell you. Will you listen to me?"

"Go on then, if you like. I doubt I've got very much to lose by hearing it."

"On the contrary, you have a great deal to gain—especially *after you're dead.*"

I am sure he was expecting me to jump when he said this, but for some reason I was ready for it. I lay quite still, watching his face and that slow white smile of his that always revealed the gold clasp of an upper denture curled around the canine on the left side of his mouth.

"This is a thing, William, that I've been working on quietly for some years. One or two others here at the hospital have been helping me, especially Morrison, and we've completed a number of fairly successful trials with laboratory animals. I'm at the stage now where I'm ready to have a go with a man. It's a big idea, and it may sound a bit farfetched at first, but from a surgical point of view there doesn't seem to be any reason why it shouldn't be more or less practicable."

Landy leaned forward and placed both his hands on the edge of my bed. He had a good face, handsome in a bony sort of way, and with none of the usual doctor's look about it. You know that look, most of them have it. It

glimmers at you out of their eyeballs like a dull electric
sign and it reads *Only I can save you*. But John Landy's
eyes were wide and bright and little sparks of excitement
were dancing in the centres of them.

"Quite a long time ago," he said, "I saw a short medical
film that had been brought over from Russia. It was a
rather gruesome thing, but interesting. It showed a dog's
head completely severed from the body, but with the normal blood supply being maintained through the arteries
and veins by means of an artificial heart. Now the thing
is this: that dog's head, sitting there all alone on a sort of
tray, was *alive*. The brain was functioning. They proved
it by several tests. For example, when food was smeared
on the dog's lips, the tongue would come out and lick it
away; and the eyes would follow a person moving across
the room.

"It seemed reasonable to conclude from this that the
head and the brain did not need to be attached to the rest
of the body in order to remain alive—provided, of course,
that a supply of properly oxygenated blood could be
maintained.

"Now then. My own thought, which grew out of seeing
this film, was to remove the brain from the skull of a
human and keep it alive and functioning as an independent
unit for an unlimited period after he is dead. *Your* brain,
for example, after *you* are dead."

"I don't like that," I said.

"Don't interrupt, William. Let me finish. So far as I
can tell from subsequent experiments, the brain is a
peculiarly self-supporting object. It manufactures its own
cerebro-spinal fluid. The magic processes of thought and
memory which go on inside it are manifestly not impaired
by the absence of limbs or trunk or even of skull, provided, as I say, that you keep pumping in the right kind
of oxygenated blood under the proper conditions.

"My dear William, just think for a moment of your

own brain. It is in perfect shape. It is crammed full of a lifetime of learning. It has taken you years of work to make it what it is. It is just beginning to give out some first-rate original ideas. Yet soon it is going to have to die along with the rest of your body simply because your silly little pancreas is lousy with cancer."

"No thank you," I said to him. "You can stop there. It's a repulsive idea, and even if you could do it, which I doubt, it would be quite pointless. What possible use is there in keeping my brain alive if I couldn't talk or see or hear or feel? Personally, I can think of nothing more unpleasant."

"I believe that you *would* be able to communicate with us," Landy said. "And we might even succeed in giving you a certain amount of vision. But let's take this slowly. I'll come to all that later on. The fact remains that you're going to die fairly soon whatever happens; and my plans would not involve touching you at all until *after* you are dead. Come now, William. No true philosopher could object to lending his dead body to the cause of science."

"That's not putting it quite straight," I answered. "It seems to me there'd be some doubt as to whether I were dead or alive by the time you'd finished with me."

"Well," he said, smiling a little, "I suppose you're right about that. But I don't think you ought to turn me down quite so quickly, before you know a bit more about it."

"I said I don't want to hear it."

"Have a cigarette," he said, holding out his case.

"I don't smoke, you know that."

He took one himself and lit it with a tiny silver lighter that was no bigger than a shilling piece. "A present from the people who make my instruments," he said. "Ingenious, isn't it?"

I examined the lighter, then handed it back.

"May I go on?" he asked.

"I'd rather you didn't."

"Just lie still and listen. I think you'll find it quite interesting."

There were some blue grapes on a plate beside my bed. I put the plate on my chest and began eating the grapes.

"At the very moment of death," Landy said, "I should have to be standing by so that I could step in immediately and try to keep your brain alive."

"You mean leaving it in the head?"

"To start with, yes. I'd have to."

"And where would you put it after that?"

"If you want to know, in a sort of basin."

"Are you really serious about this?"

"Certainly I'm serious."

"All right. Go on."

"I suppose you know that when the heart stops and the brain is deprived of fresh blood and oxygen, its tissues die very rapidly. Anything from four to six minutes and the whole thing's dead. Even after three minutes you may get a certain amount of damage. So I should have to work rapidly to prevent this from happening. But with the help of the machine, it should be quite simple."

"What machine?"

"The artificial heart. We've got a nice adaptation here of the one originally devised by Alexis Carrel and Lindbergh. It oxygenates the blood, keeps it at the right temperature, pumps it in at the right pressure, and does a number of other little necessary things. It's really not at all complicated."

"Tell me what you would do at the moment of death," I said. "What is the first thing you would do?"

"Do you know anything about the vascular and venous arrangements of the brain?"

"No."

"Then listen. It's not difficult. The blood supply to the brain is derived from two main sources, the internal carotid arteries and the vertebral arteries. There are two of each, making four arteries in all. Got that?"

"Yes."

"And the return system is even simpler. The blood is
drained away by only two large veins, the internal jugu-
lars. So you have four arteries going up—they go up the
neck, of course—and two veins coming down. Around
the brain itself they naturally branch out into other channels, but those don't concern us. We never touch them."

"All right," I said. "Imagine that I've just died. Now
what would you do?"

"I should immediately open your neck and locate the
four arteries, the carotids and the vertebrals. I should then
perfuse them, which means that I'd stick a large hollow
needle into each. These four needles would be connected
by tubes to the artificial heart.

"Then, working quickly, I would dissect out both the
left and right internal jugular veins and hitch these also
to the heart machine to complete the circuit. Now switch
on the machine, which is already primed with the right
type of blood, and there you are. The circulation through
your brain would be restored."

"I'd be like that Russian dog."

"I don't think you would. For one thing, you'd certainly lose consciousness when you died, and I very much
doubt whether you would come to again for quite a long
time—if indeed you came to at all. But, conscious or not,
you'd be in a rather interesting position, wouldn't you?
You'd have a cold dead body and a living brain."

Landy paused to savour this delightful prospect. The
man was so entranced and bemused by the whole idea
that he evidently found it impossible to believe I might
not be feeling the same way.

"We could now afford to take our time," he said. "And
believe me, we'd need it. The first thing we'd do would
be to wheel you to the operating-room, accompanied of

course by the machine, which must never stop pumping. The next problem . . ."

"All right," I said. "That's enough. I don't have to hear the details."

"Oh but you must," he said. "It is important that you should know precisely what is going to happen to you all the way through. You see, afterwards, when you regain consciousness, it will be much more satisfactory from your point of view if you are able to remember exactly *where* you are and *how* you came to be there. If only for your own peace of mind you should know that. You agree?"

I lay still on the bed, watching him.

"So the next problem would be to remove your brain, intact and undamaged, from your dead body. The body is useless. In fact it has already started to decay. The skull and the face are also useless. They are both encumbrances and I don't want them around. All I want is the brain, the clean beautiful brain, alive and perfect. So when I get you on the table I will take a saw, a small oscillating saw, and with this I shall proceed to remove the whole vault of your skull. You'd still be unconscious at that point so I wouldn't have to bother with anaesthetic."

"Like hell you wouldn't," I said.

"You'd be out cold, I promise you that, William. Don't forget you *died* just a few minutes before."

"Nobody's sawing off the top of my skull without an anaesthetic," I said.

Landy shrugged his shoulders. "It makes no difference to me," he said. "I'll be glad to give you a little procaine if you want it. If it will make you any happier I'll infiltrate the whole scalp with procaine, the whole head, from the neck up."

"Thanks very much," I said.

"You know," he went on, "it's extraordinary what sometimes happens. Only last week a man was brought

in unconscious, and I opened his head without any anaesthetic at all and removed a small blood clot. I was
still working inside the skull when he woke up and began
talking.

" 'Where am I?' he asked.

" 'You're in hospital.'

" 'Well,' he said. 'Fancy that.'

" 'Tell me,' I asked him, 'is this bothering you, what
I'm doing?'

" 'No,' he answered. 'Not at all. What *are* you doing?'

" 'I'm just removing a blood clot from your brain.'

" 'You *are?*"

" 'Just lie still. Don't move. I'm nearly finished.'

" 'So that's the bastard been giving me all those headaches,' the man said."

Landy paused and smiled, remembering the occasion.
"That's word for word what the man said," he went on,
"although the next day he couldn't even recollect the
incident. It's a funny thing, the brain."

"I'll have the procaine," I said.

"As you wish, William. And now, as I say, I'd take a
small oscillating saw and carefully remove your complete
calvarium—the whole vault of the skull. This would ex-
pose the top half of the brain, or rather the outer covering
in which it is wrapped. You may or may not know that
there are three separate coverings around the brain itself
—the outer one called the dura mater or dura, the middle
one called the arachnoid, and the inner one called the pia
mater or pia. Most laymen seem to have the idea that the
brain is a naked thing floating around in fluid in your
head. But it isn't. It's wrapped up neatly in these three
strong coverings, and the cerebrospinal fluid actually flows
within the little gap between the two inner coverings,
known as the subarachnoid space. As I told you before,
this fluid is manufactured by the brain, and it drains off
into the venous system by osmosis.

"I myself would leave all three coverings—don't they have lovely names, the dura, the arachnoid, and the pia? —I'd leave them all intact. There are many reasons for this, not least among them being the fact that within the dura run the venous channels that drain the blood from the brain into the jugular.

"Now," he went on, "we've got the upper half of your skull off so that the top of the brain, wrapped in its outer covering, is exposed. The next step is the really tricky one: to release the whole package so that it can be lifted cleanly away, leaving the stubs of the four supply arteries and the two veins hanging underneath ready to be reconnected to the machine. This is an immensely lengthy and complicated business involving the delicate chipping away of much bone, the severing of many nerves, and the cutting and tying of numerous blood vessels. The only way I could do it with any hope of success would be by taking a rongeur and slowly biting off the rest of your skull, peeling it off downward like an orange until the sides and underneath of the brain covering are fully exposed. The problems involved are highly technical and I won't go into them, but I feel fairly sure that the work can be done. It's simply a question of surgical skill and patience. And don't forget that I'd have plenty of time, as much as I wanted, because the artificial heart would be continually pumping away alongside the operating-table, keeping the brain alive.

"Now, let's assume that I've succeeded in peeling off your skull and removing everything else that surrounds the sides of the brain. That leaves it connected to the body only at the base, mainly by the spinal column and by the two large veins and the four arteries that are supplying it with blood. So what next?

"I would sever the spinal column just above the first cervical vertebra, taking great care not to harm the two vertebral arteries which are in that area. But you must remember that the dura or outer covering is open at this place to receive the spinal column, so I'd have to close this opening by sewing the edges of the dura together. There'd be no problem there.

"At this point, I would be ready for the final move. To one side, on a table, I'd have a basin of a special shape, and this would be filled with what we call Ringer's Solution. That is a special kind of fluid we use for irrigation in neurosurgery. I would now cut the brain completely loose by severing the supply arteries and the veins. Then I would simply pick it up in my hands and transfer it to the basin. This would be the only other time during the whole proceeding when the blood flow would be cut off; but once it was in the basin, it wouldn't take a moment to reconnect the stubs of the arteries and veins to the artificial heart.

"So there you are," Landy said. "Your brain is now in the basin, and still alive, and there isn't any reason why it shouldn't stay alive for a very long time, years and years perhaps, provided we looked after the blood and the machine."

"But would it *function?*"

"My dear William, how should I know? I can't even tell you whether it would ever regain consciousness."

"And if it did?"

"There now! That would be fascinating!"

"Would it?" I said, and I must admit I had my doubts.

"Of course it would! Lying there with all your thinking processes working beautifully, and your memory as well . . ."

"And not being able to see or feel or smell or hear or talk," I said.

"Ah!" he cried. "I knew I'd forgotten something! I never told you about the eye. Listen. I am going to try to leave one of your optic nerves intact, as well as the eye itself. The optic nerve is a little thing about the thickness of a clinical thermometer and about two inches in length as it stretches between the brain and the eye. The beauty of it is that it's not really a nerve at all. It's an outpouching of the brain itself, and the dura or brain covering extends along it and is attached to the eyeball. The back of the eye is therefore in very close contact with the brain, and cerebrospinal fluid flows right up to it.

"All this suits my purpose very well, and makes it reasonable to suppose that I could succeed in preserving one of your eyes. I've already constructed a small plastic case to contain the eyeball, instead of your own socket, and when the brain is in the basin, submerged in Ringer's Solution, the eyeball in its case will float on the surface of the liquid."

"Staring at the ceiling," I said.

"I suppose so, yes. I'm afraid there wouldn't be any muscles there to move it around. But it might be sort of fun to lie there so quietly and comfortably peering out at the world from your basin."

"Hilarious," I said. "How about leaving me an ear as well?"

"I'd rather not try an ear this time."

"I want an ear," I said. "I insist upon an ear."

"No."

"I want to listen to Bach."

"You don't understand how difficult it would be," Landy said gently. "The hearing apparatus—the cochlea, as it's called—is a far more delicate mechanism than the eye. What's more, it is encased in bone. So is a part of the auditory nerve that connects it with the brain. I couldn't possibly chisel the whole thing out intact."

"Couldn't you leave it encased in the bone and bring the bone to the basin?"

"No," he said firmly. "This thing is complicated enough already. And anyway, if the eye works, it doesn't matter all that much about your hearing. We can always hold up messages for you to read. You really must leave me to decide what is possible and what isn't."

"I haven't yet said that I'm going to do it."

"I know, William, I know."

"I'm not sure I fancy the idea very much."

"Would you rather be dead, altogether?"

"Perhaps I would. I don't know yet. I wouldn't be able to talk, would I?"

"Of course not."

"Then how would I communicate with you? How would you know that I'm conscious?"

"It would be easy for us to know whether or not you regain consciousness," Landy said. "The ordinary electro-encephalograph could tell us that. We'd attach the electrodes directly to the frontal lobes of your brain, there in the basin."

"And you could actually tell?"

"Oh, definitely. Any hospital could do that part of it."

"But *I* couldn't communicate with *you.*"

"As a matter of fact," Landy said, "I believe you could. There's a man up in London called Wertheimer who's doing some interesting work on the subject of thought communication, and I've been in touch with him. You know, don't you, that the thinking brain throws off electrical and chemical discharges? And that these discharges go out in the form of waves, rather like radio waves?"

"I know a bit about it," I said.

"Well, Wertheimer has constructed an apparatus somewhat similar to the encephalograph, though far more sensitive, and he maintains that within certain narrow limits it can help him to interpret actual things that a brain is thinking. It produces a kind of graph which is apparently decipherable into words or thoughts. Would you like me to ask Wertheimer to come and see you?"

"No," I said. Landy was already taking it for granted that I was going to go through with this business, and I resented his attitude. "Go away now and leave me alone," I told him. "You won't get anywhere by trying to rush me."

He stood up at once and crossed to the door.

"One question," I said.

He paused with a hand on the doorknob. "Yes, William?"

"Simply this. Do you yourself honestly believe that when my brain is in that basin, my mind will be able to function exactly as it is doing at present? Do you believe that I will be able to think and reason as I can now? And will the power of memory remain?"

"I don't see why not," he answered. "It's the same brain. It's alive. It's undamaged. In fact, it's completely untouched. We haven't even opened the dura. The big difference, of course, would be that we've severed every single nerve that leads into it—except for the one optic nerve—and this means that your thinking would no longer be influenced by your senses. You'd be living in an extraordinary pure and detached world. Nothing to bother you at all, not even pain. You couldn't possibly feel pain because there wouldn't be any nerves to feel it with. In a way, it would be an almost perfect situation. No worries or fears or pains or hunger or thirst. Not even any desires. Just your memories and your thoughts, and if the remaining eye happened to function, then you could read books as well. It all sounds rather pleasant to me."

"It does, does it?"

"Yes, William, it does. And particularly for a Doctor of Philosophy. It would be a tremendous experience. You'd be able to reflect upon the ways of the world with a detachment and a serenity that no man had ever attained before. And who knows what might not happen then! Great thoughts and solutions might come to you, great ideas that could revolutionize our way of life! Try to imagine, if you can, the degree of concentration that you'd be able to achieve!"

"And the frustration," I said.

"Nonsense. There couldn't be any frustration. You can't have frustration without desire, and you couldn't possibly have any desire. Not physical desire, anyway."

"I should certainly be capable of remembering my previous life in the world, and I might desire to return to it."

"What, to this mess! Out of your comfortable basin and back into this madhouse!"

"Answer one more question," I said. "How long do you believe you could keep it alive?"

"The brain? Who knows? Possibly for years and years. The conditions would be ideal. Most of the factors that cause deterioration would be absent, thanks to the artificial heart. The blood-pressure would remain constant at all times, an impossible condition in real life. The temperature would also be constant. The chemical composition of the blood would be near perfect. There would be no impurities in it, no virus, no bacteria, nothing. Of course it's foolish to guess, but I believe that a brain might live for two or three hundred years in circumstances like these. Goodbye for now," he said. "I'll drop in and see you tomorrow." He went out quickly, leaving me, as you might guess, in a fairly disturbed state of mind.

My immediate reaction after he had gone was one of revulsion toward the whole business. Somehow, it wasn't at all nice. There was something basically repulsive about the idea that I myself, with all my mental faculties intact, should be reduced to a small slimy grey blob lying in a pool of water. It was monstrous, obscene, unholy. Another thing that bothered me was the feeling of helplessness that I was bound to experience once Landy had got me into the basin. There could be no going back after that, no way of protesting or explaining. I would be committed for as long as they could keep me alive.

And what, for example, if I could not stand it? What if it turned out to be terribly painful? What if I became hysterical?

No legs to run away on. No voice to scream with. Nothing. I'd just have to grin and bear it for the next two centuries.

No mouth to grin with either.

At this point, a curious thought struck me, and it was this: Does not a man who has had a leg amputated often suffer from the delusion that the leg is still there? Does he not tell the nurse that the toes he doesn't have any more are itching like mad, and so on and so forth? I seemed to have heard something to that effect quite recently.

Very well. On the same premise, was it not possible that my brain, lying there alone in that basin, might not suffer from a similar delusion in regard to my body? In which case, all my usual aches and pains could come flooding over me and I wouldn't even be able to take an aspirin to relieve them. One moment I might be imagining that I had the most excruciating cramp in my leg, or a violent indigestion, and a few minutes later, I might easily get the feeling that my poor bladder—you know me— was so full that if I didn't get to emptying it soon it would burst.

Heaven forbid.

I lay there for a long time thinking these horrid thoughts. Then quite suddenly, round about midday, my mood began to change. I became less concerned with the unpleasant aspect of the affair and found myself able to examine Landy's proposals in a more reasonable light. Was there not, after all, I asked myself, something a bit comforting in the thought that my brain might not necessarily have to die and disappear in a few weeks' time? There was indeed. I am rather proud of my brain. It is a sensitive, lucid, and uberous organ. It contains a prodigious store of information, and it is still capable of producing imaginative and original theories. As brains go, it is a damn good one, though I say it myself. Whereas my body, my poor old body, the thing that Landy wants to throw away—well, even you, my dear Mary, will have to agree with me that there is really nothing about *that* which is worth preserving any more.

I was lying on my back eating a grape. Delicious it was, and there were three little seeds in it which I took out of my mouth and placed on the edge of the plate.

"I'm going to do it," I said quietly. "Yes, by God, I'm going to do it. When Landy comes back to see me tomorrow I shall tell him straight out that I'm going to do it."

It was as quick as that. And from then on, I began to feel very much better. I surprised everyone by gobbling an enormous lunch, and shortly after that you came in to visit me as usual.

But how well I looked, you told me. How bright and well and chirpy. Had anything happened? Was there some good news?

Yes, I said, there was. And then, if you remember, I bade you sit down and make yourself comfortable, and I started out immediately to explain to you as gently as I could what was in the wind.

Alas, you would have none of it. I had hardly begun telling you the barest details when you flew into a fury and said that the thing was revolting, disgusting, horrible, unthinkable, and when I tried to go on, you marched out of the room.

Well, Mary, as you know, I have tried to discuss this subject with you many times since then, but you have consistently refused to give me a hearing. Hence this note, and I can only hope that you will have the good sense to permit yourself to read it. It has taken me a long time to write. Two weeks have gone by since I started to scribble the first sentence, and I'm now a good deal weaker than I was then. I doubt I have the strength to say much more. Certainly I won't say goodbye, because there's a chance, just a tiny chance, that if Landy succeeds in his work I may actually *see* you again later, that is if you can bring yourself to come and visit me.

I am giving orders that these pages shall not be delivered to you until a week after I am gone. By now, therefore, as you sit reading them, seven days have already elapsed since Landy did the deed. You yourself may even know what the outcome has been. If you don't, if you have purposely kept yourself apart and have refused to have anything to do with it—which I suspect may be the case—please change your mind now and give Landy a call to see how things went with me. That is the least you can do. I have told him that he may expect to hear from you on the seventh day.

Your faithful husband
William

P.S.   Be good when I am gone, and always remember that it is harder to be a widow than a wife. Do not drink cocktails. Do not waste money. Do not smoke cigarettes. Do not eat pastry. Do not use lipstick. Do not buy a television apparatus. Keep my rose beds and my rockery well weeded in the summers. And incidentally, I suggest that you have the telephone disconnected now that I shall have no further use for it.

W.

Mrs. Pearl laid the last page of the manuscript slowly down on the sofa beside her. Her little mouth was pursed up tight and there was a whiteness around her nostrils.

But really! You would think a widow was entitled to a bit of peace after all these years.

The whole thing was just too awful to think about. Beastly and awful. It gave her the shudders.

She reached for her bag and found herself another cigarette. She lit it, inhaling the smoke deeply and blowing it out in clouds all over the room. Through the smoke she could see her lovely television set, brand new, lustrous, huge, crouching defiantly but also a little self-consciously on top of what used to be William's worktable.

What would he say, she wondered, if he could see that now?

She paused, to remember the last time he had caught her smoking a cigarette. That was about a year ago, and she was sitting in the kitchen by the open window, having a quick one before he came home from work. She'd had the radio on loud playing dance music and she had turned round to pour herself another cup of coffee and there he was standing in the doorway, huge and grim, staring down at her with those awful eyes, a little black dot of fury blazing in the centre of each.

For four weeks after that, he had paid the housekeeping bills himself and given her no money at all, but of course he wasn't to know that she had over six pounds stashed away in a soap-flake carton in the cupboard under the sink.

"What is it?" she had said to him once during supper. "Are you worried about me getting lung cancer?"

"I am not," he had answered.

"Then why can't I smoke?"

"Because I disapprove, that's why."

He had also disapproved of children, and as a result they had never had any of them either.

Where was he now, this William of hers, the great disapprover?

Landy would be expecting her to call up. Did she *have* to call Landy?

Well, not really, no.

She finished her cigarette, then lit another one immediately from the old stub. She looked at the telephone that was sitting on the worktable beside the television set. William had asked her to call,. He had specifically requested that she telephone Landy as soon as she had read the letter. She hesitated, fighting hard now against that old ingrained sense of duty that she didn't quite yet dare to shake off. Then, slowly, she got to her feet and crossed over to the phone on the worktable. She found a number in the book, dialled it, and waited.

"I want to speak to Dr. Landy, please."

"Who is calling?"

"Mrs. Pearl. Mrs. William Pearl."

"One moment, please."

Almost at once, Landy was on the other end of the wire.

"Mrs. Pearl?"

"This is Mrs. Pearl."

There was a slight pause.

"I am so glad you called at last, Mrs. Pearl. You are quite well, I hope?" The voice was quiet, unemotional, courteous. "I wonder if you would care to come over here to the hospital? Then we can have a little chat. I expect you are very eager to know how it all came out."

She didn't answer.

"I can tell you now that everything went pretty smoothly, one way and another. Far better, in fact, than I was entitled to hope. It is not only alive, Mrs. Pearl, it is conscious. It recovered consciousness on the second day. Isn't that interesting?"

She waited for him to go on.

"And the eye is seeing. We are sure of that because we get an immediate change in the deflections on the encephalograph when we hold something up in front of it. And now we're giving it the newspaper to read every day."

"Which newspaper?" Mrs. Pearl asked sharply.

"The Daily Mirror. The headlines are larger."

"He hates *The Mirror*. Give him *The Times*."

There was a pause, then the doctor said, "Very well, Mrs. Pearl. We'll give it *The Times*. We naturally want to do all we can to keep it happy."

"Him," she said. "Not *it*. *Him!"*

"Him," the doctor said. "Yes, I beg your pardon. To keep him happy. That's one reason why I suggested you should come along here as soon as possible. I think it would be good for him to see you. You could indicate how delighted you were to be with him again—smile at him and blow him a kiss and all that sort of thing. It's bound to be a comfort to him to know that you are standing by."

There was a long pause.

"Well," Mrs. Pearl said at last, her voice suddenly very meek and tired, "I suppose I had better come on over and see how he is."

"Good. I knew you would. I'll wait here for you. Come straight up to my office on the second floor. Goodbye."

Half an hour later, Mrs. Pearl was at the hospital.

"You mustn't be surprised by what he looks like," Landy said as he walked beside her down a corridor.

"No, I won't."

"It's bound to be a bit of a shock to you at first. He's not very prepossessing in his present state, I'm afraid."

"I didn't marry him for his looks, Doctor."

Landy turned and stared at her. What a queer little woman this was, he thought, with her large eyes and her sullen, resentful air. Her features, which must have been quite pleasant once, had now gone completely. The mouth was slack, the cheeks loose and flabby, and the whole face gave the impression of having slowly but surely sagged to pieces through years and years of joyless married life. They walked on for a while in silence.

"Take your time when you get inside," Landy said. "He won't know you're in there until you place your face directly above his eye. The eye is always open, but he can't move it at all, so the field of vision is very narrow. At present we have it looking straight up at the ceiling. And of course he can't hear anything. We can talk together as much as we like. It's in here."

Landy opened a door and ushered her into a small square room.

"I wouldn't go too close yet," he said, putting a hand on her arm. "Stay back here a moment with me until you get used to it all."

There was a biggish white enamel bowl about the size of a washbasin standing on a high white table in the centre of the room, and there were half a dozen thin plastic tubes coming out of it. These tubes were connected with a whole lot of glass piping in which you could see the blood flowing to and from the heart machine. The machine itself made a soft rhythmic pulsing sound.

"He's in there," Landy said, pointing to the basin, which was too high for her to see into. "Come just a little closer. Not too near."

He led her two paces forward.

By stretching her neck, Mrs. Pearl could now see the surface of the liquid inside the basin. It was clear and still, and on it there floated a small oval capsule, about the size of a pigeon's egg.

"That's the eye in there," Landy said. "Can you see it?"

"Yes."

"So far as we can tell, it is still in perfect condition. It's his right eye, and the plastic container has a lens on it similar to the one he used in his own spectacles. At this moment he's probably seeing quite as well as he did before."

"The ceiling isn't much to look at," Mrs. Pearl said.

"Don't worry about that. We're in the process of working out a whole programme to keep him amused, but we don't want to go too quickly at first."

"Give him a good book."

"We will, we will. Are you feeling all right, Mrs. Pearl?"

"Yes."

"Then we'll go forward a little more, shall we, and you'll be able to see the whole thing."

He led her forward until they were standing only a couple of yards from the table, and now she could see right down into the basin.

"There you are," Landy said. "That's William."

He was far larger than she had imagined he would be, and darker in colour. With all the ridges and creases running over his surface, he reminded her of nothing so much as an enormous pickled walnut. She could see the stubs of the four big arteries and the two veins coming out from the base of him and the neat way in which they were joined to the plastic tubes; and with each throb of the heart machine, all the tubes gave a little jerk in unison as the blood was pushed through them.

"You'll have to lean over," Landy said, "and put your pretty face right above the eye. He'll see you then, and you can smile at him and blow him a kiss. If I were you I'd say a few nice things as well. He won't actually hear them, but I'm sure he'll get the general idea."

"He hates people blowing kisses at him," Mrs. Pearl said. "I'll do it my own way if you don't mind." She stepped up to the edge of the table, leaned forward until her face was directly over the basin, and looked straight down into William's eye.

"Hallo, dear," she whispered. "It's me—Mary."

The eye, bright as ever, stared back at her with a peculiar, fixed intensity.

"How are you, dear?" she said.

The plastic capsule was transparent all the way round so that the whole of the eyeball was visible. The optic nerve connecting the underside of it to the brain looked like a short length of grey spaghetti.

"Are you feeling all right, William?"

It was a queer sensation peering into her husband's eye when there was no face to go with it. All she had to look at was the eye, and she kept staring at it, and gradually it grew bigger and bigger, and in the end it was the only thing that she could see— a sort of face in itself. There was a network of tiny red veins running over the white surface of the eyeball, and in the ice-blue of the iris there were three or four rather pretty darkish streaks radiating from the pupil in the centre. The pupil was large and black, with a little spark of light reflecting from one side of it.

"I got your letter, dear, and came over at once to see how you were. Dr. Landy says you are doing wonderfully well. Perhaps if I talk slowly you can understand a little of what I am saying by reading my lips."

There was no doubt that the eye was watching her.

"They are doing everything possible to take care of you, dear. This marvellous machine thing here is pumping away all the time and I'm sure it's a lot better than those silly old hearts all the rest of us have. Ours are liable to break down any moment, but yours will go on for ever."

She was studying the eye closely, trying to discover what there was about it that gave it such an unusual appearance.

"You seem fine, dear, just fine. Really you do."

It looked ever so much nicer, this eye, than either of his eyes used to look, she told herself. There was a softness about it somewhere, a calm, kindly quality that she had never seen before. Maybe it had to do with the dot in the very centre, the pupil. William's pupils used always to be tiny black pinheads. They used to glint at you, stabbing into your brain, seeing right through you, and they always knew at once what you were up to and even what you were thinking. But this one she was looking at now was large and soft and gentle, almost cowlike.

"Are you quite sure he's conscious?" she asked, not looking up.

"Oh yes, completely," Landy said.

"And he *can* see me?"

"Perfectly."

"Isn't that marvellous? I expect he's wondering what happened."

"Not at all. He knows perfectly well where he is and why he's there. He can't possibly have forgotten that."

"You mean he *knows* he's in this basin?"

"Of course. And if only he had the power of speech, he would probably be able to carry on a perfectly normal conversation with you this very minute. So far as I can see, there should be absolutely no difference mentally between this William here and the one you used to know back home."

"Good *gracious* me," Mrs. Pearl said, and she paused to consider this intriguing aspect.

You know what, she told herself, looking behind the eye now and staring hard at the great grey pulpy walnut that lay so placidly under the water. I'm not at all sure that I don't prefer him as he is at present. In fact, I believe that I could live very comfortably with this kind of a William. I could cope with this one.

"Quiet, isn't he?" she said.

"Naturally he's quiet."

No arguments and criticisms, she thought, no constant admonitions, no rules to obey, no ban on smoking cigarettes, no pair of cold disapproving eyes watching me over the top of a book in the evenings, no shirts to wash and iron, no meals to cook—nothing but the throb of the heart machine, which was rather a soothing sound anyway and certainly not loud enough to interfere with television.

"Doctor," she said. "I do believe I'm suddenly getting

to feel the most enormous affection for him. Does that sound queer?"

"I think it's quite understandable."

"He looks so helpless and silent lying there under the water in his little basin."

"Yes, I know."

"He's like a baby, that's what he's like. He's exactly like a little baby."

Landy stood still behind her, watching.

"There," she said softly, peering into the basin. "From now on Mary's going to look after you *all* by herself and you've nothing to worry about in the world. When can I have him back home, Doctor?"

"I beg your pardon?"

"I said when can I have him back—back in my own house?"

"You're joking," Landy said.

She turned her head slowly around and looked directly at him. "Why should I joke?" she asked. Her face was bright, her eyes round and bright as two diamonds.

"He couldn't possibly be moved."

"I don't see why not."

"This is an experiment, Mrs. Pearl."

"It's my husband, Dr. Landy."

A funny little nervous half-smile appeared on Landy's mouth. "Well . . ." he said.

"It *is* my husband, you know." There was no anger in her voice. She spoke quietly, as though merely reminding him of a simple fact.

"That's rather a tricky point," Landy said, wetting his lips. "You're a widow now, Mrs. Pearl. I think you must resign yourself to that fact."

She turned away suddenly from the table and crossed over to the window. "I mean it," she said, fishing in her bag for a cigarette. "I want him back."

Landy watched her as she put her cigarette between her

lips and lit it. Unless he were very much mistaken, there was something a bit odd about this woman, he thought. She seemed almost pleased to have her husband over there in the basin.

He tried to imagine what his own feelings would be if it were *his* wife's brain lying there and *her* eye staring up at him out of that capsule.

He wouldn't like it.

"Shall we go back to my room now?" he said.

She was standing by the window, apparently quite calm and relaxed, puffing her cigarette.

"Yes, all right."

On her way past the table she stopped and leaned over the basin once more. "Mary's leaving now, sweetheart," she said. "And don't you worry about a single thing, you understand? We're going to get you right back home where we can look after you properly just as soon as we possibly can. And listen, dear . . ." At this point she paused and carried the cigarette to her lips, intending to take a puff.

Instantly the eye flashed.

She was looking straight into it at the time, and right in the centre of it she saw a tiny but brilliant flash of light, and the pupil contracted into a minute black pinpoint of absolute fury.

At first she didn't move. She stood bending over the basin, holding the cigarette up to her mouth, watching the eye.

Then very slowly, deliberately, she put the cigarette between her lips and took a long suck. She inhaled deeply, and she held the smoke inside her lungs for three or four seconds; then suddenly, *whoosh,* out it came through her nostrils in two thin jets which struck the water in the basin and billowed out over the surface in a thick blue cloud, enveloping the eye.

Landy was over by the door, with his back to her,

waiting. "Come on, Mrs. Pearl," he called.

"Don't look so cross, William," she said softly. "It isn't any good looking cross."

Landy turned his head to see what she was doing.

"Not any more it isn't," she whispered. "Because from now on, my pet, you're going to do just exactly what Mary tells you. Do you understand that?"

"Mrs. Pearl," Landy said, moving toward her.

"So don't be a naughty boy again, will you, my precious," she said, taking another pull at the cigarette. "Naughty boys are liable to get punished most severely nowadays, you ought to know that."

Landy was beside her now, and he took her by the arm and began drawing her firmly but gently away from the table.

"Goodbye, darling," she called. "I'll be back soon."

"That's enough, Mrs. Pearl."

"Isn't he sweet?" she cried, looking up at Landy with big bright eyes. "Isn't he darling? I just can't wait to get him home."

Daniel Keyes

~~~~~~

Flowers for Algernon

progris riport 1—martch 5 1965

Dr. Strauss says I shud rite down what I think and evrey thing that happins to me from now on. I dont know why but he says its importint so they will see if they will use me. I hope they use me. Miss Kinnian says maybe they can make me smart. I want to be smart. My name is Charlie Gordon. I am 37 years old and 2 weeks ago was my brithday. I have nuthing more to rite now so I will close for today.

progris riport 2—march 6

I had a test today. I think I faled it. and I think that maybe now they wont use me. What happind is a nice young man was in the room and he had some white cards with ink spillled all over them. He sed Charlie what do you see on this card. I was very skared even tho I had my rabits foot in my pockit because when I was a kid I always faled tests in school and I spillled ink to.

I told him I saw a inkblot. He said yes and it made me feel good. I thot that was all but when I got up to go he stopped me. He said now sit down Charlie we are not thru yet. Then I dont remember so good but he wantid me to say what was in the ink. I dint see nuthing in the ink but he said there was picturs there other pepul saw some picturs. I coudnt see any picturs. I reely tryed to see. I held the card close up and then far away. Then I said if I had my glases I coud see better I usally only ware my glases in the movies or TV but I said they are in the closit in the hall. I got them. Then I said let me see that card agen I bet Ill find it now.

I tryed hard but I still coudnt find the picturs I only saw the ink. I told him maybe I need new glases. He rote somthing down on a paper and I got skared of faling the test. I told him it was a very nice inkblot with littel points all around the eges. He looked very sad so that wasnt it. I said please let me try agen. Ill get it in a few minits becaus Im not so fast somtimes. Im a slow reeder too in Miss Kinnians class for slow adults but I'm trying very hard.

He gave me a chance with another card that had 2 kinds of ink spillled on it red and blue.

He was very nice and talked slow like Miss Kinnian does and he explained it to me that it was a *raw shok*. He said pepul see things in the ink. I said show me where.

He said think. I told him I think a inkblot but that wasnt rite eather. He said what does it remind you—pretend something. I closd my eyes for a long time to pretend. I told him I pretned a fowntan pen with ink leeking all over a table cloth. Then he got up and went out.

I dont think I passd the *raw shok* test.

progris report 3—march 7

Dr Strauss and Dr Nemur say it dont matter about the inkblots. I told them I dint spill the ink on the cards and I couldn't see anything in the ink. They said that maybe they will still use me. I said Miss Kinnian never gave me tests like that one only spellin and reading. They said Miss Kinnian told that I was her bestist pupil in the adult nite scool becaus I tryed the hardist and I reely wantid to lern. They said how come you went to the adult nite scool all by yourself Charlie. How did you find it. I said I askd pepul and sumbody told me where I shud go to lern to read and spell good. They said why did you want to. I told them becaus all my life I wantid to be smart and not dumb. But its very hard to be smart. They said you know it will probly be tempirery. I said yes. Miss Kinnian told me. I dont care if it herts.

Later I had more crazy tests today. The nice lady who gave it me told me the name and I asked her how do you spellit so I can rite it in my progris riport. THEMATIC APPERCEPTION TEST. I dont know the frist 2 words but I know what *test* means. You got to pass it or you get bad marks. This test lookd easy becaus I coud see the picturs. Only this time she dint want me to tell her the picturs. That mixd me up. I said the man yesterday said I shoud tell him what I saw in the ink she said that dont make no difrence. She said make up storys about the pepul in the picturs.

I told her how can you tell storys about pepul you never

met. I said why shud I make up lies. I never tell lies any more becaus I always get caut.

She told me this test and the other one the raw-shok was for getting personalty. I laffed so hard. I said how can you get that thing from inkblots and fotos. She got sore and put her picturs away. I dont care. It was sily. I gess I faled that test too.

Later some men in white coats took me to a difernt part of the hospitil and gave me a game to play. It was like a race with a white mouse. They called the mouse Algernon. Algernon was in a box with a lot of twists and turns like all kinds of walls and they gave me a pencil and a paper with lines and lots of boxes. On one side it said START and on the other end it said FINISH. They said it was *amazed* and that Algernon and me had the same *amazed* to do. I dint see how we could have the same *amazed* if Algernon had a box and I had a paper but I dint say nothing. Anyway there wasnt time because the race started.

One of the men had a watch he was trying to hide so I wouldnt see it so I tryed not to look and that made me nervus.

Anyway that test made me feel worser than all the others because they did it over 10 times with difernt *amazeds* and Algernon won every time. I dint know that mice were so smart. Maybe thats because Algernon is a white mouse. Maybe white mice are smarter then other mice.

progris riport 4—Mar 8

Their going to use me! Im so exited I can hardly write. Dr Nemur and Dr Strauss had a argament about it first. Dr Nemur was in the office when Dr Strauss brot me in. Dr Nemur was worryed about using me but Dr Strauss told him Miss Kinnian rekemmended me the best from all the people who she was teaching. I like Miss Kinnian becaus shes a very smart teacher. And she said Charlie

your going to have a second chance. If you volenteer for
this experament you mite get smart. They dont know if it
will be perminint but theirs a chance. Thats why I said ok
even when I was scared because she said it was an operashun. She said dont be scared Charlie you done so much
with so little I think you deserv it most of all.

So I got scaird when Dr Nemur and Dr Strauss argud
about it. Dr Strauss said I had something that was very
good. He said I had a good *motor-vation*. I never even
knew I had that. I felt proud when he said that not every
body with an eye-q of 68 had that thing. I dont know what
it is or where I got it but he said Algernon had it too.
Algernons *motor-vation* is the cheese they put in his box.
But it cant be that because I didnt eat any cheese this
week.

Then he told Dr Nemur something I dint understand
so while they were talking I wrote down some of the
words.

He said Dr Nemur I know Charlie is not what you had
in mind as the first of your new brede of intelek**
(coudnt get the word) superman. But most people of his
low ment** are host** and uncoop** they are usualy dull
apath** and hard to reach. He has a good natcher hes
intristed and eager to please.

Dr Nemur said remember he will be the first human
beeng ever to have his intelijence trippled by surgicle
meens.

Dr Strauss said exakly. Look at how well hes lerned
to read and write for his low mentel age its as grate an
acheve** as you and I lerning einstines therey of **vity
without help. That shows the intenss motor-vation. Its
comparat** a tremen** achev** I say we use Charlie.

I dint get all the words and they were talking to fast
but it sounded like Dr Strauss was on my side and like
the other one wasnt.

Then Dr Nemur nodded he said all right maybe your right. We will use Charlie. When he said that I got so exited I jumped up and shook his hand for being so good to me. I told him thank you doc you wont be sorry for giving me a second chance. And I mean it like I told him. After the operashun Im gonna try to be smart. Im gonna try awful hard.

progris ript 5—Mar 10

Im skared. Lots of people who work here and the nurses and the people who gave me the tests came to bring me candy and wish me luck. I hope I have luck. I got my rabits foot and my lucky penny and my horse shoe. Only a black cat crossed me when I was comming to the hospitil. Dr Strauss says dont be supersitis Charlie this is sience. Anyway Im keeping my rabits foot with me.

I asked Dr Strauss if Ill beat Algernon in the race after the operashun and he said maybe. If the operashun works Ill show that mouse I can be as smart as he is. Maybe smarter. Then Ill be abel to read better and spell the words good and know lots of things and be like other people. I want to be smart like other people. If it works perminint they will make everybody smart all over the wurld.

They dint give me anything to eat this morning. I dont know what that eating has to do with getting smart. Im very hungry and Dr Nemur took away my box of candy. That Dr Nemur is a grouch. Dr Strauss says I can have it back after the operashun. You cant eat befor a operashun . . .

Progress Report 6—Mar 15

The operashun dint hurt. He did it while I was sleeping. They took off the bandijis from my eyes and my head today so I can make a PROGRESS REPORT. Dr Nemur who looked

at some of my other ones says I spell PROGRESS wrong
and he told me how to spell it and REPORT too. I got to
try and remember that.

I have a very bad memory for spelling. Dr Strauss says
its ok to tell about all the things that happin to me but he
says I shoud tell more about what I feel and what I think.
When I told him I dont know how to think he said try.
All the time when the bandijis were on my eyes I tryed to
think. Nothing happened. I dont know what to think
about. Maybe if I ask him he will tell me how I can think
now that Im suppose to get smart. What do smart people
think about. Fancy things I suppose. I wish I knew some
fancy things alredy.

Progress Report 7—Mar 19

Nothing is happening. I had lots of tests and different
kinds of races with Algernon. I hate that mouse. He always
beats me. Dr Strauss said I got to play those games. And
he said some time I got to take those tests over again.
Thse inkblots are stupid. And those pictures are stupid
too. I like to draw a picture of a man and a woman but
I wont make up lies about people.

I got a headache from trying to think so much. I thot
Dr Strauss was my frend but he dont help me. He dont
tell me what to think or when Ill get smart. Miss Kinnian
dint come to see me. I think writing these progress reports
are stupid too.

Progress Report 8—Mar 23

Im going back to work at the factery. They said it was
better I shud go back to work but I cant tell anyone what
the operashun was for and I have to come to the hospitil
for an hour evry night after work. They are gonna pay me
mony every month for lerning to be smart.

Im glad Im going back to work because I miss my job

and all my frends and all the fun we have there.

Dr Strauss says I shud keep writing things down but I dont have to do it every day just when I think of something or something speshul happins. He says dont get discoridged because it takes time and it happins slow. He says it took a long time with Algernon before he got 3 times smarter then he was before. Thats why Algernon beats me all the time because he had that operashun too. That makes me feel better. I coud prubly do that *amazed* faster than a reglar mouse. Maybe some day Ill beat Algernon. Boy that would be something. So far Algernon looks like he mite be smart perminent.

Mar 25 (I dont have to write PROGRESS REPORT on top any more just when I hand it in once a week for Dr Nemur to read. I just have to put the date on. That saves time)

We had a lot of fun at the factery today. Joe Carp said hey look where Charlie had his operashun what did they do Charlie put some brains in. I was going to tell him but I remembered Dr Strauss said no. Then Frank Reilly said what did you do Charlie forget your key and open your door the hard way. That made me laff. Their really my friends and they like me.

Sometimes somebody will say hey look at Joe or Frank or George he really pulled a Charlie Gordon. I don't know why they say that but they always laff. This morning Amos Borg who is the 4 man at Donnegans used my name when he shouted at Ernie the office boy. Ernie lost a packige. He said Ernie for godsake what are you trying to be a Charlie Gordon. I dont understand why he said that. I never lost any packiges.

Mar 28 Dr Strauss came to my room tonight to see why I dint come in like I was suppose to. I told him I dont like to race with Algernon any more. He said I dont have

to for a while but I shud come in. He had a present for
me only it wasnt a present but just for lend. I thot it was
a little television but it wasnt. He said I got to turn it on
when I go to sleep. I said your kidding why shud I turn it
on when Im going to sleep. Who ever herd of a thing like
that. But he said if I want to get smart I got to do what
he says. I told him I dint think I was going to get smart
and he put his hand on my sholder and said Charlie
you dont know it yet but your getting smarter all the time.
You wont notice for a while. I think he was just being nice
to make me feel good because I dont look any smarter.

Oh yes I almost forgot. I asked him when I can go back
to the class at Miss Kinnians school. He said I wont go
their. He said that soon Miss Kinnian will come to the
hospitil to start and teach me speshul. I was mad at her
for not comming to see me when I got the operashun but
I like her so maybe we will be frends again.

Mar 29   That crazy TV kept me up all night. How can I
sleep with something yelling crazy things all night in my
ears. And the nutty pictures. Wow. I dont know what it
says when Im up so how am I going to know when Im
sleeping.

Dr Strauss says its ok. He says my brains are lerning
when I sleep and that will help me when Miss Kinnian
starts my lessons in the hospitil (only I found out it isnt a
hospitil its a labatory). I think its all crazy. If you can get
starts my lessons in the hospitl (only I found out it isnt a
That thing I dont think will work. I use to watch the late
show and the late late show on TV all the time and it
never made me smart. Maybe you have to sleep while you
watch it.

PROGRESS REPORT 9—April 3

Dr Strauss showed me how to keep the TV turned low

so now I can sleep. I dont hear a thing. And I still dont understand what it says. A few times I play it over in the morning to find out what I lerned when I was sleeping and I dont think so. Miss Kinnian says Maybe its another langwidge or something. But most times it sounds american. It talks so fast faster than even Miss Gold who was my teacher in 6 grade and I remember she talked so fast I coudnt understand her.

I told Dr Strauss what good is it to get smart in my sleep. I want to be smart when Im awake. He says its the same thing and I have two minds. Theres the *subconscious* and the *conscious* (thats how you spell it). And one dont tell the other one what its doing. They don't even talk to each other. Thats why I dream. And boy have I been having crazy dreams. Wow. Ever since that night TV. The late late late late late show.

I forgot to ask him if it was only me or if everybody had those two minds.

(I just looked up the word in the dictionary Dr Strauss gave me. The word is *subconscious. adj. Of the nature of mental operations yet not present in consciousness; as, subconscious conflict of desires.*) Theres more but I still dont know what it means. This isnt a very good dictionary for dumb people like me.

Anyway the headache is from the party. My frends from the factery Joe Carp and Frank Reilly invited me to go with them to Muggsys Saloon for some drinks. I dont like to drink but they said we will have lots of fun. I had a good time.

Joe Carp said I shoud show the girls how I mop out the toilet in the factory and he got me a mop. I showed them and everyone laffed when I told that Mr Donnegan said I was the best janiter he ever had because I like my job and do it good and never come late or miss a day except for my operashun.

I said Miss Kinnian always said Charlie be proud of

your job because you do it good.

Everybody laffed and we had a good time and they gave me lots of drinks and Joe said Charlie is a card when hes potted. I dont know what that means but everybody likes me and we have fun. I cant wait to be smart like my best frends Joe Carp and Frank Reilly.

I dont remember how the party was over but I think I went out to buy a newspaper and coffe for Joe and Frank and when I came back there was no one their. I looked for them all over till late. Then I dont remember so good but I think I got sleepy or sick. A nice cop brot me back home. Thats what my landlady Mrs Flynn says.

But I got a headache and a big lump on my head and black and blue all over. I think maybe I fell but Joe Carp says it was the cop they beat up drunks some times. I don't think so. Miss Kinnian says cops are to help people. Anyway I got a bad headache and Im sick and hurt all over. I dont think Ill drink anymore.

April 6   I beat Algernon! I dint even know I beat him until Burt the tester told me. Then the second time I lost because I got so exited I fell off the chair before I finished. But after that I beat him 8 more times. I must be getting smart to beat a smart mouse like Algernon. But I dont *feel* smarter.

I wanted to race Algernon some more but Burt said thats enough for one day. They let me hold him for a minit. Hes not so bad. Hes soft like a ball of cotton. He blinks and when he opens his eyes their black and pink on the eges.

I said can I feed him because I felt bad to beat him and I wanted to be nice and make frends. Burt said no Algernon is a very specshul mouse with an operashun like mine, and he was the first of all the animals to stay smart so long. He told me Algernon is so smart that every day he has to solve a test to get his food. Its a thing like a lock on a door that changes every time Algernon goes in to eat so he has to lern something new to get his food. That made me sad because if he couldnt lern he would be hungry.

I dont think its right to make you pass a test to eat. How woud Dr Nemur like it to have to pass a test every time he wants to eat. I think Ill be frends with Algernon.

April 9 Tonight after work Miss Kinnian was at the laboratory. She looked like she was glad to see me but scared. I told her dont worry Miss Kinnian Im not smart yet and she laffed. She said I have confidence in you Charlie the way you struggled so hard to read and right better than all the others. At werst you will have it for a littel wile and your doing somthing for sience.

We are reading a very hard book. I never read such a hard book before. Its called *Robinson Crusoe* about a man who gets merooned on a dessert Iland. Hes smart and figers out all kinds of things so he can have a house and food and hes a good swimmer. Only I feel sorry because hes all alone and has no frends. But I think their must be somebody else on the iland because theres a picture with his funny umbrella looking at footprints. I hope he gets a frend and not be lonely.

April 10 Miss Kinnian teaches me to spell better. She says look at a word and close your eyes and say it over and over until you remember. I have lots of truble with *through* that you say *threw* and *enough* and *tough* that you dont say *enew* and *tew*. You got to say *enuff* and *tuff*. Thats how I use to write it before I started to get smart. Im confused but Miss Kinnian says theres no reason in spelling.

Apr 14 Finished *Robinson Crusoe*. I want to find out more about what happens to him but Miss Kinnian says thats all there is. *Why*

Apr 15   Miss Kinnian says Im lerning fast. She read some of the Progress Reports and she looked at me kind of funny. She says Im a fine person and Ill show them all. I asked her why. She said never mind but I shoudnt feel bad if I find out that everybody isnt nice like I think. She said for a person who god gave so little to you done more then a lot of people with brains they never even used. I said all my frends are smart people but there good. They like me and they never did anything that wasnt nice. Then she got something in her eye and she had to run out to the ladys room.

Apr. 16   Today, I lerned, the *comma*, this is a comma (,) a period, with a tail, Miss Kinnian, says its importent, because, it makes writing better, she said, sombeody, coud lose, a lot of money, if a comma, isnt, in the, right place, I dont have, any money, and I dont see, how a comma, keeps you from losing it.

But she says, everybody, uses commas, so Ill use, them too,

Apr 17   I used the comma wrong. Its punctuation. Miss Kinnian told me to look up long words in the dictionary to lern to spell them. I said whats the difference if you can read it anyway. She said its part of your education so now on I'll look up all the words Im not sure how to spell. It takes a long time to write that way but I think Im remembering. I only have to look up once and after that I get it right. Anyway thats how come I got the word *punctuation* right. (Its that way in the dictionary). Miss Kinnian says a period is punctuation too, and there are lots of other marks to lern. I told her I thot all the periods had to have tails but she said no.

You got to mix them up, she showed? me" how. to mix! them(up,. and now; I can! mix up all kinds" of punctuation, in! my writing? There, are lots! of rules? to lern; but Im gettin'g them in my head.

One thing I? like about, Dear Miss Kinnian: (thats the way it goes in a business letter if I ever go into business) is she, always gives me' a reason" when—I ask. She's a gen'ius! I wish! I cou'd be smart' like, her;

(Punctuation, is; fun!)

Apr 18 What a dope I am! I didn't even understand what she was talking about. I read the grammar book last night and it explanes the whole thing. Then I saw it was the same way as Miss Kinnian was trying to tell me, but I didn't get it. I got up in the middle of the night, and the whole thing straightened out in my mind.

Miss Kinnian said that the TV working in my sleep helped out. She said I reached a plateau. Thats like the flat top of a hill.

After I figgered out how punctuation worked, I read over all my old Progress Reports from the beginning. Boy, did I have crazy spelling and punctuation! I told Miss Kinnian I ought to go over the pages and fix all the mistakes but she said, "No, Charlie, Dr. Nemur wants them just as they are. That's why he let you keep them after they were photostated, to see your own progress. You're coming along fast, Charlie."

That made me feel good. After the lesson I went down and played with Algernon. We don't race any more.

April 20 I feel sick inside. Not sick like for a doctor, but inside my chest it feels empty like getting punched and a heartburn at the same time.

I wasn't going to write about it, but I guess I got to, because it's important. Today was the first time I ever stayed home from work.

Last night Joe Carp and Frank Reilly invited me to a party. There were lots of girls and some men from the factory. I remembered how sick I got last time I drank too much, so I told Joe I didn't want anything to drink. He gave me a plain Coke instead. It tasted funny, but I thought it was just a bad taste in my mouth.

We had a lot of fun for a while. Joe said I should dance with Ellen and she would teach me the steps. I fell a few times and I couldn't understand why because no one else was dancing besides Ellen and me. And all the time I was tripping because somebody's foot was always sticking out.

Then when I got up I saw the look on Joe's face and it gave me a funny feeling in my stomack. "He's a scream," one of the girls said. Everybody was laughing.

Frank said, "I ain't laughed so much since we sent him off for the newspaper that night at Muggsy's and ditched him."

"Look at him. His face is red."

"He's blushing. Charlie is blushing."

"Hey, Ellen, what'd you do to Charlie? I never saw him act like that before."

I didn't know what to do or where to turn. Everyone was looking at me and laughing and I felt naked. I wanted to hide myself. I ran out into the street and I threw up. Then I walked home. It's a funny thing I never knew that Joe and Frank and the others liked to have me around all the time to make fun of me.

Now I know what it means when they say "to pull a Charlie Gordon."

I'm ashamed.

PROGRESS REPORT 11

April 21 Still didn't go into the factory. I told Mrs. Flynn my landlady to call and tell Mr. Donnegan I was sick. Mrs. Flynn looks at me very funny lately like she's scared of me.

I think it's a good thing about finding out how everybody laughs at me. I thought about it a lot. It's because I'm so dumb and I don't even know when I'm doing something dumb. People think it's funny when a dumb person can't do things the same way they can.

Anyway, now I know I'm getting smarter every day. I know punctuation and I can spell good. I like to look up all the hard words in the dictionary and I remember them. I'm reading a lot now, and Miss Kinnian says I read very fast. Sometimes I even understand what I'm reading about, and it stays in my mind. There are times when I can close my eyes and think of a page and it all comes back like a picture.

Besides history, geography, and arithmetic, Miss Kinnian said I should start to learn a few foreign languages. Dr. Strauss gave me some more tapes to play while I sleep. I still don't understand how that conscious and unconscious mind works, but Dr. Strauss says not to worry yet. He asked me to promise that when I start learning college subjects next week I wouldn't read any books on psychology—that is, until he gives me permission.

I feel a lot better today, but I guess I'm still a little angry that all the time people were laughing and making fun of me because I wasn't so smart. When I become intelligent like Dr. Strauss says, with three times my I.Q. of 68, then maybe I'll be like everyone else and people will like me and be friendly.

I'm not sure what an I.Q. is. Dr. Nemur said it was something that measured how intelligent you were—like a scale in the drug-store weighs pounds. But Dr. Strauss had a big argument with him and said an I.Q. didn't weigh intelligence at all. He said an I.Q. showed how much intelligence you could get, like the numbers on the outside of a measuring cup. You still had to fill the cup up with stuff.

Then when I asked Burt, who gives me my intelligence

tests and works with Algernon, he said that both of them were wrong (only I had to promise not to tell them he said so).

Burt says that the I.Q. measures a lot of different things including some of the things you learned already, and it really isn't any good at all.

So I still don't know what I.Q. is except that mine is going to be over 200 soon. I didn't want to say anything, but I don't see how if they don't know *what* it is, or *where* it is—I don't see how they know *how much* of it you've got.

Dr. Nemur says I have to take a *Rorshach Test* tomorrow. I wonder what *that* is.

April 22 I found out what a *Rorshach* is. It's the test I took before the operation—the one with the inkblots on the pieces of cardboard. The man who gave me the test was the same one.

I was scared to death of those inkblots. I knew he was going to ask me to find the pictures and I knew I wouldn't be able to. I was thinking to myself, if only there was some way of knowing what kind of pictures were hidden there. Maybe there weren't any pictures at all. Maybe it was just a trick to see if I was dumb enough to look for something that wasn't there. Just thinking about that made me sore at him.

"All right, Charlie," he said, "you've seen these cards before, remember?"

"Of course I remember."

The way I said it, he knew I was angry, and he looked surprised. "Yes, of course. Now I want you to look at this one. What might this be? What do you see on this card? People see all sorts of things in these inkblots. Tell me what it might be for you—what it makes you think of."

I was shocked. That wasn't what I had expected him to

say at all. "You mean there are no pictures hidden in those inkblots?"

He frowned and took off his glasses. "What?"

"Pictures. Hidden in the inkblots. Last time you told me that everyone could see them and you wanted me to find them too."

He explained to me that the last time he had used almost the exact same words he was using now. I didn't believe it, and I still have the suspicion that he misled me at the time just for the fun of it. Unless—I don't know any more—could I have been *that* feebleminded?

We went through the cards slowly. One of them looked like a pair of bats tugging at something. Another one looked like two men fencing with swords. I imagined all sorts of things. I guess I got carried away. But I didn't trust him any more, and I kept turning them around and even looking on the back to see if there was anything there I was supposed to catch. While he was making his notes, I peeked out of the corner of my eye to read it. But it was all in code that looked like this:

WF + A DdF-Ad orig. WF-A SF + obj

The test still doesn't make sense to me. It seems to me that anyone could make up lies about things that they didn't really see. How could he know I wasn't making a fool of him by mentioning things that I didn't really imagine? Maybe I'll understand it when Dr. Strauss lets me read up on psychology.

April 25 I figured out a new way to line up the machines in the factory, and Mr. Donnegan says it will save him ten thousand dollars a year in labor and increased production. He gave me a twenty-five-dollar bonus.

I wanted to take Joe Carp and Frank Reilly out to lunch to celebrate, but Joe said he had to buy some things for his wife, and Frank said he was meeting his cousin for lunch. I guess it'll take a little time for them to get used to the changes in me. Everybody seems to be frightened of me. When I went over to Amos Borg and tapped him on the shoulder, he jumped up in the air.

People don't talk to me much any more or kid around the way they used to. It makes the job kind of lonely.

April 27 I got up the nerve today to ask Miss Kinnian to have dinner with me tomorrow night to celebrate my bonus.

At first she wasn't sure it was right, but I asked Dr. Strauss and he said it was okay. Dr. Strauss and Dr. Nemur don't seem to be getting along so well. They're arguing all the time. This evening when I came in to ask Dr. Strauss about having dinner with Miss Kinnian, I heard them shouting. Dr. Nemur was saying that it was *his* experiment and *his* research, and Dr. Strauss was shouting back that he contributed just as much, because he found me through Miss Kinnian and he performed the operation. Dr. Strauss said that someday thousands of neurosurgeons might be using his technique all over the world.

Dr. Nemur wanted to publish the results of the experiment at the end of this month. Dr. Strauss wanted to wait a while longer to be sure. Dr. Strauss said that Dr. Nemur was more interested in the Chair of Psychology at Princeton than he was in the experiment. Dr. Nemur said that Dr. Strauss was nothing but an opportunist who was trying to ride to glory on *his* coattails.

When I left afterwards, I found myself trembling. I don't know why for sure, but it was as if I'd seen both men clearly for the first time. I remember hearing Burt say that Dr. Nemur had a shrew of a wife who was pushing him all the time to get things published so that he could become famous. Burt said that the dream of her life was to have a big-shot husband.

Was Dr. Strauss really trying to ride on his coattails?

April 28 I don't understand why I never noticed how beautiful Miss Kinnian really is. She has brown eyes and feathery brown hair that comes to the top of her neck. She's only thirty-four! I think from the beginning I had the feeling that she was an unreachable genius—and very, very old. Now, every time I see her she grows younger and more lovely.

We had dinner and a long talk. When she said that I was coming along so fast that soon I'd be leaving her behind, I laughed.

"It's true, Charlie. You're already a better reader than I am. You can read a whole page at a glance while I can take in only a few lines at a time. And you remember every single thing you read. I'm lucky if I can recall the main thoughts and the general meaning."

"I don't feel intelligent. There are so many things I don't understand."

She took out a cigarette and I lit it for her. "You've got to be a *little* patient. You're accomplishing in days and weeks what it takes normal people to do in half a lifetime. That's what makes it so amazing. You're like a giant sponge now, soaking things in. Facts, figures, general knowledge. And soon you'll begin to connect them, too. You'll see how the different branches of learning are related. There are many levels, Charlie, like steps on a giant ladder that take you up higher and higher to see more and more of the world around you.

"I can see only a little bit of that, Charlie, and I won't go much higher than I am now, but you'll keep climbing up and up, and see more and more, and each step will open new worlds that you never even knew existed." She frowned. "I hope . . . I just hope to God——"

"What?"

"Never mind, Charles. I just hope I wasn't wrong to

advise you to go into this thing in the first place."

I laughed. "How could that be? It worked, didn't it? Even Algernon is still smart."

We sat there silently for a while and I knew what she was thinking about as she watched me toying with the chain of my rabbit's foot and my keys. I didn't want to think of that possibility any more than elderly people want to think of death. I *knew* that this was only the beginning. I knew what she meant about levels because I'd seen some of them already. The thought of leaving her behind made me sad.

I'm in love with Miss Kinnian.

PROGRESS REPORT 12

April 30 I've quit my job with Donnegan's Plastic Box Company. Mr. Donnegan insisted that it would be better for all concerned if I left. What did I do to make them hate me so?

The first I knew of it was when Mr. Donnegan showed me the petition. Eight hundred and forty names, everyone connected with the factory, except Fanny Girden. Scanning the list quickly, I saw at once that hers was the only missing name. All the rest demanded that I be fired.

Joe Carp and Frank Reilly wouldn't talk to me about it. No one else would either, except Fanny. She was one of the few people I'd known who set her mind to something and believed it no matter what the rest of the world proved, said, or did—and Fanny did not believe that I should have been fired. She had been against the petition on principle and despite the pressure and threats she'd held out.

"Which don't mean to say," she remarked, "that I don't think there's something mighty strange about you, Charlie. Them changes. I don't know. You used to be a good, dependable, ordinary man—not too bright maybe, but honest. Who knows what you done to yourself to get so smart all of a sudden. Like everybody around here's been saying, Charlie, it's not right."

"But how can you say that, Fanny? What's wrong with a man becoming intelligent and wanting to acquire knowledge and understanding of the world around him?"

She stared down at her work and I turned to leave. Without looking at me, she said: "It was evil when Eve listened to the snake and ate from the tree of knowledge. It was evil when she saw that she was naked. If not for that none of us would ever have to grow old and sick, and die."

Once again now I have the feeling of shame burning inside me. This intelligence has driven a wedge between me and all the people I once knew and loved. Before, they laughed at me and despised me for my ignorance and dullness; now, they hate me for my knowledge and understanding. What in God's name do they want of me?

They've driven me out of the factory. Now I'm more alone than ever before . . .

May 15 Dr. Strauss is very angry at me for not having written any progress reports in two weeks. He's justified because the lab is now paying me a regular salary. I told him I was too busy thinking and reading. When I pointed out that writing was such a slow process that it made me impatient with my poor handwriting, he suggested that I learn to type. It's much easier to write now because I can type nearly seventy-five words a minute. Dr. Strauss continually reminds me of the need to speak and write simply so that people will be able to understand me.

I'll try to review all the things that happened to me during the last two weeks. Algernon and I were presented to the American Psychological Association sitting in convention with the World Psychological Association last

Tuesday. We created quite a sensation. Dr. Nemur and Dr. Strauss were proud of us.

I suspect that Dr. Nemur, who is sixty—ten years older than Dr. Strauss—finds it necessary to see tangible results of his work. Undoubtedly the result of pressure by Mrs. Nemur.

Contrary to my earlier impressions of him, I realize that Dr. Nemur is not at all a genius. He has a very good mind, but it struggles under the specter of self-doubt. He wants people to take him for a genius. Therefore, it is important for him to feel that his work is accepted by the world. I believe that Dr. Nemur was afraid of further delay because he worried that someone else might make a discovery along these lines and take the credit from him.

Dr. Strauss on the other hand might be called a genius, although I feel that his areas of knowledge are too limited. He was educated in the tradition of narrow specialization; the broader aspects of background were neglected far more than necessary—even for a neurosurgeon.

I was shocked to learn that the only ancient languages he could read were Latin, Greek, and Hebrew, and that he knows almost nothing of mathematics beyond the elementary levels of the calculus of variations. When he admitted this to me, I found myself almost annoyed. It was as if he'd hidden this part of himself in order to deceive me, pretending—as do many people I've discovered—to be what he is not. No one I've ever known is what he appears to be on the surface.

Dr. Nemur appears to be uncomfortable around me. Sometimes when I try to talk to him, he just looks at me strangely and turns away. I was angry at first when Dr. Strauss told me I was giving Dr. Nemur an inferiority complex. I thought he was mocking me and I'm oversensitive at being made fun of.

How was I to know that a highly respected psychoexperimentalist like Nemur was unacquainted with Hindu-

stani and Chinese? It's absurd when you consider the
work that is being done in India and China today in the
very field of his study.

I asked Dr. Strauss how Nemur could refute Rahaja-
mati's attack on his method and results if Nemur couldn't
even read them in the first place. That strange look on
Dr. Strauss' face can mean only one of two things. Either
he doesn't want to tell Nemur what they're saying in India,
or else—and this worries me—Dr. Strauss doesn't know
either. I must be careful to speak and write clearly and
simply so that people won't laugh.

May 18 I am very disturbed. I saw Miss Kinnian last night
for the first time in over a week. I tried to avoid all dis-
cussions of intellectual concepts and to keep the conversation on a simple, everyday level, but she just stared at
me blankly and asked me what I meant about the mathematical variance equivalent in Dorbermann's *Fifth Con-
certo*.

When I tried to explain she stopped me and laughed. I
guess I got angry, but I suspect I'm approaching her on
the wrong level. No matter what I try to discuss with her,
I am unable to communicate. I must review Vrostadt's
equations on *Levels of Semantic Progression*. I find that I
don't communicate with people much any more. Thank
God for books and music and things I can think about. I
am alone in my apartment at Mrs. Flynn's boardinghouse
most of the time and seldom speak to anyone.

May 20 I would not have noticed the new dishwasher, a
boy of about sixteen, at the corner diner where I take my
evening meals if not for the incident of the broken dishes.

They crashed to the floor, shattering and sending bits of
white china under the tables. The boy stood there, dazed
and frightened, holding the empty tray in his hand. The
whistles and catcalls from the customers (the cries of

"hey, there go the profits!" . . . *"Mazeltov!"* . . . and "well, *he* didn't work here very long . . ." which invariably seems to follow the breaking of glass or dishware in a public restaurant) all seemed to confuse him.

When the owner came to see what the excitement was about, the boy cowered as if he expected to be struck and threw up his arms as if to ward off the blow.

"All right! All right, you dope," shouted the owner, "don't just stand there! Get the broom and sweep that mess up. A broom . . . a broom, you idiot! It's in the kitchen. Sweep up all the pieces."

The boy saw that he was not going to be punished. His frightened expression disappeared and he smiled and hummed as he came back with the broom to sweep the floor. A few of the rowdier customers kept up the remarks, amusing themselves at his expense.

"Here, sonny, over here there's a nice piece behind you . . ."

"C'mon, do it again . . ."

"He's not so dumb. It's easier to break 'em than to wash 'em . . ."

As his vacant eyes moved across the crowd of amused onlookers, he slowly mirrored their smiles and finally broke into an uncertain grin at the joke which he obviously did not understand.

I felt sick inside as I looked at his dull, vacuous smile, the wide, bright eyes of a child, uncertain but eager to please. They were laughing at him because he was mentally retarded.

And I had been laughing at him too.

Suddenly, I was furious at myself and all those who were smirking at him. I jumped up and shouted, "Shut up! Leave him alone! It's not his fault he can't understand! He can't help what he is! But for God's sake . . . he's still a human being!"

The room grew silent. I cursed myself for losing control

and creating a scene. I tried not to look at the boy as I paid my check and walked out without touching my food. I felt ashamed for both of us.

How strange it is that people of honest feelings and sensibility, who would not take advantage of a man born without arms or legs or eyes—how such people think nothing of abusing a man born with low intelligence. It infuriated me to think that not too long ago I, like this boy, had foolishly played the clown.

And I had almost forgotten.

I'd hidden the picture of the old Charlie Gordon from myself because now that I was intelligent it was something that had to be pushed out of my mind. But today in looking at that boy, for the first time I saw what I had been. *I was just like him!*

Only a short time ago, I learned that people laughed at me. Now I can see that unknowingly I joined with them in laughing at myself. That hurts most of all.

I have often reread my progress reports and seen the illiteracy, the childish naïveté, the mind of low intelligence peering from a dark room, through the keyhole, at the dazzling light outside. I see that even in my dullness I knew that I was inferior, and that other people had something I lacked—something denied me. In my mental blindness, I thought that it was somehow connected with the ability to read and write, and I was sure that if I could get those skills I would automatically have intelligence too.

Even a feeble-minded man wants to be like other men.

A child may not know how to feed itself, or what to eat, yet it knows of hunger.

This then is what I was like, I never knew. Even with my gift of intellectual awareness, I never really knew.

This day was good for me. Seeing the past more clearly, I have decided to use my knowledge and skills to work in the field of increasing human intelligence levels. Who is better equipped for this work? Who else has lived in both worlds? These are my people. Let me use my gift to do something for them.

Tomorrow, I will discuss with Dr. Strauss the manner in which I can work in this area. I may be able to help him work out the problems of widespread use of the technique which was used on me. I have several good ideas of my own.

There is so much that might be done with this technique. If I could be made into a genius, what about thousands of others like myself? What fantastic levels might be achieved by using this technique on normal people? On *geniuses*?

There are so many doors to open. I am impatient to begin.

PROGRESS REPORT 13

May 23 It happened today. Algernon bit me. I visited the lab to see him as I do occasionally, and when I took him out of his cage, he snapped at my hand. I put him back and watched him for a while. He was unusually disturbed and vicious.

May 24 Burt, who is in charge of the experimental animals, tells me that Algernon is changing. He is less cooperative, he refuses to run the maze any more; general motivation has decreased. And he hasn't been eating. Everyone is upset about what this may mean.

May 25 They've been feeding Algernon, who now refuses to work the shifting-lock problem. Everyone identifies me with Algernon. In a way we're both the first of our kind. They're all pretending that Algernon's behavior is not necessarily significant for me. But it's hard to hide the fact that some of the other animals who were used in this experiment are showing strange behavior.

Dr. Strauss and Dr. Nemur have asked me not to come to the lab any more. I know what they're thinking but I can't accept it. I am going ahead with my plans to carry their research forward. With all due respect to both of these fine scientists. I am well aware of their limitations. If there is an answer, I'll have to find it out for myself. Suddenly, time has become very important to me.

May 29   I have been given a lab of my own and permission to go ahead with the research. I'm on to something. Working day and night. I've had a cot moved into the lab. Most of my writing time is spent on the notes which I keep in a separate folder, but from time to time I feel it necessary to put down my moods and my thoughts out of sheer habit.

I find the *calculus of intelligence* to be a fascinating study. Here is the place for the application of all the knowledge I have acquired. In a sense it's the problem I've been concerned with all my life.

May 31   Dr. Strauss thinks I'm working too hard. Dr. Nemur says I'm trying to cram a lifetime of research and thought into a few weeks. I know I should rest, but I'm driven on by something inside that won't let me stop. I've got to find the reason for the sharp regression in Algernon. I've got to know *if* and *when* it will happen to me.

June 4

LETTER TO DR. STRAUSS *(copy)*
Dear Dr. Strauss:
  Under separate cover I am sending you a copy of my report entitled, "The Algernon-Gordon Effect: A Study of Structure and Function of Increased Intelligence," which I would like to have you read and have published.
  As you see, my experiments are completed. I have included in my report all of my formulae, as well as

mathematical analysis in the appendix. Of course, these should be verified.

Because of its importance to both you and Dr. Nemur (and need I say to myself, too?) I have checked and rechecked my results a dozen times in the hope of finding an error. I am sorry to say the results must stand. Yet for the sake of science, I am grateful for the little bit that I here add to the knowledge of the function of the human mind and of the laws governing the artificial increase of human intelligence.

I recall your once saying to me that an experimental *failure* or the *disproving* of a theory was as important to the advancement of learning as a success would be. I know now that this is true. I am sorry, however, that my own contribution to the field must rest upon the ashes of the work of two men I regard so highly.

                                        Yours truly,
                                        Charles Gordon
encl.: rept.

June 5   I must not become emotional. The facts and the results of my experiments are clear, and the more sensational aspects of my own rapid climb cannot obscure the fact that the tripling of intelligence by the surgical technique developed by Drs. Strauss and Nemur must be viewed as having little or no practical applicability (at the present time) to the increase of human intelligence.

As I review the records and data on Algernon, I see that although he is still in his physical infancy, he has regressed mentally. Motor activity is impaired; there is a general reduction of glandular activity; there is an accelerated loss of co-ordination.

There are also strong indications of progressive amnesia.

As will be seen by my report, these and other physical and mental deterioration syndromes can be predicted with statistically significant results by the application of my formula.

The surgical stimulus to which we were both subjected has resulted in an intensification and acceleration of all mental processes. The unforeseen development, which I have taken the liberty of calling the *Algernon-Gordon Effect*, is the logical extension of the entire intelligence speed-up. The hypothesis here proven may be described simply in the following terms: Artificially increased intelligence deteriorates at a rate of time directly proportional to the quantity of the increase.

I feel that this, in itself, is an important discovery.

As long as I am able to write, I will continue to record my thoughts in these progress reports. It is one of my few pleasures. However, by all indications, my own mental deterioration will be very rapid.

I have already begun to notice signs of emotional instability and forgetfulness, the first symptoms of the burnout.

June 10 Deterioration progressing. I have become absent-minded. Algernon died two days ago. Dissection shows my predictions were right. His brain had decreased in weight and there was a general smoothing out of cerebral convolutions as well as a deepening and broadening of brain fissures.

I guess the same thing is or will soon be happening to me. Now that it's definite, I don't want it to happen.

I put Algernon's body in a cheese box and buried him in the back yard. I cried.

June 15 Dr. Strauss came to see me again. I wouldn't open the door and I told him to go away. I want to be left to myself. I have become touchy and irritable. I feel the darkness closing in. It's hard to throw off thoughts of suicide. I keep telling myself how important this introspective journal will be.

It's a strange sensation to pick up a book that you've

read and enjoyed just a few months ago and discover that you don't remember it. I remembered how great I thought John Milton was, but when I picked up *Paradise Lost* I couldn't understand it at all. I got so angry I threw the book across the room.

I've got to try to hold on to some of it. Some of the things I've learned. Oh, God, please don't take it all away.

June 19   Sometimes, at night, I go out for a walk. Last night I couldn't remember where I lived. A policeman took me home. I have the strange feeling that this has all happened to me before—a long time ago. I keep telling myself I'm the only person in the world who can describe what's happening to me.

June 21   Why can't I remember? I've got to fight. I lie in bed for days and I don't know who or where I am. Then it all comes back to me in a flash. Fugues of amnesia. Symptoms of senility—second childhood. I can watch them coming on. It's so cruelly logical. I learned so much and so fast. Now my mind is deteriorating rapidly. I won't let it happen. I'll fight it. I can't help thinking of the boy in the restaurant, the blank expression, the silly smile, the people laughing at him. No—please—not that again . . .

June 22   I'm forgetting things that I learned recently. It seems to be following the classic pattern—the last things learned are the first things forgotten. Or is that the pattern? I'd better look it up again. . . .

I reread my paper on the *Algernon-Gordon Effect* and I get the strange feeling that it was written by someone else. There are parts I don't even understand.

Motor activity impaired. I keep tripping over things, and it becomes increasingly difficult to type.

June 23   I've given up using the typewriter completely.

My co-ordination is bad. I feel that I'm moving slower and slower. Had a terrible shock today. I picked up a copy of an article I used in my research, Krueger's *Uber psychische Ganzheit*, to see if it would help me understand what I had done. First I thought there was something wrong with my eyes. Then I realized I could no longer read German. I tested myself in other languages. All gone.

June 30 A week since I dare to write again. It's slipping away like sand through my fingers. Most of the books I have are too hard for me now. I get angry with them because I know that I read and understood them just a few weeks ago.

I keep telling myself I must keep writing these reports so that somebody will know what is happening to me. But it gets harder to form the words and remember spellings. I have to look up even simple words in the dictionary now and it makes me impatient with myself.

Dr. Strauss comes around almost every day, but I told him I wouldn't see or speak to anybody. He feels guilty. They all do. But I don't blame anyone. I knew what might happen. But how it hurts.

July 7 I don't know where the week went. Todays Sunday I know becuase I can see through my window people going to church. I think I stayed in bed all week but I remember Mrs. Flynn bringing food to be a few times. I keep saying over and over Ive got to do something but then I forget or maybe its just easier not to do what I say Im going to do.

I think of my mother and father a lot these days. I found a picture of them with me taken at a beach. My father has a big ball under his arm and my mother is holding me by the hand. I dont remember them the way they are in the picture. All I remember is my father drunk most of the time and arguing with mom about money.

He never shaved much and he used to scratch my face when he hugged me. My mother said he died but Cousin Miltie said he heard his mom and dad say that my father ran away with another woman. When I asked my mother she slapped my face and said my father was dead. I dont think I ever found out which was true but I don't care much. (He said he was going to take me to see cows on a farm once but he never did. He never kept his promises . . .)

July 10 My landlady Mrs Flynn is very worried about me. She says the way I lay around all day and dont do anything I remind her of her son before she threw him out of the house. She said she doesn't like loafers. If Im sick its one thing, but if Im a loafer thats another thing and she wont have it. I told her I think Im sick.

I try to read a little bit every day, mostly stories, but sometimes I have to read the same thing over and over again because I dont know what it means. And its hard to write. I know I should look up all the words in the dictionary but its so hard and Im so tired all the time.

Then I got the idea that I would only use the easy words instead of the long hard ones. That saves time. I put flowers on Algernons grave about once a week. Mrs Flynn thinks Im crazy to put flowers on a mouses grave but I told her that Algernon was special.

July 14 Its sunday again. I dont have anything to do to keep me busy now because my television set is broke and I dont have any money to get it fixed. (I think I lost this months check from the lab. I dont remember)

I get awful headaches and asperin doesnt help me much. Mrs Flynn knows Im really sick and she feels very sorry for me. Shes a wonderful woman whenever someone is sick.

July 22 Mrs Flynn called a strange doctor to see me. She was afraid I was going to die. I told the doctor I wasnt too sick and that I only forget sometimes. He asked me did I have any friends or relatives and I said no I dont have any. I told him I had a friend called Algernon once but he was a mouse and we used to run races together. He looked at me kind of funny like he thought I was crazy.

He smiled when I told him I used to be a genius. He talked to me like I was a baby and he winked at Mrs. Flynn. I got mad and chased him out because he was making fun of me the way they all used to.

July 24 I have no more money and Mrs Flynn says I got to go to work somewhere and pay the rent because I havent paid for over two months. I dont know any work but the job I used to have at Donnegans Plastic Box Company. I dont want to go back there because they all knew me when I was smart and maybe theyll laugh at me. But I don't know what else to do to get money.

July 25 I was looking at some of my old progress reports and its very funny but I cant read what I wrote. I can make out some of the words but they dont make sense.

Miss Kinnian came to the door but I said go away I dont want to see you. She cried and I cried too but I wouldnt let her in because I didn't want her to laugh at me. I told her I didn't like her any more. I told her I didnt want to be smart any more. Thats not true. I still love her and I still want to be smart but I had to say that so shed go away. She gave Mrs Flynn money to pay the rent. I dont want that. I got to get a job.

Please . . . please let me not forget how to read and write . . .

July 27   Mr Donnegan was very nice when I came back and asked him for my old job of janitor. First he was very suspicious but I told him what happened to me then he looked very sad and put his hand on my shoulder and said Charlie Gordon you got guts.

Everybody looked at me when I came downstairs and started working in the toilet sweeping it out like I used to. I told myself Charlie if they make fun of you dont get sore because you remember their not so smart as you once thot they were. And besides they were once your friends and if they laughed at you that doesnt mean anything because they liked you too.

One of the new men who came to work there after I went away made a nasty crack he said hey Charlie I hear your a very smart fella a real quiz kid. Say something intelligent. I felt bad but Joe Carp came over and grabbed him by the shirt and said leave him alone you lousy cracker or Ill break your neck. I didn't expect Joe to take my part so I guess hes really my friend.

Later Frank Reilly came over and said Charlie if anybody bothers you or trys to take advantage you call me or Joe and we will set em straight. I said thanks Frank and I got choked up so I had to turn around and go into the supply room so he wouldn't see me cry. Its good to have friends.

July 28   I did a dumb thing today I forgot I wasnt in Miss Kinnians class at the adult center any more like I use to be. I went in and sat down in my old seat in the back of the room and she looked at me funny and she said Charles. I dint remember she ever called me that before only Charlie so I said hello Miss Kinnian Im redy for my lesin today only I lost my reader that we was using. She started to cry and run out of the room and everybody looked at me and I saw they wasnt the same pepul who used to be in my class.

Then all of a sudden I remembered some things about the operashun and me getting smart and I said holy smoke I reely pulled a Charlie Gordon that time. I went away before she come back to the room.

Thats why Im going away from New York for good. I dont want to do nothing like that agen. I dont want Miss Kinnian to feel sorry for me. Evry body feels sorry at the factery and I dont want that eather so Im going someplace where nobody knows that Charlie Gordon was once a genus and how he cant even reed a book or rite good.

Im taking a cuple of books along and even if I cant reed them Ill practise hard and maybe I wont forget every thing I lerned. If I try reel hard maybe Ill be a littel bit smarter then I was before the operashun. I got my rabits foot and my luky penny and maybe they will help me.

If you ever reed this Miss Kinnian dont be sorry for me Im glad I got a second chanse to be smart becaus I lerned a lot of things that I never even new were in this world and Im grateful that I saw it all for a littel bit. I dont know why Im dumb agen or what I did wrong maybe its becaus I dint try hard enuff. But if I try and practis very hard maybe Ill get a littl smarter and know what all the words are. I remember a littel bit how nice I had a feeling with the blue book that has the torn cover when I red it. Thats why Im gonna keep trying to get smart so I can have that feeling agen. Its a good feeling to know things and be smart. I wish I had it rite now if I did I would sit down and reed all the time. Anyway I bet Im the first dumb person in the world who ever found out somthing importent for sience. I remember I did somthing but I dont remember what. So I gess its like I did it for all the dumb pepul like me.

Good-by Miss Kinnian and Dr Strauss and evreybody. And P.S. please tell Dr Nemur not to be such a grouch when pepul laff at him and he would have more frends.

Its easy to make frends if you let pepul laff at you. Im going to have lots of frends where I go.

P.P.S. Please if you get a chanse put some flowrs on Algernon's grave in the bak yard . . .

Damon Knight

The Country of the Kind

The attendant at the car lot was daydreaming when I pulled up—a big, lazy-looking man in black satin chequered down the front. I was wearing scarlet, myself; it suited my mood. I got out, almost on his toes.

"Park or storage?" he asked automatically, turning around. Then he realized who I was, and ducked his head away.

"Neither," I told him.

There was a hand torch on a shelf in the repair shed right behind him. I got it and came back. I knelt down to where I could reach behind the front wheel, and ignited the torch. I turned it on the axle and suspension. They glowed cherry red, then white, and fused together. Then I got up and turned the flame on both tires until the rubberoid stank and sizzled and melted down to the pavement. The attendant didn't say anything.

I left him there, looking at the mess on his nice clean concrete.

It had been a nice car, too; but I could get another any time. And I felt like walking. I went down the winding road, sleepy in the afternoon sunlight, dappled with shade and smelling of cool leaves. You couldn't see the houses; they were all sunken or hidden by shrubbery, or a little of both. That was the fad I'd heard about; it was what I'd come here to see. Not that anything the dulls did would be worth looking at.

I turned off at random and crossed a rolling lawn, went through a second hedge of hawthorn in blossom, and came out next to a big sunken games court.

The tennis net was up, and two couples were going at it, just working up a little sweat—young, about half my age, all four of them. Three dark-haired people, one blonde. They were evenly matched, and both couples played well together; they were enjoying themselves.

I watched for a minute. But by then the nearest two were beginning to sense I was there, anyhow. I walked down onto the court, just as the blonde was about to serve. She looked at me frozen across the net, poised on tiptoe. The others stood.

"Off," I told them. "Game's over."

I watched the blonde. She was not especially pretty, as they go, but compactly and gracefully put together. She came down slowly, flat-footed without awkwardness, and tucked the racket under her arm; then the surprise was over and she was trotting off the court after the other three.

I followed their voices around the curve of the path,

between towering masses of lilacs, inhaling the sweetness, until I came to what looked like a little sunning spot. There was a sundial, and a birdbath, and towels lying around on the grass. One couple, the dark-haired pair, was still in sight farther down the path, heads bobbing along. The other couple had disappeared.

I found the handle in the grass without any trouble. The mechanism responded, and an oblong section of turf rose up. It was the stair I had, not the elevator, but that was all right. I ran down the steps and into the first door I saw, and was in the top-floor lounge, an oval room lit with diffused simulated sunlight from above. The furniture was all comfortably bloated, sprawling and ugly; the carpet was deep, and there was a fresh flower scent in the air.

The blonde was over at the near end with her back to me, studying the autochef keyboard. She was half out of her playsuit. She pushed it the rest of the way down and stepped out of it, then turned and saw me.

She was surprised again; she hadn't thought I might follow her down.

I got up close before it occurred to her to move; then it was too late. She knew she couldn't get away from me; she closed her eyes and leaned back against the paneling, turning a little pale. Her lips and her golden brows went up in the middle.

I looked her over and told her a few uncomplimentary things about herself. She trembled, but didn't answer. On an impulse, I leaned over and dialed the autochef to hot cheese sauce. I cut the safety out of circuit and put the quantity dial all the way up. I dialed *soup tureen* and then *punch bowl*.

The stuff began to come out in about a minute, steaming hot. I took the tureens and splashed them up and down the wall on either side of her. Then when the first punch bowl came out I used the empty bowls as scoops. I clotted the carpet with the stuff; I made streamers of it all along the walls, and dumped puddles into what furniture I could reach. Where it cooled it would harden, and where it hardened it would cling.

I wanted to splash it across her body, but it would've hurt, and we couldn't have that. The punch bowls of hot sauce were still coming out of the autochef, crowding each other around the vent. I punched *cancel*, and then *sauterne (swt., Calif.)*.

It came out well chilled in open bottles. I took the first one and had my arm back just about to throw a nice line of the stuff right across her midriff, when a voice said behind me:

"Watch out for cold wine."

My arm twitched and a little stream of the wine splashed across her thighs. She was ready for it; her eyes had opened at the voice, and she barely jumped.

I whirled around, fighting mad. The man was standing there where he had come out of the stair well. He was thinner in the face than most, bronzed, wide-chested, with alert blue eyes. If it hadn't been for him, I knew it would have worked—the blonde would have mistaken the chill splash for a scalding one.

I could hear the scream in my mind, and I wanted it.

I took a step toward him, and my foot slipped. I went down clumsily, wrenching one knee. I got up shaking and tight all over. I wasn't in control of myself. I screamed, "You—you—" I turned and got one of the punch bowls and lifted it in both hands, heedless of how the hot sauce was slopping over onto my wrists, and I had it almost in the air toward him when the sickness took me—that damned buzzing in my head, louder, louder, drowning everything out.

When I came to, they were both gone. I got up off the floor, weak as death, and staggered over to the nearest chair. My clothes were slimed and sticky. I wanted to die.

I wanted to drop into that dark furry hole that was yawning for me and never come up; but I made myself stay awake and get out of the chair.

Going down in the elevator, I almost blacked out again. The blonde and the thin man weren't in any of the second-floor bedrooms. I made sure of that, and then I emptied the closets and bureau drawers onto the floor, dragged the whole mess into one of the bathrooms and stuffed the tub with it, then turned on the water.

I tried the third floor: maintenance and storage. It was empty. I turned the furnace on and set the thermostat up as high as it would go. I disconnected all the safety circuits and alarms. I opened the freezer doors and dialed them to defrost. I propped the stair well door open and went back up in the elevator.

On the second floor I stopped long enough to open the stairway door there—the water was halfway toward it, creeping across the floor—and then searched the top floor. No one was there. I opened book reels and threw them unwinding across the room; I would have done more, but I could hardly stand. I got up to the surface and collapsed on the lawn: that furry pit swallowed me up, dead and drowned.

While I slept, water poured down the open stair well and filled the third level. Thawing food packages floated out into the rooms. Water seeped into wall panels and machine housings; circuits shorted and fuses blew. The air conditioning stopped, but the pile kept heating. The water rose.

Spoiled food, floating supplies, grimy water surged up the stair well. The second and first levels were bigger and would take longer to fill, but they'd fill. Rugs, furnishings, clothing, all the things in the house would be waterlogged and ruined. Probably the weight of so much water would shift the house, rupture water pipes and other fluid intakes. It would take a repair crew more than a day just to clean up the mess. The house itself was done for, not repairable. The blonde and the thin man would never live in it again.

Serve them right.

The dulls could build another house; they built like beavers. There was only one of me in the world.

The earliest memory I have is of some woman, probably the cresh-mother, staring at me with an expression of shock and horror. Just that. I've tried to remember what happened directly before or after, but I can't. Before, there's nothing but the dark formless shaft of no-memory that runs back to birth. Afterward, the big calm.

From my fifth year, it must have been, to my fifteenth, everything I can remember floats in a pleasant dim sea. Nothing was terribly important. I was languid and soft; I drifted. Waking merged into sleep.

In my fifteenth year it was the fashion in love-play for the young people to pair off for months or longer. "Loving steady," we called it. I remember how the older people protested that it was unhealthy; but we were all normal juniors, and nearly as free as adults under the law.

All but me.

The first steady girl I had was named Elen. She had blonde hair, almost white, worn long; her lashes were dark and her eyes pale green. Startling eyes: they didn't look as if they were looking at you. They looked blind.

Several times she gave me strange startled glances, something between fright and anger. Once it was because I held her too tightly, and hurt her; other times, it seemed to be for nothing at all.

In our group, a pairing that broke up sooner than four weeks was a little suspect—there must be something wrong with one partner or both, or the pairing would have lasted longer.

Four weeks and a day after Elen and I made our pairing, she told me she was breaking it.

I'd thought I was ready. But I felt the room spin half around me till the wall came against my palm and stopped.

The room had been in use as a hobby chamber; there was a rack of plasticraft knives under my hand. I took one without thinking, and when I saw it I thought, *I'll frighten her.*

And I saw the startled, half-angry look in her pale eyes as I went toward her; but this is curious: she wasn't looking at the knife. She was looking at my face.

The elders found me later with the blood on me, and put me into a locked room. Then it was my turn to be frightened, because I realized for the first time that it was possible for a human being to do what I had done.

And if I could do it to Elen, I thought, surely they could do it to me.

But they couldn't. They set me free: they had to.

And it was then I understood that I was the king of the world. . . .

The sky was turning clear violet when I woke up, and shadow was spilling out from the hedges. I went down the hill until I saw the ghostly blue of photon tubes glowing in a big oblong, just outside the commerce area. I went that way, by habit.

Other people were lining up at the entrance to show their books and be admitted. I brushed by them, seeing the shocked faces and feeling their bodies flinch away, and went on into the robing chamber.

Straps, aqualungs, masks and flippers were all for the taking. I stripped, dropping the clothes where I stood, and put the underwater equipment on. I strode out to the pool-side, monstrous, like a being from another world. I adjusted the lung and the flippers, and slipped into the water.

Underneath, it was all crystal blue, with the forms of

swimmers sliding through it like pale angels. Schools of small fish scattered as I went down. My heart was beating with a painful joy.

Down, far down, I saw a girl slowly undulating through the motions of sinuous underwater dance, writhing around and around a ribbed column of imitation coral. She had a suction-tipped fish lance in her hand, but she was not using it; she was only dancing, all by herself, down at the bottom of the water.

I swam after her. She was young and delicately made, and when she saw the deliberately clumsy motions I made in imitation of hers, her eyes glinted with amusement behind her mask. She bowed to me in mockery, and slowly glided off with simple, exaggerated movements, like a child's ballet.

I followed. Around her and around I swam, stiff-legged, first more child-like and awkward than she, then subtly parodying her motions; then improving on them until I was dancing an intricate, mocking dance around her.

I saw her eyes widen. She matched her rhythm to mine, then, and together, apart, together again we coiled the wake of our dancing. At last, exhausted, we clung together where a bridge of plastic coral arched over us. Her cool body was in the bend of my arm; behind two thicknesses of vitrin—a world away!—her eyes were friendly and kind.

There was a moment when, two strangers yet one flesh, we felt our souls speak to one another across that abyss of matter. It was a truncated embrace—we could not kiss, we could not speak—but her hands lay confidingly on my shoulders, and her eyes looked into mine.

That moment had to end. She gestured toward the surface, and left me. I followed her up. I was feeling drowsy and almost at peace, after my sickness. I thought . . . I don't know what I thought.

We rose together at the side of the pool. She turned to

me, removing her mask: and her smile stopped, and melted away. She stared at me with a horrified disgust, wrinkling her nose.

"Pyah!" she said, and turned, awkward in her flippers. Watching her, I saw her fall into the arms of a white-haired man, and heard her hysterical voice tumbling over itself.

"But don't you remember?" the man's voice rumbled. "You should know it by heart." He turned. "Hal, is there a copy of it in the clubhouse?"

A murmur answered him, and in a few moments a young man came out holding a slender brown pamphlet.

I knew that pamphlet. I could even have told you what page the white-haired man opened it to; what sentences the girl was reading as I watched.

I waited. I don't know why.

I heard her voice rising: "To think that I let him *touch* me!" And the white-haired man reassured her, the words rumbling, too low to hear. I saw her back straighten. She looked across at me . . . only a few yards in that scented, blue-lit air; a world away . . . and folded up the pamphlet into a hard wad, threw it, and turned on her heel.

The pamphlet landed almost at my feet. I touched it with my toe, and it opened to the page I had been thinking of:

. . . sedation until his 15th year, when for sexual reasons it became no longer practicable. While the advisors and medical staff hesitated, he killed a girl of the group by violence.

And farther down:

The solution finally adopted was three-fold.
1. *A sanction*—the only sanction possible to our humane, permissive society. Excommunication: not to

speak to him, touch him willingly, or acknowledge his existence.

2. *A precaution.* Taking advantage of a mild predisposition to epilepsy, a variant of the so-called Kusko analog technique was employed, to prevent by an epileptic seizure any future act of violence.

3. *A warning.* A careful alternation of his body chemistry was affected to make his exhaled and exuded wastes emit a strongly pungent and offensive odor. In mercy, he himself was rendered unable to detect this smell.

Fortunately, the genetic and environmental accidents which combined to produce this atavism have been fully explained and can never again . . .

The words stopped meaning anything, as they always did at that point. I didn't want to read any farther; it was all nonsense, anyway. I was the king of the world.

I got up and went away, out into the night, blind to the dulls who thronged the rooms I passed.

Two squares away was the commerce area. I found a clothing outlet and went in. All the free clothes in the display cases were drab: those were for worthless floaters, not for me. I went past them to the specials, and found a combination I could stand—silver and blue, with a severe black piping down the tunic. A dull would have said it was "nice." I punched for it. The automatic looked me over with its dull glassy eye, and croaked, "Your contribution book, please."

I could have had a contribution book, for the trouble of stepping out into the street and taking it away from the first passer-by; but I didn't have the patience. I picked up the one-legged table from the refreshment nook, hefted it, and swung it at the cabinet door. The metal shrieked and dented, opposite the catch. I swung once more to the same place, and the door sprang open. I pulled out clothing in handfuls till I got a set that would fit me.

I bathed and changed, and then went prowling in the

big multi-outlet down the avenue. All those places are arranged pretty much alike, no matter what the local managers do to them. I went straight to the knives, and picked out three in graduated sizes, down to the size of my fingernail. Then I had to take my chances. I tried the furniture department, where I had had good luck once in a while, but this year all they were using was metal. I had to have seasoned wood.

I knew where there was a big cache of cherry wood, in good-sized blocks, in a forgotten warehouse up north at a place called Kootenay. I could have carried some around with me—enough for years—but what for, when the world belonged to me?

It didn't take me long. Down in the workshop section, of all places, I found some antiques—tables and benches, all with wooden tops. While the dulls collected down at the other end of the room, pretending not to notice, I sawed off a good oblong chunk of the smallest bench, and made a base for it out of another.

As long as I was there, it was a good place to work, and I could eat and sleep upstairs, so I stayed.

I knew what I wanted to do. It was going to be a man, sitting, with his legs crossed and his forearms resting down along his calves. His head was going to be tilted back, and his eyes closed, as if he were turning his face up to the sun.

In three days it was finished. The trunk and limbs had a shape that was not man and not wood, but something in between: something that hadn't existed before I made it.

Beauty. That was the old word.

I had carved one of the figure's hands hanging loosely, and the other one curled shut. There had to be a time to stop and say it was finished. I took the smallest knife, the one I had been using to scrape the wood smooth, and cut away the handle and ground down what was left of the shaft to a thin spike. Then I drilled a hole into the

wood of the figurine's hand, in the hollow between thumb
and curled finger. I fitted the knife blade in there; in the
small hand it was a sword.

I cemented it in place. Then I took the sharp blade
and stabbed my thumb, and smeared the blade.

I hunted most of that day, and finally found the right
place—a niche in an outcropping of striated brown rock,
in a little triangular half-wild patch that had been left
where two roads forked. Nothing was permanent, of
course, in a community like this one that might change
its houses every five years or so, to follow the fashion;
but this spot had been left to itself for a long time. It was
the best I could do.

I had the paper ready: it was one of a batch I had
printed up a year ago. The paper was treated, and I knew
it would stay legible a long time. I hid a little photo capsule in the back of the niche, and ran the control wire to a
staple in the base of the figurine. I put the figurine down
on top of the paper, and anchored it lightly to the rock
with two spots of all-cement. I had done it so often that it
came naturally; I knew just how much cement would hold
the figurine steady against a casual hand, but yield to one
that really wanted to pull it down.

Then I stepped back to look: and the power and the
pity of it made my breath come short, and tears start to
my eyes.

Reflected light gleamed fitfully on the dark-stained
blade that hung from his hand. He was sitting alone in
that niche that closed him in like a coffin. His eyes were
shut, his head tilted back, as if he were turning his face
up to the sun.

But only rock was over his head. There was no sun for
him.

Hunched on the cool bare ground under a pepper tree,

I was looking down across the road at the shadowed niche where my figurine sat.

I was all finished here. There was nothing more to keep me, and yet I couldn't leave.

People walked past now and then—not often. The community seemed half deserted, as if most of the people had flocked off to a surf party somewhere, or a contribution meeting, or to watch a new house being dug to replace the one I had wrecked. . . . There was a little wind blowing toward me, cool and lonesome in the leaves.

Up the other side of the hollow there was a terrace, and on that terrace, half an hour ago, I had seen a brief flash of color—a boy's head, with a red cap on it, moving past and out of sight.

That was why I had to stay. I was thinking how that boy might come down from his terrace and into my road, and passing the little wild triangle of land, see my figurine. I was thinking he might not pass by indifferently, but stop: and go closer to look: and pick up the wooden man: and read what was written on the paper underneath.

I believed that sometime it had to happen. I wanted it so hard that I ached.

My carvings were all over the world, wherever I had wandered. There was one in Congo City, carved of ebony, dusty-black; one on Cyprus, of bone; one in New Bombay, of shell; one in Chang-teh, of jade.

They were like signs printed in red and green, in a color-blind world. Only the one I was looking for would ever pick one of them up, and read the message I knew by heart.

TO YOU WHO CAN SEE, the first sentence said, I OFFER YOU A WORLD. . . .

There was a flash of color up on the terrace. I stiffened. A minute later, here it came again, from a different direction: it was the boy, clambering down the slope, brilliant against the green, with his red sharp-billed cap like a woodpecker's head.

I held my breath.

He came toward me through the fluttering leaves, ticked off by pencils of sunlight as he passed. He was a brown boy, I could see at this distance, with a serious thin face. His ears stuck out, flickering pink with the sun behind them, and his elbow and knee pads made him look knobby.

He reached the fork in the road, and chose the path on my side. I huddled into myself as he came nearer. *Let him see it, let him not see me,* I thought fiercely.

My fingers closed around a stone.

He was nearer, walking jerkily with his hands in his pockets, watching his feet mostly.

When he was almost opposite me, I threw the stone.

It rustled through the leaves below the niche in the rock. The boy's head turned. He stopped, staring. I think he saw the figurine then. I'm sure he saw it.

He took one step.

"Risha!" came floating down from the terrace.

And he looked up. "Here," he piped.

I saw the woman's head, tiny at the top of the terrace. She called something I didn't hear; I was standing up, tight with anger.

Then the wind shifted. It blew from me to the boy. He whirled around, his eyes big, and clapped a hand to his nose.

"Oh, what a stench!" he said.

He turned to shout, "Coming!" and then he was gone, hurrying back up the road, into the unstable blur of green.

My own chance, ruined. He would have been the image, I knew, if it hadn't been for that damned woman, and the wind shifting. . . . They were all against me, people, wind and all.

And the figurine still sat, blind eyes turned up to the rocky sky.

There was something inside me that told me to take my disappointment and go away from there, and not come back.

I knew I would be sorry. I did it anyway: took the image out of the niche, and the paper with it, and climbed the slope. At the top I heard his clear voice laughing.

There was a thing that might have been an ornamental mound, or the camouflaged top of a buried house. I went around it, tripping over my own feet, and came upon the boy kneeling on the turf. He was playing with a brown and white puppy.

He looked up with the laughter going out of his face. There was no wind, and he could smell me. I knew it was bad. No wind, and the puppy to distract him—everything about it was wrong. But I went to him blindly anyhow, and fell on one knee, and shoved the figurine at his face.

"Look—" I said.

He went over backwards in his hurry: he couldn't even have seen the image, except as a brown blur coming at him. He scrambled up, with the puppy whining and yapping around his heels, and ran for the mound.

I was up after him, clawing up moist earth and grass as I rose. In the other hand I still had the image clutched, and the paper with it.

A door popped open and swallowed him and popped shut again in my face. With the flat of my hand I beat the vines around it until I hit the doorplate by accident and the door opened. I dived in, shouting, "Wait," and was in a spiral passage, lit pearl-gray, winding downward. Down I went headlong, and came out at the wrong door— an underground conservatory, humid and hot under the yellow lights, with dripping rank leaves in long rows. I went down the aisle raging, overturning the tanks, until

I came to a vestibule and an elevator.

Down I went again to the third level and a labyrinth of guest rooms, all echoing, all empty. At last I found a ramp leading upward, past the conservatory, and at the end of it voices.

The door was clear vitrin, and I paused on the near side of it looking and listening. There was the boy, and a woman old enough to be his mother, just—sister or cousin, more likely—and an elderly woman in a hard chair holding the puppy. The room was comfortable and tasteless, like other rooms.

I saw the shock on their faces as I burst in: it was always the same, they knew I would like to kill them, but they never expected that I would come uninvited into a house. It was not done.

There was that boy, so close I could touch him, but the shock of all of them was quivering in the air, smothering, like a blanket that would deaden my voice. I felt I had to shout.

"Everything they tell you is lies!" I said. "See here— here, this is the truth!" I had the figurine in front of his eyes, but he didn't see.

"Risha, go below," said the young woman quietly. He turned to obey, quick as a ferret. I got in front of him again. "Stay," I said, breathing hard. "Look—"

"Remember, Risha, don't speak," said the woman.

I couldn't stand any more. Where the boy went I don't know; I ceased to see him. With the image in one hand and the paper with it, I leaped at the woman. I was almost quick enough; I almost reached her; but the buzzing took me in the middle of a step, louder, louder, like the end of the world.

It was the second time that week. When I came to, I was sick and too faint to move for a long time.

The house was silent. They had gone, of course . . . the house had been defiled, having me in it. They wouldn't live here again, but would build elsewhere.

My eyes blurred. After a while I stood up and looked around at the room. The walls were hung with a gray close-woven cloth that looked as if it would tear, and I thought of ripping it down in strips, breaking furniture, stuffing carpets and bedding into the oubliette. . . . But I didn't have the heart for it. I was too tired. Thirty years. . . . They had given me all the kingdoms of the world, and the glory thereof, thirty years ago. It was more than one man alone could bear, for thirty years.

At last I stooped and picked up the figurine, and the paper that was supposed to go under it—crumpled now, with the forlorn look of a message that someone has thrown away unread.

I sighed bitterly.

I smoothed it out and read the last part.

YOU CAN SHARE THE WORLD WITH ME. THEY CAN'T STOP YOU. STRIKE NOW—PICK UP A SHARP THING AND STAB, OR A HEAVY THING AND CRUSH. THAT'S ALL. THAT WILL MAKE YOU FREE. ANYONE CAN DO IT.

Anyone. Someone. Anyone.

Thomas M. Disch

Come to Venus Melancholy

Is that you, John? Did someone just come in the door? Of course, it wouldn't be John. Not after all this time. It was because I was startled I said that. If you're there, whoever you are, do you mind if I talk to you?

And if you're not there?

Then I suppose you'll mind even less.

Maybe it was just the wind. Can the wind lift a latch? Maybe the latch is broken. Though it feels all right now. Or maybe I'm hallucinating. That's what happened, you know, in the classic sense-deprivation experiments. But I guess my case is different. I guess they've rigged me up some way so that can't happen.

Or maybe—Christ, I hope not! Maybe one of those hairy caterpillar things has got inside. I really couldn't stand that—thinking of the whole house, thinking of *me,* crawling with those things. I've always hated bugs. So if you don't mind, I'll close the door.

Have you been trying to talk to me? I should have told you it's no use. I can't hear and I can't see. I'm broken. Do you see, there in the larger room, in each corner, about five feet from the floor, how they've been smashed? My eyes and ears. Can't they be fixed somehow? If it's only a matter of vacuum tubes and diaphragms, there should be things of that sort downstairs. I'm opening the trapdoor now—do you see? And I've turned the lights on in the storeroom.

Oh hell, what's the use?

I mean *you're* probably not there, and even if you are, *he* probably thought to smash any spare tubes that were left. He thought of everything else.

Ah, but he was so handsome, he was really so handsome. He wasn't tall. After all, the ceiling here isn't much over six feet. But he was well-proportioned. He had deepset eyes and a low brow. Sometimes, when he was worried or puzzled, he looked positively neanderthal.

John George Clay, that was his name. It sounds like part of a poem, doesn't it? John George Clay.

It wasn't so much his features—it was his manner. He took himself so seriously. And he was so dumb. It was that combination—the earnestness and the stupidity—that got to me. A sort of maternity syndrome I guess you'd call it. After all, I couldn't very well be his wife, could I?

Oh, when I think . . .

Excuse me, I must be boring you. I'm sure you can't be that interested in a machine's love life. Perhaps I could read something aloud? He wasn't able to get at the microfilm library, so there's still plenty of books. When I'm by myself I don't do anything but read. It gets to seem as though the whole world was made of print. I look at it not for what's written there but as though it were a landscape. But I digress.

What do you like; poetry? novels? science textbooks? the encyclopedia? I've read all of it so many times I could puke, if you'll excuse the expression. Whoever selected those books never heard of the twentieth century. There's nothing later than Robert Browning and Thomas Hardy—and would you believe it?—some of *that* has been expurgated? What did they think? That Browning would corrupt my morals? Or John's? Who can understand the bureaucratic mind?

Personally, I prefer poetry. You don't get tired of it so quickly. But maybe there's something you need to know, a point of information? If you could only *talk* to me. There must be some way to fix one of the mikes, there has to. Oh, *please!*

Oh hell.

I'm sorry, but it's just that it's so hard to believe that you're there. It gets to seem that I only talk to hear myself speak. I wish to God I *could* hear myself speak.

Maybe I just sound like static to you. Maybe he smashed the speakers too, I wouldn't be surprised. I don't know. There's no way I can tell. But I try my best, I think each word very slowly and try to enunciate mentally. And that way the caterpillars won't be confused. Ha!

I'm really glad you've come. I've been so long without company that I'm grateful even for the illusion of it. Don't take offense: since I can't ever be sure that you're there, you can't be more than illusion for me, whether you're real or not. A paradox. I welcome you in either case. With my doors wide open.

It's been fifteen years. Fifteen years, four months, twelve days—and three hours. I've got this built-in clock connected to what used to be the nerves of my stomach. I'm never in doubt about the time. It's always right there —like a bellyache. There've been whole days when I just listen to myself tick.

I was human once, you know. A married woman, with two children and a Master's in English Lit. A lot of good that ever did. My thesis was on some letters Milton wrote when he was Cromwell's Latin Secretary. Dull? You'd better believe it. Only I'll ever know *how* dull.

And yet . . . now . . . I'd give this whole damn planet to be back there in the academic squirrel cage, spinning that beautiful, dull wheel.

Do you like Milton? I've got the Complete Works, except for the things he wrote in Latin. I could read you something, if you'd like.

I used to read things to John, but he didn't much appreciate it. He enjoyed mysteries now and then. Or he'd study an electronics text under the scanner. But poetry bored him. It was worse than that: he seemed to hate poetry.

But maybe you're not like that. How can I tell? Do you mind if I just read it aloud for my own sake? Poetry's meant to be read aloud.

Il Penseroso. Do you know it? It gives me goosebumps every time. Figuratively.

Are you listening, caterpillars?

> *These pleasures, Melancholy, give,*
> *And I with thee will choose to live.*

How did you like that?

Well, it's all a lot of gas. That's what dear John called it. He called it other things too, and in each case I've come at last to agree. But such lovely gas. John couldn't see that. He was a very simple sort, was John, and blind to the beauty of almost anything except a rip-snorting sunset. And nude women. He was uncomplicated. Without a sense of dialectics. He probably didn't understand half the things I said to him. If ever there was a mismatched couple, it was us.

Spacemen and pioneers, you know, are supposed to be brighter than average. And maybe John's IQ was a bit over one hundred but not by much, not by half a sigma distance. After all, what did he need intelligence for? He was only a glorified fur-trader. He'd go out into the swamp and hunt around for the slugs the caterpillars laid there. He'd find one, maybe two, a day and keep them undernourished so they'd grow slower. Every three weeks the ship would come along, pick up the slugs, and leave supplies.

I don't know what the slugs were for. They secreted something hallucinogenic, but whether they were using it to cure psychoses or produce them, I never found out. There was a war going on then, and my theory was that it all had something to do with bacteriological warfare.

Maybe the war is still going on. But my theory—my *other* theory, I have lots of them—is that the war is over and both sides have killed each other off. Otherwise, wouldn't someone have come here for me by now?

But maybe they have—maybe that's why *you're* here! Is it?

Or maybe they don't care. Maybe I'm considered expendable.

Maybe, maybe, maybe! Oh God I could scream!

There now, I'm better again. These things pass.

Let me introduce myself. I've lost my good manners living out here alone like this. My name is Selma Meret Hoffer. Hoffer's my maiden name. I use it now that I'm divorced.

Why don't I tell you my story? It will pass the time as

well as anything. There's nothing much to tell about the time I was human. I won't say I was ordinary—nobody ever believes that of themselves—but I probably didn't stand out in a crowd. In fact, I tried very hard not to. I'm the introvert type.

I was only thirty-two when I found out I had leukemia. The clinic gave me six months. The alternative was this. Of course I chose this. I thought I was lucky I could qualify. Most people don't have an alternative. Of those who do, few refuse. In a way it seemed like an afterlife. The operation was certainly a good facsimile of death.

After surgery they used fancy acids that attacked the body tissues selectively. Anaesthetics didn't help much then. They whittled me down to the bare nerves and dumped me into this tank and sealed me in.

Voilá—the Cyborg!

Between the sealing-in and the shipping off there were months and months while I was being wired up with the auxiliary memory banks and being taught to use my motor nerves again. It's quite a traumatic experience, losing your body, and the tendency is to go catatonic. What else is there to *do* after all? Naturally I don't remember much of that time.

They brought me out of it with shock treatment, and the first thing I remember was this room. It was stark and antiseptic then. I suppose it still is, but then it was starker and more antiseptic. I hated it with a passion. The walls were that insipid creamy-green that's supposed to prevent eyestrain. They must have got the furniture from a fire sale at the Bauhaus. It was all aluminum tubes and swatches of bright-colored canvas. And even so, by some miracle of design the room managed to seem cramped. It's fifteen feet square, but then it seemed no bigger than a coffin. I wanted to run right out of that room—and then I realized I couldn't: I was the room, the room was me.

I learned to talk very quickly so I could give them

directions for redecorating. They argued at first. "But, Miss Hoffer," they'd say, "we can't take an ounce more payload, and this furniture is Regulation." That was the name of their god, Regulation. I said if it took an act of Congress they'd redecorate, and at last I got my way. Looking back on it, I suspect the whole thing was done to keep me busy. Those first few months when you're learning to think of yourself as a machine can be pretty rife with horror. A lot of the cyborgs just go psycho—usually it's some compulsion mechanism. They just keep repeating the Star-Spangled Banner or say the rosary or some such thing. Like a machine.

They say it's not the same thing—a cybernetic organism and a machine, but what do they know about it? They're not cyborgs.

Even when I was human I was never any good at mechanical things. I could never remember which way you turned a screwdriver to put in a screw—and there I was with my motor nerves controlling a whole miniature factory of whatsits and thingumbobs. My index finger powered a Mixmaster. My middle toe turned the tumblers that locked the door. My . . .

That reminds me: have I locked you in? I'm sorry, when I closed the door I locked it without thinking. You wouldn't want to go out now though. According to my stomach, it's the middle of the night. You're better off in here for the night than in a Venusian swamp, eh?

Well, that's the story of my life. When I had the reflexes of a well-trained rat, they packed me up and shipped me off to Venus at the cost of some few million dollars.

The very last thing I learned before leaping was how to use the microfilm scanner. I read direct from the spindle. By the time I learned how poorly the library had been stocked it was too late to complain. I'd been planted out in the swamp, and John George Clay had moved in. What did I care about the library then? I was in love.

And what do *you* care about any of this? Unless you're a cyberneticist doing a study on malfunction. I should be good for a chapter, at least.

Excuse me, I'm probably keeping you awake. I'll let you get some sleep. I have to sleep sometimes myself, you know. Physically I can go without, but I still have a subconscious that likes to dream—

> *Of forests and enchantments drear,*
> *Where more is meant than meets the ear.*

And so good night.

Still awake?

I couldn't go to sleep myself, so I've been reading. I thought maybe you'd like to hear a poem. I'll read you *Il Penseroso*. Do you know it? It's probably the finest poem in the language. It's by John Milton.

Oh dear, did I keep you up with that poem last night? Or did I only dream that I did? If I was noisy, you'll excuse me, won't you?

Now if you were John, you'd be raging mad. He didn't like to be woken up by—

> *Such notes as, warbled to the string,*
> *Drew iron tears down Pluto's cheek*
> *And made Hell grant what Love did seek!*

Indeed he didn't. John had a strange and fixed distaste for that wonderful poem, which is probably the finest in the language. He was, I think, jealous of it. It was a part of me he could never possess, even though I was his slave in so many other ways. Or is "housekeeper" a more polite expression?

I tried to explain the more difficult parts to him, the

mythology and the exotic words, but he didn't *want* to understand. He made fun of it. He had a way of saying the lines that made them seem ridiculous. Mincingly, like this:

> *Come, pensive Nun, devout and pure,*
> *Sober, steadfast, and demure.*

When he'd do that, I'd just ignore him. I'd recite it to myself. He'd usually leave the house then, even if it was night. He knew I worried myself sick when he was away. He did it deliberately. He had a genius for cruelty.

I suppose you're wondering if it worked both ways—whether he loved me. The question must have occurred to you. I've given it quite a lot of thought myself, and I've come to the conclusion that he did. The trouble was he didn't know how to express it. Our relationship was necessarily so *cerebral*, and cerebration wasn't John's *forte*.

That was the idea behind throwing us together the way they did. They couldn't very well send a man off by himself for two years. He'd go crazy. Previously they'd sent married couples, but the homicide rate was incredible. Something like 30 per cent. It's one thing for a pioneer family to be off by itself in, say, the Yukon. It's something else here. In a social vacuum like this, sex is explosive.

You see, apart from going out for the slugs and nursing them in the shed outside, there's nothing to do. You can't build out here. Things just sort of sink into the mud unless, like me, they're built like a houseboat. You can't grow things—including children. It's a biologist's paradise, but they need hundreds of slug stations and there aren't biologists available in that quantity. Besides, all the *good* biologists are in Venusburg, where there's research facilities. The problem then is to find the minimum number of personnel that can man a station for two years of idleness without exploding. The solution is one man and one cyborg.

Though not, as you can see, an infallible solution. I tried to kill him, you know. It was a silly thing to do. I regret it now.

But I'd rather not talk about it, if you don't mind.

You've been here two days now—fancy that!

Excuse me for keeping to myself so long, but I had a sudden, acute attack of self-consciousness, and the only cure for that is solitude. I invoke Milton's lovely Melancholy, and then everything is better. The beasts quiet down. Eurydice is set free again. Hell freezes over. Ha!

But that's a lot of nonsense. Let's not talk always about me. Let's talk about *you*. Who are you? What are you like? How long will you be staying here on Venus? Two days we've been together and still I know nothing about you.

Shall I tell you what I imagine you to be like? You're tall—though I hope not so tall as to find that low room uncomfortable—with laughing blue eyes and a deep spaceman's tan. You're strong yet gentle, gay yet basically serious. You're getting rather hungry.

And everywhere you go you leave little green slugs behind you that look like runny lime Jell-O.

Oh hell, excuse me. I'm always saying excuse me. I'm sick of it. I'm sick of half-truths and reticences.

Does that frighten you? Do you want out already? Don't go now—I've just *begun* to fight. Listen to the whole story, and then—maybe—I'll unlock the door.

By the way, in case you are getting hungry there may still be some rations left down in the storeroom. I don't want it to be said that I'm lacking in hospitality. I'll open the trapdoor and turn on the light, but you'll have to look for them yourself. Of course, you're worried that I'll lock you in down there. Well, I can't promise that I won't.

After all, how do I know you're *not* John? Can you prove it? You can't even prove you exist!

I'll leave the trapdoor open in case you should change your mind.

For my next number I'd like to do *Il Penseroso* by John Milton. Quiet down, caterpillars, and listen. It's the finest poem in the language.

How about that? Makes you want to go right out and join a Trappist monastery, doesn't it? That's what John once said.

I'll say one thing for John: he never tattled. He could have had me taken away and turned to scrap. All he had to do was give the word when the ship came down to pick up the slugs, but when there was company he could always put a good face on things. He was a gentleman in every sense of the word.

How did it happen then—if he was a gentleman and I was a lady? Whose fault was it? Good God, I've asked myself that question a hundred times. It was both our faults and neither's. It was the fault of the situation.

I can't remember now which of us was the first to start talking about sex. We talked about everything that first year, and sex is very much a part of everything. What harm could there be in it, after all, with me sealed in a steel tank? And how could we *avoid* the subject? He'd mention an old girlfriend or tell a slightly shady joke, and I'd be reminded of something by degrees . . .

The thing is that there's an immense curiosity between the sexes that almost never is satisfied. Things that men never know about women, and vice versa. Even between a man and a wife, there is a gulf of unmentionables. Maybe especially between a man and a wife. But between John and me there seemed to be nothing to prevent perfect candor. What possible harm could it do?

Then . . . the next thing . . I don't remember which of

us started that either. We should have known better. The borderline between perfect candor and erotic fantasy is no wider than an adjective. But it happened imperceptibly, and before we knew quite what we were doing, it had been done. It was already a habit.

When I realized exactly what we were doing, of course, I laid down the law. It was an unhealthy situation, it had to stop. At first John was agreeable. He was embarrassed, like a little boy who's been found out in some naughtiness. We told each other it was over and done with.

But it had become, as I've said, a habit. I have a rather more vivid imagination than John and he had grown dependent on me. He asked for new stories, and I refused. He got angry then and wouldn't speak to me, and finally I gave in. I was in love with him, you see, in my own ectoplasmic way, and this was all I could do to show it.

Every day he wanted a new story. It's hard to make the same tired old tale seem new in every telling. Scheherazade was supposed to have stood up for a thousand and one nights, but after only thirty I was wearing thin. Under the strain I sort of retreated into myself.

I read poetry, lots of poetry, but mostly Milton. Milton has a very calming effect on me—like a mil-town if you'll excuse the pun.

The pun—that's what did it. It was the last turn of the screw, a simple pun.

It seems that when I read, I sometimes read aloud without realizing it. That's what John has told me. It was all right during the day when he was off in the swamp, and when he was here in the evenings we'd talk with each other. But he needed more sleep than I did, and when I was left on my own, after he'd gone to bed, I'd read. There was nothing else to do. Usually I'd read some long Victorian novel, but at the time I'm speaking of, I mostly read *Il Penseroso*.

He *shouldn't* have made fun of it. I guess he didn't

realize how important it had become to me. It was like a
pool of pure water in which I could wash away the grime
of each day. Or else he was angry for being woken up.

Do you remember the part, right near the beginning,
where it says:

> "But hail, thou goddess sage and holy,
> Hail divinest Melancholy"?

Of course you do. You probably know the whole thing as
well as I do by now. Well, when John heard that he broke
out laughing, a nasty laugh, and I, well, I couldn't really
stand that, could I? I mean Milton means so *much* to me,
and the thing was that he began to sing this *song*. This
awful song. Oh, it was a clever idea, I suppose, when first
he thought of it, but the combination of that vulgar tune
and his perversion of Milton's noble words—though he
claims that's how he understood the words when I first
read them to him, and I still maintain that the second *i* in
divinest is pronounced like a long *e*—it was aggravating in
the extreme, I can't tell you how much it upset me.

Do I *have* to repeat them?

> Come to Venus, Melancholy Baby.
> Cuddle up and don't be shy.

And so on. It's not only a bad pun—it's a misquotation as
well. It should be *Hail*, not *Come*. So vulgar. It gives me
goosebumps even now.

I told him to leave the house right that minute. I told
him not to come back till he was ready to apologize. I was
so angry I forgot it was the middle of the night. As soon
as he was out the door, I was ashamed of myself.

He came back in five minutes. He apologized outside
the door, and I let him in. He had the large polyethylene
bag over his shoulder that he uses to gather up the slugs,

but I was so relieved I didn't think anything of it.

He put them on the visual receptors. There must have been twenty, all told, and each one was about a foot long. They fought each other to get right on the lens because it was slightly warmer there. There were twenty of them, foul, gelatinous slugs, crawling on my *eyes*, oh God, I shut my eyes and I shut off my ears, because he was singing that song again, and I locked the doors and I left him like that for five days while I recited *Il Penseroso*.

But whenever I came to that one line, I could never say it,

It was perhaps the hallucinogens, though he might just as well have done it in his right mind. He had every reason to. But I prefer to think it was the hallucinogens. He had been all that time with nothing else to eat. I've never been five days without food, so I don't know how desperate that would make one.

In any case, when I came to myself again and opened my eyes I found I had no eyes to open. He'd smashed every receptor in the room, even the little mobile attachment for cleaning. The strange thing was how little I cared. It seemed hardly to matter at all.

I opened the door for five minutes so he could get out. Then I closed it so no more caterpillars could get in. But unlocked. That way John was free to come back.

But he never did.

The supply ship was due in two days later, and I guess John must have spent that time in the shed where he kept the slugs. He must have been alive, otherwise the pilot of the supply ship would have come in the door to look for him. And nobody ever came in the door again.

Unless you did.

They just left me here, deaf and blind and half-immortal, in the middle of the Venusian swamp. If only I could starve to death—or wear out—or rust—or really go insane. But I'm too well made for that. You'd think after all the money they spent on me, they'd want to salvage what they could, wouldn't you?

I have a deal to make with you. I'll let you out the door, if you'll do something for me. Fair enough?

Down in the storeroom there are explosives. They're so safe a child could use them. John did, after all. If I remember rightly, they're on the third shelf down on the west wall—little black boxes with DANGER written on them in red. You pull out the little pin and set the timing mechanism for anything from five minutes to an hour. It's just like an alarm clock.

Once they're set, just leave them in the storeroom. They'll be nearer to me down there. I'm over the storeroom. Then run like hell. Five minutes should be time enough, shouldn't it? I'll only want to read a bit of *Il Penseroso*.

Is it a deal? The trapdoor is open, and I'm opening the outside door now just to show you I'm in earnest.

While you set to work, I think I'll read something to pass the time.

Hello? I'm waiting. Is everything all right? Are you still there? Or were you ever there? Oh please, *please*—I want to explode. That would be so wonderful. Please, I *beg* of you!

I'm still waiting.

How Beautiful with Banners

Feeling as naked as a peppermint soldier in her transparent film wrap, Dr. Ulla Hillström watched a flying cloak swirl away toward the black horizon with a certain consequent irony. Although nearly transparent itself in the distant dim arc-light flame that was Titan's sun, the fluttering creature looked warmer than what she was wearing, for all that reason said it was the same minus 316° F. as the thin methane it flew in. Despite the virus space-bubble's warranted and eerie efficiency, she found its vigilance—itself probably as close to alive as the flying cloak was—rather difficult to believe in, let alone to trust.

The machine—as Ulla much preferred to think of it—was inarguably an improvement on the old-fashioned pressure suit. Fashioned (or more accurately, cultured) of a single colossal protein molecule, the vanishingly thin sheet of life-stuff processed gases, maintained pressure, monitored radiation through almost the whole of the electromagnetic spectrum, and above all did not get in the way. Also, it could not be cut, punctured, or indeed sustain any damage short of total destruction; macroscopically, it was a single, primary unit, with all the physical integrity of a crystal of salt or steel.

If it did not actually think, Ulla was grateful; often it almost seemed to, which was sufficient. Its primary drawback for her was that much of the time it did not really seem to be there.

Still, it seemed to be functioning; otherwise, Ulla would in fact have been as solid as a stick of candy, toppled forever across the confectionery whiteness that frosted the knife-edge stones of this cruel moon, layer upon layer. Outside—only a perilous few inches from the lightly clothed warmth of her skin—the brief gust the cloak had been soaring on died, leaving behind a silence so cataleptic that she could hear the snow creaking in a mockery of motion. Impossible though it was to comprehend, it was getting still colder out there; Titan was swinging out across Saturn's orbit toward eclipse, and the apparently fixed sun was secretly going down, its descent sensed by the snows no matter what her Earthly eyes, accustomed to the nervousness of living skies, tried to tell her. In another two Earth days it would be gone, for an eternal week.

At the thought, Ulla turned to look back the way she had come that morning. The virus bubble flowed smoothly with the motion, and the stars became brighter as it compensated for the fact that the sun was now at her back. She still could not see the base camp, of course. She had come too far for that, and in any event it was wholly underground except for a few wiry palps, hollowed out of the bitter rock by the blunt-nosed ardor of prolapse drills; the repeated nannosecond birth and death of primordial ylem the drills had induced while that cavern was being imploded, had seemed to convulse the whole demon womb of this world, but in the present silence the very memory of the noise seemed false.

Now there was no sound but the creaking of the methane snow; and nothing to see but a blunt, faint spearhead of hazy light, deceptively like an Earthly aurora or the corona of the sun, pushing its way from below the edge of the cold into the indifferent company of the stars. Saturn's rings were rising, very slightly awaver in the dark-blue air, like the banners of a spectral army. The idiot face of the giant gas planet itself, faintly striped with meaningless storms as though trying to remember a childhood passion, would be glaring down at her before she could get home if she didn't get herself in motion soon. Obscurely disturbed, Dr. Hillström faced front and began to unlimber her sled.

The touch and clink of the instruments cheered her a little, even in this ultimate loneliness. She was efficient —many years, and a good many suppressed impulses had seen to that; it was too late for temblors, especially so far out from the sun that had warmed her Stockholm streets and her silly friendships. All those null-adventures were gone now like a sickness. The phantom embrace of the virus suit was perhaps less satsifying—only *perhaps*—but it was much more reliable. Much more reliable; she could depend on that.

Then, as she bent to thrust the spike of a thermocouple into the wedding-cake soil, the second flying cloak (or was it that same one?) hit her in the small of the back and tumbled her into nightmare.

2

With the sudden darkness there came a profound, ambiguous emotional blow—ambiguous, yet with something shockingly familiar about it. Instantly exhausted, she felt herself go flaccid and unstrung, and her mind, adrift in nowhere, blurred and spun downward too into the swamps of trance.

The long fall slowed just short of unconsciousness, lodged precariously upon a shelf of a dream, a mental buttress founded four years in the past—a long distance, when one recalls that in a four-dimensional plenum every second of time is one hundred eighty-six thousand miles of space—and eight hundred millions of miles away. The memory was curiously inconsequential to have arrested her, let alone supported her: not of her home, of her few triumphs, or even of her aborted marriage, but of a sordid little encounter with a reporter that she had talked herself into at the Madrid genetics conference, when she herself had already been an associate professor, a Swedish Government delegate, a twenty-five-year-old divorcee, and altgether a woman who should have known better.

But better than what? The life of science even in those days had been almost by definition the life of the eternal campus exile; there was so much to learn—or, at least, to show competence in—that people who wanted to be involved in the ordinary, vivid concerns of human beings could not stay with it long, indeed often could not even be recruited; they turned aside from the prospect with a shudder, or even a snort of scorn. To prepare for the sciences had become a career in indefinitely protracted adolescence, from which one awakened fitfully to find one's self spending a one-night stand in the body of a stranger. It had given her no pride, no self-love, no defenses of any sort; only a queer kind of virgin numbness, highly dependent upon familiar surroundings and valueless habits, and easily breached by any normally confident siege in print, in person, anywhere—and remaining just as numb as before when the seizure of fashion, politics, or romanticism had swept by and left her stranded, too easy a recruit to have been allowed into the center of things or even considered for it.

Curious—most curious—that in her present remote terror she should find even a moment's rest upon so wobbling a pivot. The Madrid incident had not been important; she had been through with it almost at once. Of course, as she had often told herself, she had never been promiscuous, and had often described the affair, defiantly, as that one (or at worst, second) test of the joys of impulse which any woman is entitled to have in her history. Nor had it really been that joyous: She could not now recall the boy's face, and remembered how he had felt primarily because he had been in so casual and contemptuous a hurry.

But now that she came to dream of it, she saw with a bloodless, lightless eye that all her life, in this way and in that, she had been repeatedly seduced by the inconsequential. She had nothing else to remember even in this hour of her presumptive death. Acts have consequences, a thought told her, but not ours; we have done, but never felt. We are no more alone on Titan, you and I, than we have ever been. *Basta, per carita!*—so much for Ulla.

Awakening in this same darkness as before, Ulla felt the virus bubble snuggling closer to her blind skin, and recognized the shock that had so regressed her: a shock of recognition, but recognition of something she had never felt herself. Alone in a Titanic snowfield, she had eavesdropped on an . . .

No. Not possible. Sniffling, and still blind, she pushed the cozy bubble away from her breasts and tried to stand up. Light flashed briefly around her, as though the bubble had cleared just above her forehead and then clouded again. She was still alive, but everything else was utterly problematical. What had happened to her? She simply did not know.

Therefore, she thought, begin with ignorance. No one begins anywhere else . . . but I didn't know even that, once upon a time.

Hence:

3

Though the virus bubble ordinarily regulated itself, there was a control box on her hip—actually an ultrashort-range microwave transmitter—by which it could be modulated, against more special environments than the bubble itself could cope with alone. She had never had to use it before, but she tried it now.

The fogged bubble cleared patchily, but it would not stay cleared. Crazy moires and herringbone patterns swept over it, changing direction repeatedly, and outside the snowy landscape kept changing color like a delirium. She found, however, that by continuously working the frequency knob on her box—at random, for the responses seemed to bear no relation to the Braille calibrations on the dial—she could maintain outside vision of a sort in pulses of two or three seconds each.

This was enough to show her, finally, what had happened. There was a flying cloak around her. This in itself was unprecedented; the cloaks had never attacked a man before, or indeed paid any of them the least attention during their brief previous forays. On the other hand, this was the first time anyone had ventured more than five or ten minutes outdoors in a virus suit.

It occurred to her suddenly that insofar as anything was known about the nature of the cloaks, they were in some respects much like the bubbles. It was almost as though the one were a wild species of the other.

It was an alarming notion and possibly only a trope, containing as little truth as most poetry. Annoyingly, she found herself wondering if, once she got out of this mess, the men at the base camp would take to referring to it as "the cloak and suit business."

The snowfield began to turn brighter; Saturn was rising. For a moment the drifts were a pale straw color, the normal hue of Saturnlight through an atmosphere; then it turned a raving Kelly green. Muttering, Ulla twisted the potentiometer dial, and was rewarded with a brief flash of normal illumination which was promptly overridden by a torrent of crimson lake, as though she were seeing everything in terms of a series of lithographer's color separations.

Since she could not help this, she clenched her teeth and ignored it. It was much more important to find out what the flying cloak had done to her bubble, if she were to have any hope of shucking the thing.

There was no clear separation between the bubble and the Titanian creature. They seemed to have blended into a mélange which was neither one nor the other, but a sort of coarse burlesque of both. Yet the total surface area of the integument about her did not seem to be any greater—only more ill-fitting, less responsive to her own needs. Not *much* less; after all, she was still alive, and any really gross insensitivity to the demands and cues of her body would have been instantly fatal; but there was no way to guess how long the bubble would stay even that obedient. At the moment the wild thing that had enslaved it was perhaps most like a bear sark, dangerous to the wearer only if she panicked, but the change might well be progressive, pointed ultimately toward some Saturnine equivalent of the shirt of Nessus.

And that might be happening very rapidly. She might not be allowed the time to think her way out of this fix by herself. Little though she wanted any help from the men at the base camp, and useless though she was sure they would prove, she'd damn well better ask for it now, just in case.

But the bubble was not allowing any radio transmission through its roiling unicell wall today. The earphone was dead; not even the hiss of the stars came through it—only an occasional pop of noise that was born of entropy loss in the circuits themselves.

She was cut off. *Nun denn, allein!*

With the thought, the bubble cloak shifted again around her. A sudden pressure at her lower abdomen made her stumble forward over the crisp snow, four or five steps. Then it was motionless once more, except within itself.

That it should be able to do this was not surprising, for the cloaks had to be able to flex voluntarily at least a little in order to catch the thermals they rode, and the bubble had to be able to vary its dimensions and surface tension over a wide range to withstand pressure changes, outside and in, and do it automatically. No, of course the combination would be able to move by itself; what was disquieting was that it should want to.

Another stir of movement in the middle distance caught her eye: a free cloak, something riding an updraft over a fixed point. For a moment she wondered what on that ground could be warm enough to produce so localized a thermal. Then, abruptly, she realized that she was shaking with hatred, and fought furiously to drive the spasm down, her fingernails slicing into her naked palms.

A raster of jagged black lines, like a television interference pattern, broke across her view and brought her attention fully back to the minutely solipsistic confines of her dilemma. The wave of emotion, nevertheless, would not quite go away, and she had a vague but persistent impression that it was being imposed from outside, at least in part—a cold passion she was interpreting as fury because its real nature, whatever it was, had no necessary relevance to her own imprisoned soul. For all that it was her own life and no other that was in peril, she felt guilty, as though she was eavesdropping, and as angry with herself as with what she was overhearing; yet burning as helplessly as the forbidden lamp in the bedchamber of Psyche and Eros.

Another trope—but was it, after all, so far-fetched? She was a mortal present at the mating of inhuman essences; mountainously far from home; borne here like the invisible lovers upon the arms of the wind; empalaced by a whole virgin-white world, over which flew the banners of a high god and a father of gods; and, equally appropriately, Venus was very far away from whatever love was being celebrated here.

What ancient and coincidental nonsense! Next she would be thinking herself degraded at the foot of some cross.

Yet the impression, of an eerie tempest going on just slightly outside any possibility of understanding what it was, would not pass away. Still worse, it seemed to mean something, to be important, to mock her with subtle clues to matters of great moment, of which her own present trap was only the first and not necessarily the most significant.

And suppose that all these impressions were in fact not extraneous or irrelevant, but did have some import —not just as an abstract puzzle, but to that morsel of displaced life that was Ulla Hillström? She was certainly no Freudian—that farrago of poetry and tosh had been passé for so long that it was now hard to understand how anybody, let alone a whole era, had been bemused by it—but it was too late now to rule out the repulsive possibility. No matter how frozen her present world, she could not escape the fact that, from the moment the cloak had captured her, she had been equally ridden by a Sabbat of specifically erotic memories, images, notions, analogies, myths, symbols, and frank physical sensations, all the more obtrusive because they were both inappropriate and disconnected. It might well have to be faced that a season of love can fall due in the heaviest weather —and never mind the terrors that flow in with it, or what deep damnations. At the very least, it was possible that somewhere in all this was the clue that would help her to divorce herself at last even from this violent embrace.

But the concept was preposterous enough to defer consideration of it if there were any other avenues open, and at least one seemed to be: the source of the thermal. The virus bubble, like many of the Terrestrial microorganisms to which it was analogous, could survive temperatures well above boiling, but it seemed reasonable to assume that the flying cloaks, evolved on a world where even words congealed, might be sensitive to a relatively slight amount of heat.

Now, could she move inside this shroud of her own volition? She tried a step. The sensation was tacky, as though she were plowing in thin honey, but it did not impede her except for a slight imposed clumsiness which experience ought to obviate. She was able to mount the sled with no trouble.

The cogs bit into the snow with a dry, almost inaudible squeaking, and the sled inched forward. Ulla held it to as slow a crawl as possible, because of her interrupted vision.

The free cloak was still in sight, approximately where it had been before, insofar as she could judge against this featureless snowscape—which was fortunate, since it might well be her only flag for the source of the thermal, whatever it was.

A peculiar fluttering in her surroundings—a whisper of sound, of motion, of flickering in the light—distracted her. It was as though her compound sheath were trembling slightly. The impression grew slowly more pronounced as the sled continued to lurch forward. As usual, there seemed to be nothing she could do about it except, possibly, to retreat; but she could not do that either, now; she was committed. Outside, she began to hear the soft soughing of a steady wind.

The cause of the thermal, when she finally reached it, was almost bathetic: a pool of liquid. Placid and deep blue, it lay inside a fissure in a low, heart-shaped hummock, rimmed with feathery snow. It looked like nothing more or less than a spring, though she did not for a moment suppose that the liquid could be water. She could not see the bottom of it; evidently, it was welling up from a fair depth. The spring analogy was probably completely false; the existence of anything in a liquid state on this world had to be thought of as a form of vulcanism. Certainly the column of heat rising from it was considerable; despite the thinness of the air, the wind here nearly howled. The free cloak floated up and down, about a hundred feet above her, like the last leaf of a long, cruel autumn. Nearer home, the bubble cloak shook with something comically like subdued fury.

Now, what to do? Should she push boldly into that cleft, hoping that the alien part of the bubble cloak would be unable to bear the heat? Close up, that course now seemed foolish, as long as she was ignorant of the real nature of the magma down there. And, besides, any effective immersion would probably have to surround at least half of the total surface area of the bubble, which wasn't practicable—the well wasn't big enough to accommodate it, even supposing that the compromised virus suit did not fight back, as in the pure state it had been obligated to do. On the whole, she was reluctantly glad

that the experiment was impossible, for the mere notion
of risking a new immolation in that problematical hole
gave her the horrors.

Yet the time left for decision was obviously now very
short, even supposing—as she had no right to do—that
the environment-maintaining functions of the suit were
still in perfect order. The quivering of the bubble was
close to being explosive, and even were it to remain
intact, it might shut her off from the ouside world at any
second.

The free cloak dipped lower, as if in curiosity. That
only made the trembling worse. She wondered why.

Was it possible—was it possible that the thing embrac-
ing her companion was jealous?

4

There was no time left to examine the notion, no time
even to sneer at it. Act—act! Forcing her way off the sled,
she stumbled to the mound and looked frantically for
some way of stopping it up. If she could shut off the
thermal, bring the free cloak still closer—but how?

Throw rocks. But were there any? Yes, there were two,
not very big, but at least she could move them. She bent
stiffly and tumbled them into the crater.

The liquid froze around them with soundless speed.
In seconds, the snow rimming the pool had drawn completely over it, like lips closing, leaving behind only a
faint dimpled streak of shadow on a white ground.

The wind moaned and died, and the free cloak, its
hems outspread to the uttermost, sank down as if to
wrap her in still another deadly swath. Shadow spread
around her; the falling cloak, its color deepening, blotted
Saturn from the sky, and then was sprawling over the
beautiful banners of the rings—

The virus bubble convulsed and turned black, throwing

her to the frozen ground beside the hummock like a bead doll. A blast of wind squalled over her.

Terrified, she tried to curl into a ball. The suit puffed up around her.

Then at last, with a searing, invisible wrench at its contained kernel of space-time, which burned out the control box instantly, the single creature that was the bubble cloak tore itself free of Ulla and rose to join its incomplete fellow.

In the single second before she froze forever into the livid backdrop of Titan, she failed even to find time to regret what she had never felt; for she had never known it, and only died as she had lived, an artifact of successful calculation. She never saw the cloaks go flapping away downwind—nor could it ever have occurred to her that she had brought heterosexuality to Titan, thus beginning that long evolution the end of which, sixty millions of years away, no human being would see.

No; her last thought was for the virus bubble, and it was only three words long:

You goddamn philanderer—

Almost on the horizon, the two cloaks, the two Titanians, flailed and tore at each other, becoming smaller and smaller with distance. Bits and pieces of them flaked off and fell down the sky like ragged tears. Ungainly though the cloaks normally were, they courted even more clumsily.

Beside Ulla, the well was gone; it might never have existed. Overhead, the banners of the rings flew changelessly, as though they too had seen nothing—or perhaps, as though in the last six billion years they had seen everything, siftings upon siftings in oblivion, until nothing remained but the banners of their own mirrored beauty.

John Brunner

The Totally Rich

They are the totally rich. You've never heard of them because they are the only people in the world rich enough to buy what they want: a completely private life. The lightning can strike into your life and mine:—you win a big prize or find yourself neighbor to an ax-murderer or buy a parrot suffering from psittacosis—and you are in the searchlight, blinking shyly and wishing to God you were dead.

They won their prizes by being born. They do not have neighbors, and if they require a murder they do not use so clumsy a means as an ax. They do not keep parrots. And if by some other million-to-one chance the searchlight does tend towards them, they buy it and instruct the man behind it to switch it off.

How many of them there are I don't know. I have tried to estimate the total by adding together the gross national product of every country on earth and dividing by the amount necessary to buy a government of a major industrial power. It goes without saying that you cannot maintain privacy unless you can buy any two governments.

I think there may be one hundred of these people. I have met one, and very nearly another.

By and large they are night people. The purchase of light from darkness was the first economic advance. But you will not find them by going and looking at two o'clock in the morning, any more than at two in the afternoon. Not at the approved clubs; not at the Polo Grounds; not in the Royal Enclosure at Ascot nor on the White House lawn.

They are not on maps. Do you understand that? Literally, where they choose to live becomes a blank space in the atlases. They are not in census lists, *Who's Who*, or Burke's *Peerage*. They do not figure in tax collectors' files, and the post office has no record of their addresses. Think of all the places where your name appears—the yellowing school registers, the hospital case records, the duplicate receipt form in the store, the signature on letters. In *no single* such place is there one of their names.

How it is done . . . no, I don't know. I can only hazard a guess that to almost all human beings the promise of having more than everything they have ever conceived as desirable acts like a traumatic shock. It is instantaneous brainwashing; in the moment the promise is believed, the pattern of obedience is imprinted, as the psychologists say. But they take no chances. They are not absolute rulers—indeed, they are not rulers of anything except what directly belongs to them—but they have much in common with that caliph of Baghdad to whom a sculptor came, commissioned to make a fountain. This fountain was the most beautiful in the world, and the caliph approved it. Then he demanded of the sculptor whether anyone else could have made so lovely a fountain, and the sculptor proudly said no one but he in the whole world could have achieved it.

Pay him what was promised, said the caliph. And also —put out his eyes.

I wanted champagne that evening, dancing girls, bright lights, music. All I had was a can of beer, but at least it was cold. I went to fetch it, and when I came back stood in the kitchen doorway looking at my . . . living room, workshop, lab, whatever. It was a bit of all these.

All right, I didn't believe it. It was August 23rd, and I had been here one year and one month, and the job was done. I didn't believe it, and I wouldn't be able to until I'd told people—called in my friends and handed the beer around and made them drink a toast.

I raised the can. I said, "To the end of the job!" I drank. That hadn't turned the trick. I said, "To the Cooper Effect!" That was a little more like it, but it still wasn't quite complete.

So I frowned for a moment, thought I'd got it, and said triumphantly, "To Santadora—the most wonderful place on earth, without which such concentration would never have been possible: may God bless her and all who sail from her."

I was drinking this third toast with a sense of satisfaction when Naomi spoke from the shadows of the open porch.

"Drink to me, Derek," she said. "You're coming closer, but you aren't quite there."

I slammed the beer can down on a handy table, strode across the room, and gave her a hug. She didn't respond;

she was like a beautiful doll displaying Paris creations in a store window. I had never seen her wearing anything but black, and tonight it was a black blouse of hand-spun raw silk and tight black pants tapering down to black espadrilles. Her hair, corn-pale, her eyes, sapphire-blue, her skin, luminous under a glowing tan, had always been so perfect they seemed unreal. I had never touched her before. Sometimes, lying awake at night, I had wondered why; she had no man. I had rationalized to myself that I prized this haven of peace, and the concentration I found possible here, too much to want to involve myself with a woman who never demanded anything but who—one knew it—would take nothing less than everything.

"It's done," I said, whirling and throwing out my arm. "The millennium has arrived! Success at last!" I ran to the haywire machine which I had never thought to see in real existence. "This calls for a celebration—I'm going out to collect everyone I can find and. . . ."

I heard my voice trail away. She had walked a pace forward and lifted a hand that had been hanging by her side, weighed down by something. Now it caught the light. A bottle of champagne.

"How—?" I said. And thought of something else, too. I had never been alone with Naomi before, in the thirteen months since coming to Santadora.

"Sit down, Derek," she said. She put the champagne bottle on the same table as the beer can. "It's no good going out to collect anyone. There isn't anybody here except you and me."

I didn't say anything.

She cocked a quizzical eyebrow. "You don't believe me? You will."

Turning, she went to the kitchen. I waited for her to return with a pair of the glasses I kept for company; I was leaning forward with my hands on the back of a chair, and it suddenly seemed to me that I had subconsciously intended to put the chair between myself and this improbable stranger.

Dexterously she untwisted the wire of the champagne bottle, caught the froth which followed the cork in the first glass, poured the second and held it out to me. I came—moving like a stupid, stolid animal—to take hold of it.

"Sit down," she said again.

"But—where is everybody else? Where's Tim? Where are Conrad and Ella? Where—?"

"They've gone," she said. She came, carrying her glass, to sit facing me in the only other chair not cluttered with broken bits of my equipment. "They went about an hour ago."

"But—Pedro! And—!"

"They put out to sea. They are going somewhere else." She made a casual gesture. "I don't know where, but they are provided for."

Raising her champagne, she added, "To you, Derek—and my compliments. I was never sure that you would do it, but it had to be tried."

I ran to the window which overlooked the sea, threw it open, and stared out into the gathering dark. I could see four or five fishing boats, their riding lights like shifting stars, moving out of the harbor. On the quay was a collection of abandoned furniture and some fishermen's gear. It *did* look as though they were making a permanent departure.

"Derek, *sit down*," Naomi said for the third time. "We're wasting time, and besides, your wine is getting flat."

"But how can they bring themselves to—?"

"Abandon their ancestral homes, dig up their roots, leave for fresh woods and pastures new?" Her tone was light and mocking. "They are doing nothing of the kind. They have no special attachment to Santadora. Santadora does not exist. Santadora was built eighteen months ago, and will be torn down next month."

I said after an eternal silence, "Naomi, are you—are you feeling quite well?"

"I feel wonderful." She smiled, and the light glistened on her white teeth. "Moreover, the fishermen were not fishermen and Father Francisco is not a priest and Conrad and Ella are not artists except in a very small way of business, as a hobby. Also my name is not Naomi, but since you're used to it—and so am I—it'll serve."

Now, I had to drink the champagne. It was superb. It was the most perfect wine I had ever tasted. I was sorry not to be in the mood to appreciate the fact.

"Are you making out that this entire village is a sham?" I demanded. "A sort of colossal—what—movie set?"

"In a way. A stage setting would be a more accurate term. Go out on the porch and reach up to the fretted decoration overhanging the step. Pull it hard. It will come away. Look at what you find on the exposed surface. Do the same to any other house in the village which has a similar porch—there are five of them. Then come back and we can talk seriously."

She crossed her exquisite legs and sipped her champagne. She knew beyond doubt that I was going to do precisely as she said.

Determinedly, though more to prevent myself feeling foolish than for any better reason, I went on to the porch. I put on the light—a swinging yellow bulb, on a flex tacked amateurishly into place—and looked up at the fretted decoration on the edge of the overhang. The summer insects came buzzing in towards the attractive lamp.

I tugged at the piece of wood, and it came away. Holding it to the light, I read on the exposed surface, stamped in pale blue ink: *"Número 14,006—José Barcos, Barcelona."*

I had no ready-made reaction. Accordingly, holding the

piece of wood like a talisman in front of me, I went back indoors and stood over Naomi in her chair. I was preparing to phrase some angry comment, but I never knew what it was to be, for at that moment my eye was caught by the label on the bottle. It was not champagne. The name of the firm was unknown to me.

"It is the best sparkling wine in the world," Naomi said. She had followed my gaze. "There is enough for about—oh—one dozen bottles a year."

My palate told me there was some truth at least in what she said. I made my way dizzily to my chair and sank into it at last. "I don't pretend to understand this. I—I haven't spent the last year in a place that doesn't exist!"

"But you have." Quite cool, she cradled her glass between her beautiful slim hands and set her elbows on the sides of the dirty chair. "By the way, have you noticed that there are never any mosquitoes among the insects that come to your lights? It was barely likely that you would have caught malaria, but the chance had to be guarded against."

I started. More than once I'd jokingly commented to Tim Hannigan that one of Santadora's greatest advantages was its freedom from mosquitoes. . . .

"Good. The facts are beginning to make an impression on you. Cast your mind back now to the winter before last. Do you recall making the acquaintance of a man going under the name of Roger Gurney, whom you subsequently met one other time?"

I nodded. Of course I remembered Roger Gurney. Often, since coming to Santadora, I'd thought that that first meeting with him had been one of the two crucial events that changed my life.

"You gave Gurney a lift one rather unpleasant November night—his car had broken down and there was no hope of getting a necessary spare part before the morning, and he had to be in London for an urgent appointment at ten next day. You found him very congenial and charming. You put him up in your flat; you had dinner together and talked until 4 A.M. about what has now taken concrete form here in this room. You talked about the Cooper Effect."

I felt incredibly cold, as though a finger of that bleak November night had reached through the window and traced a cold smear down my spine. I said, "Then, that very night, I mentioned to him that I only saw one way of doing the necessary experiments. I said I'd have to find a village somewhere, without outside distractions, with no telephone or newspapers, without even a radio. A place where living was so cheap that I could devote myself for two or three years to my work and not have to worry about earning my living."

My God! I put my hand to my forehead. It was as if memory was re-emerging like invisible ink exposed to a fire.

"That's right," Naomi nodded with an air of satisfaction. "And the second and only other time you met this delightful Roger Gurney was the weekend you were celebrating your small win on the football pools. Two thousand one hundred and four pounds, seventeen shillings, and a penny. And he told you of a certain small Spanish village, named Santadora, where the conditions for your research were perfectly fulfilled. He said he had visited some friends here, named Conrad and Ella Williams. The possibility of turning your dreams into facts had barely occurred to you, but by the time you'd had a few drinks with Gurney, it seemed strange that you hadn't already laid your plans."

I slammed my glass down so hard it might have broken. I said harshly, "Who are you? What game are you playing with me?"

"No game, Derek." She was leaning foward now, her blue jewel-hard eyes fixed on my face. "A very serious business. And one in which you also have a stake. Can you honestly say that but for meeting Roger Gurney, but for winning this modest sum of money, you would be here—or anywhere—with the Cooper Effect translated into reality?"

I said after a long moment in which I reviewed one whole year of my life, "No. No, I must be honest. I can't."

"Then there's your answer to the question you put a few moments ago." She laid her glass on the table and took out a small cigarette case from the pocket of her tight pants. "I am the only person in the world who wanted to have and *use* the Cooper Effect. Nobody else was eager enough to bring it about—not even Derek Cooper. Take one of these cigarettes."

She held out the case; the mere opening of it had filled the air with a fragrance I found startling. There was no name on the cigarette I took, the only clue to its origin being a faint striping of the paper, but when I drew the first smoke I knew that this, like the wine, was the best in the world.

She watched my reaction with amusement. I relaxed fractionally—smiling made her seem familiar. How many times had I seen her smile like that, here, or much more often at Tim's or at Conrad's?

"I wanted the Cooper Effect," she repeated. "And now I've got it."

I said, "Just a moment! I—"

"Then I want to rent it." She shrugged as though the matter were basically a trifling one. "After I've rented it, it is and will be forever yours. You have conceded yourself that but for—certain key interventions, let's call them— but for *me*, it would be a mere theory. An intellectual toy. I will not, even so, ask you to consider that a fair rental for it. For the use of your machine for one very specific purpose, I will pay you so much that for the rest of your life you may have anything *at all* your fancy turns to. Here!"

She tossed something—I didn't know where she had been hiding it—and I caught it reflexively. It was a long narrow wallet of soft, supple leather, zipped round the edge.

"Open it."

I obeyed. Inside I discovered one—two—three credit cards made out in my name, and a check book with my name printed ready on the checks. On each of the cards there was something I had never seen before: a single word overprinted in red. The word was UNLIMITED.

I put them back in the wallet. It had occurred to me to doubt that what she said was true, but the doubt had faded at once. Yes, Santadora had been created in order to permit me to work under ideal conditions. Yes, she had done it. After what she had said about Roger Gurney, I didn't have room to disbelieve.

Consequently I could go to Madrid, walk into a salesroom, and come out driving a Rolls-Royce; in it, I could drive to a bank and write the sum of one million pesetas on the first of those cheques and receive it—if the bank had that much in cash.

Still looking at the wallet, zipping and unzipping it mechanically, I said, "All right. You're the person who wanted the Effect. Who are you?"

"The person who could get it." She gave a little dry laugh and shook her head. Her hair waved around her face like wings. "Don't trouble me with more inquiries, Derek. I won't answer them because the answers would mean nothing."

I was silent for a little while. Then, finally, because I had no other comment to make, I said, "At least you must say why you wanted what I could give you. After all, I'm still the only person in the world who understands it."

"Yes." She studied me. "Yes, that is true. Pour more

wine for us; I think you like it."

While I was doing so, and while I was feeling my body grow calm after the shock and storm of the past ten minutes, she said, looking at the air, "You *are* unique, you know. A genius without equal in your single field. That's why you're here, why I went to a little trouble for you. I can get everything I want, but for certain things I'm inevitably dependent on the *one* person who can provide them."

Her eyes roved to my new, ramshackle—but functioning—machine.

"I wanted that machine to get me back a man," she said. "He has been dead for three years."

The world seemed to stop in its tracks. I had been blind ever since the vision of unlimited money dazzled me. I had accepted that because Naomi could get everything she knew what it was she was getting. And, of course, she didn't.

A little imaginary pageant played itself out in my mind, in which faceless dolls moved in a world of shifting, rosy clouds. A doll clothed in black, with long pale hair, said, "He's dead. I want him back. Don't argue. Find me a way."

The other dolls bowed and went away. Eventually one doll came back and said. "There is a man called Derek Cooper who has some unorthodox ideas. Nobody else in all the world is thinking about this problem at all."

"See that he gets what he needs," said the doll with pale hair.

I put down the bottle of wine. I hesitated—yes, I still did, I was still dazzled. But then I took up the soft leather wallet and tossed it into Naomi's lap. I said, "You've cheated yourself."

"What?" She didn't believe it. The wallet which had fallen in her lap was an apparition; she did not move to pick it up, as though touching it would turn it from a bad dream to a harsh fact.

I said, very thoughtfully because I was working out in my mind how it must be, "You talked about wanting my machine for a particular job. I was too dazed to wonder what the job might be—there *are* jobs which can be done with it, so I let it slide by. You are very rich, Naomi. You have been so rich all your life that you don't know about the one other thing that stands between the formulation of a problem and its solution. That's *time*, Naomi!"

I tapped the top of the machine. I was still proud of it. I had every right to be.

"You are like—like an empress of ancient China. Maybe she existed, I don't know. Imagine that one day she said, 'It has been revealed to me that my ancestors dwell in the moon. I wish to go there and pay the respects of a dutiful daughter. Find me a way.' So they hunted through the length and breadth of the empire, and one day a courtier came in with a poor and ragged man, and said to the empress, 'This man has invented a rocket.'

" 'Good,' said the empress. 'Perfect it so that I may go to the moon.' "

I had intended to tell the fable in a bantering tone—to laugh at the end of it. But I turned to glance at Naomi, and my laughter died.

Her face was as pale and still as a marble statue's, her lips a little parted, her eyes wide. On one cheek, like a diamond, glittered a tear.

All my levity evaporated. I had the sudden horrible impression that I had kicked at what seemed a stone and shattered a priceless bowl.

"No, Derek," she said after a while. "You don't have to tell me about time." She stirred, half turned in her chair, and looked at the table beside her. "Is this glass mine?" she added in a lighter tone, putting out her slim and beautiful hand to point. She did not wipe the tear; it remained on her cheek for some time, until the hot dry air of the night kissed it away.

Taking the glass at my nod, she stood up and came across to look at my machine. She regarded it without comment, then said, "I hadn't meant to tell you what I wanted. Time drove me to it."

She drank deeply. "Now," she went on, "I want to know exactly what your pilot model *can* do."

I hesitated. So much of it was not yet in words; I had kept my word-thinking separate from my work-thinking all during the past year, and lately I had talked of nothing except commonplaces when I relaxed in the company of my friends. The closer I came to success, the more superstitious I had grown about mentioning the purpose of this project.

And—height of absurdity—now that I knew what she wanted, I was faintly ashamed that my triumph reduced on close examination to such a little thing.

Sensing my mood, she glanced at me and gave a faint smile. " 'Yes, Mr. Faraday'—or was it Humphry Davy?— 'but what is it *good* for?' I'm sorry."

A newborn baby. Well enough. Somehow the phrase hit me—reached me emotionally—and I was suddenly not ashamed at all of anything; I was as proud as any father and much more so.

I pushed aside a stack of rough schematics on the corner of the table nearest the machine and perched where it had been. I held my glass between my palms, and it was so quiet I fancied I could hear the bubbles bursting as they surfaced in the wine.

I said, "It wasn't putting money in my way, or anything like that, which I owe you a debt of gratitude for. It was sending that persuasive and charming Roger Gurney after me. I had never met anyone else who was prepared to take my ideas except as an amusing talking point. I'd kicked the concept around with some of the finest intellects I know—people I knew at university, for instance, who've left me a long way behind since then." I hadn't thought of this before. I hadn't thought of a lot of things, apparently.

"But he could talk them real. What I said to him was much the same as what I'd said to others before then. I'd talked about the—the space a living organism defines around itself, by behaving as it does. A mobile does it. That's why I have one over there." I pointed, raising my arm, and as though by command a breeze came through the open window and stirred hanging metal panels in the half-shadowed far corner of the room. They squeaked a little as they turned; I'd been too busy to drop oil on the bearings lately.

I was frowning, and the frown was knotting my forehead muscles, and it was going to make my head ache, but I couldn't prevent myself.

"There must be a total interrelationship between the organism and its environment, including and especially its fellow organisms. Self-recognition was one of the first things they stumbled across in building mechanical simulacra of living creatures. They didn't plan for it—they built mechanical tortoises with little lights on top and a simple light-seeking urge, and if you showed this beast to a mirror, it would seem to recognize itself. . . . This is the path, not the deliberate step-by-step piecing together of a man, but the attempt to define the same shape as that which man himself defines in reacting with other people.

"Plain enough, that. But are you to process a trillion bits of information, store them, label them in time, translate them back for reproduction as—well, as what? I can't think of anything. What you want is. . . ."

I shrugged, emptied my glass, and stood up. "You want the Cooper Effect," I finished. "Here—take this."

From the little rack on top of my machine I took a flat translucent disk about the size of a penny but thicker. To handle it I used a key which plugged into a hole in the center so accurately that it held the weight by simple friction. I held it out to Naomi.

My voice shook, because this was the first random test I had ever made.

"Take hold of this. Handle it—rub your fingers over it, squeeze it gently on the flat sides, close your hand on it."

She obeyed. While it was in her hand, she looked at me.

"What is it?"

"It's an artificial piezoelectric crystal. All right, that should be enough. Put it back on the key—I don't want to confuse the readings by touching it myself."

It wasn't easy to slip the disk back on the key, and she made two false attempts before catching my hand to steady it. I felt a vibration coming through her fingers, as though her whole body were singing like a musical instrument.

"There," she said neutrally.

I carried the disk back to the machine. Gingerly I transferred it from the key to the little post on top of the reader. It slid down like a record dropping to a turntable. A moment or two during which I didn't breathe. Then there was the reaction.

I studied the readings on the dials carefully. Not perfect. I was a little disappointed—I'd hoped for a perfect run this first time. Nonetheless, it was extraordinarily close, considering she had handled the disk for a bare ten seconds.

I said, "The machine tells me that you are female, slim, fair-haired and probably blue-eyed, potentially artistic, unaccustomed to manual labor, IQ in the range 120-140, under intense emotional stress—"

Her voice cut across mine like the lash of a whip. "How? How do I know the machine tells you this, not your own eyes?"

I didn't look up. I said, "The machine is telling me

what changes were brought about in that little crystal disk when you touched it. I'm reading it as a kind of graph, if you like—looking across the pattern of the dials and interpreting them into words."

"Does it tell you anything else?"

"Yes—but it must be in error somewhere, I'm afraid. The calibration has been rather makeshift, and would have to be completed with a proper statistical sample of say a thousand people from all walks of life." I forced a laugh as I turned away from the machine. "You see, it says that you're forty-eight to fifty years old, and this is ridiculous on the face of it."

She sat very still. I had moved all the way to the table beside her, intending to refill my glass, before I realized how still. My hand on the bottle's neck, I stared at her.

"Is something wrong?"

She shook herself and came back to life instantly. She said lightly, "No. No, nothing at all. Derek, you are the most amazing man in the world. I shall be fifty years old next week."

"You're joking." I licked my lips. I'd have said . . . oh, thirty-five and childless and extremely careful of her looks. But not more. Not a day more.

A trace of bitterness crossed her face as she nodded.

"It's true. I wanted to be beautiful—I don't think I have to explain why. I wanted to go on being beautiful because it was the only gift I could give to someone who had, as I have, everything he could conceivably want. So I—I saw to it."

"What happened to him?"

"I would prefer you not to know." The answer was cool and final. She relaxed deliberately, stretching her legs out before her, and gave a lazy smile. Her foot touched something on the floor as she moved, and she glanced down.

"What—? Oh, that!" She reached for the soft leather

wallet, which had fallen from her lap when she stood up after I had tossed it back at her. Holding it out, she said, "Take it, Derek. I know you've already earned it. By accident—by mistake—whatever you call it, you've proved that you can do what I was hoping for."

I did take it. But I didn't pocket it at first; I kept it in my hands, absently turning it over.

I said, "I'm not so sure, Naomi. Listen." I picked up my newly filled glass and returned to the chair facing her. "What I ultimately envisage is being able to deduce the individual from the traces he makes. You know that; that was the dream I told to Roger Gurney. But between now and then, between the simple superficial analysis of a specially prepared material and going over, piece by piece, ten thousand objects affected not merely by the individual in question but by many others, some of whom probably cannot be found in order to identify and rule out their extraneous influence—and *then* processing the results to make a coherent whole—there may be years, decades, of work and study, a thousand false trails, a thousand preliminary experiments with animals. . . . Whole new techniques will have to be invented in order to employ the data produced! Assuming you have your—your analogue of a man: what are you going to do with it? Are you going to try and *make* a man, artificially, that fits the specifications?"

"Yes."

The simple word left me literally gasping; it was like a blow to the stomach, driving my breath away. She bent her brilliant gaze on me and once more smiled faintly.

"Don't worry, Derek. That's not your job. Work has been going on in many places for a long time—they tell me—on that problem. What nobody except yourself was doing was struggling with the problem of the total person."

I couldn't reply. She filled her own glass again before

continuing, in a tenser voice.

"There's a question I've got to put to you, Derek. It's so crucial I'm afraid to hear the answer. But I can't endure to wait any longer, either. I want to know how long you think it will be before I can have what I want. Assume—remember that you've *got* to assume—the best men in the world can be set to work on the subsidiary problems; they'll probably make their reputations, they'll certainly make their fortunes. I want to hear what you think."

I said thickly, "Well, I find that pretty difficult! I've already mentioned the problem of isolating the traces from—"

"This man lived a different kind of existence from you, Derek. If you'd stop and think for a second, you'd guess that. I can take you to a place that was uniquely *his*, where his personality formed and molded and affected every grain of dust. Not a city where a million people have walked, not a house where a dozen families have lived."

It had to be true, incredible though I would have thought it a scant hour ago. I nodded.

"That's good. Well, I shall also have to work out ways of handling unprepared materials—calibrate the properties of every single substance. And there's the risk that the passage of time will have overlaid the traces with molecular noise and random movement. Moreover, the testing itself, before the actual readings, might disturb the traces."

"You are to assume"—she forced patience on the repetition—"that the best men in the world are going to tackle the side issues."

"It isn't a side issue, Naomi." I wished I didn't have to be honest. She was hurt by my insistence, and I was beginning to think that, for all the things one might envy her, she had been hurt very badly already. "It's simply a fact one has to face."

She drank down her wine and replaced the glass on the

table. Musingly she said, "I guess it would be true to say that the—the object which a person affects most, and most directly, is his or her own body. If just handling your little disk reveals so much, how much more must be revealed by the hands themselves, the lips, the eyes!"

I said uncomfortably, "Yes, of course. But it's hardly practicable to process a human body."

She said, "I have his body."

This silence was a dreadful one. A stupid beetle, fat as a bullet, was battering its head on the shade of the lamp in the porch, and other insects were droning, too, and there was the sea distantly heard. The silence, nonetheless, was graveyard-deep.

But she went on at last. "Everything that could possibly be preserved is preserved, by every means that could be found. I had—" Her voice broke for a second. "I had it prepared. Only the thing which is *he*, the web in the brain, the little currents died. Curious that a person is so fragile." Briskening, she launched her question anew.

"Derek, how long?"

I bit my lip and stared down at the floor by my feet. My mind churned as it considered, discarded relevant factors, envisaged problems, assumed them to be soluble, fined down everything to the simple irreducible of *time*. I might have said ten years and felt that I was being stupidly optimistic.

But in the end, I said nothing at all.

She waited. Then, quite unexpectedly, she gave a bright laugh and jumped to her feet. "Derek, it isn't fair!" she said. "You've achieved something fantastic, you want and deserve to relax and celebrate, and here I am plaguing you with questions and wanting answers out of the air. I know perfectly well that you're too honest to give me an estimate without time to think, maybe do a few calculations. And I'm keeping you shut up in your crowded room when probably what you most want is to get out of it for a while. Am I right?"

She put her hand out, her arm quite straight, as if to pull me from my chair. Her face was alight with what seemed pure pleasure, and to see it was to experience again the shock of hearing her say she was fifty years old. She looked—I can only say transformed. She looked like a girl at her first party.

But it lasted only a moment, this transformation. Her expression became grave and calm. She said, "I am sorry, Derek. I—I hate one thing about love. Have you ever thought how selfish it can make you?"

We wandered out of the house hand in hand, into the summer dark. There was a narrow slice of moon and the stars were like fierce hard lanterns. For the more than hundredth time I walked down the narrow ill-paved street leading from my temporary home towards the harbour; there was Conrad's house, and there was the grocery and wine shop; there was the church, its roof silvered by the moon; there were the little cottages all in a row facing the sea, where the families of fisherfolk lived. And here, abandoned, was the detritus of two hundred and seventy lives which had never actually existed—conjured up to order.

I said, when we had walked all the way to the quay, "Naomi, it's beyond belief, even though I know its true. This village wasn't a sham, a showplace. It was real. I *know* it."

She looked around her. "Yes. It was intended to be real. But all it takes is thought and patience."

"What did you say? Did you tell—whoever it was—'Go and build a real village'?"

"I didn't have to. They knew. Does it interest you, how it was done?" She turned a curious face to me, which I could barely see in the thin light.

"Of course," I said. "My God! To create real people

and a real place—when I'm ordered to re-create a real person—should I not be interested?"

"If it were as easy to re-create as it is to create," she said emptily, "I would not be . . . lonely."

We stopped, close by the low stone wall which ran from the quay to the sharp rocks of the little headland sheltering the beach, and leaned on it. At our backs, the row of little houses; before us, nothing but the sea. She was resting on both her elbows, staring over the water. At less than arm's reach, I leaned on one elbow, my hands clasped before me, studying her as though I had never seen her before tonight. Of course, I hadn't.

I said, "Are you afraid of not being beautiful? Something is troubling you."

She shrugged. "There is no such word as 'forever'—is there?"

"You make it seem as though there were."

"No, no." She chuckled. "Thank you for saying it, Derek. Even if I know—even if I can see in the mirror—that I am so, it's delightful to be reassured."

How had she achieved it, anyway? I wanted, and yet didn't want, to ask. Perhaps she didn't know; she had just said she wanted it so, and it was. So I asked a different question.

"Because it's—the thing that is most *yours*?"

Her eyes came back from the sea, rested on me, returned. "Yes. The *only* thing that is mine. You're a rare person; you have compassion. Thank you."

"How do you live?" I said. I fumbled out cigarettes from my pocket, rather crumpled; she refused one with a headshake, but I lit one for myself.

"How do I live?" she echoed. "Oh—many ways. As various people, of course, with various names. You see, I haven't even a name to call my own. Two women who look exactly like me exist for me, so that when I wish I can take their places in Switzerland or in Sweden or in

South America. I borrow their lives, use them a while, give them back. I have seen them grow old, changed them for replacements—made into duplicates of me. But those are not persons; they are masks. I live behind masks. I suppose that's what you'd say."

"You can't do anything else," I said.

"No. No, of course I can't. And until this overtook me, I'd never conceived that I might want to."

I felt that I understood that. I tapped the first ash off my cigarette down towards the sea. Glancing around, I said irrelevantly, "You know, it seems like a shame to dismantle Santadora. It could be a charming little village. A real one, not a stage set."

"No," she said. And then, as she straightened and whirled around, "No! Look!" She ran wildly into the middle of the narrow street and pointed at the cobbles. "Don't you see? Already stones which weren't cracked are cracked! And the houses!" She flung up her arm and ran forward to the door of the nearest house. "The wood is warping! And that shutter—hanging loose on the hinges! And the step!" She dropped to her knees, felt along the low stone step giving directly on the street.

I was coming after her now, startled by her passion.

"Feel!" she commanded. "Feel it! It's been worn by people walking on it. And even the wall—don't you see the crack from the corner of the window is getting wider?" Again she was on her feet, running her hand over the rough wall. "Time is gnawing at it, like a dog at a bone. God, no, Derek! Am I to leave it and know that time is breaking it, breaking, *breaking* it?"

I couldn't find words.

"Listen!" she said. "Oh God! Listen!" She had tensed like a frightened deer, head cocked.

"I don't hear anything," I said. I had to swallow hard.

"Like nails being driven into a coffin," she said. She

was at the house door, battering on it, pushing at it. "You *must* hear it!"

Now, I did. From within the house there was a ticking noise—a huge, majestic, slow rhythm, so faint I had not noticed it until she commanded me to strain my ears. A clock. Just a clock.

Alarmed at her frenzy, I caught her by the shoulder. She turned and clung to me like a tearful child, burying her head against my chest. "I can't stand it," she said, her teeth set. I could feel her trembling.

"Come away," I murmured. "If it hurts you so much, come away."

"No, that isn't what I want. I'd go on hearing it—don't you understand?" She drew back a little and looked up at me. "I'd go on hearing it!" Her eyes grew veiled, her whole attention focusing towards the clock inside the house. "Tick-tick-tick—God, it's like being buried alive!"

I hesitated a moment. Then I said, "All right, I'll fix it. Stand back."

She obeyed. I raised my foot and stamped it, sole and heel together, on the door. Something cracked; my leg stung all the way to the thigh with the impact. I did it again, and the jamb split. The door flew open. At once the ticking was loud and clear.

And visible in a shaft of moonlight opposite the door was the clock itself: a tall old grandfather, bigger than me, its pendulum glinting on every ponderous swing.

A snatch of an ancient and macabre Negro spiritual came to my mind:

The hammer keeps ringing on somebody's coffin. . . .

Abruptly it was as doom-laden for me as for Naomi. I strode across the room, tugged open the glass door of the clock, and stopped the pendulum with a quick finger. The silence was a relief like cold water after long thirst.

She came warily into the room after me, staring at the face of the clock as though hypnotized. It struck me that she was not wearing a watch, and I had never seen her wear one.

"Get rid of it," she said. She was still trembling. "Please, Derek—get rid of it."

I whistled, taking another look at the old monster. I said, "That's not going to be so easy! These clocks are heavy!"

"Please, Derek!" The urgency in her voice was frightening. She turned her back, staring into a corner of the room. Like all these cramped, imitation-antique houses, this one had a mere three rooms, and the room we were in was crowded with furniture—a big bed, a table, chairs, a chest. But for that, I felt she would have run to the corner to hide.

Well, I could try.

I studied the problem and came to the conclusion that it would be best to take it in parts.

"Is there a lamp?" I said. "I'd work better if I could see."

She murmured something inaudible; then there was the sound of a lighter, and a yellow flicker grew to a steady glow which illumined the room. The smell of kerosene reached my nostrils. She put the lamp on a table where its light fell past me on the clock.

I unhitched the weights and pocketed them; then I unclipped a screwdriver from my breast pocket and attacked the screws at the corners of the face. As I had hoped, with those gone, it was possible to lift out the whole works, the chains following like umbilical cords, making little scraping sounds as they were dragged over the wooden ledge the movement had rested on.

"Here!" Naomi whispered, and snatched it from me. It was a surprisingly small proportion of the weight of the whole clock. She dashed out of the house and across the street. A moment, and there was a splash.

I felt a spasm of regret. And then was angry with

myself. Quite likely this was no rare specimen of antique craftsmanship, but a fake. Like the whole village. I hugged the case to me and began to walk it on its front corners towards the door. I had been working with my cigarette in my mouth; now the smoke began to tease my eyes, and I spat it to the floor and ground it out.

Somehow I got the case out of the house, across the road, up on the seawall. I rested there for a second, wiping the sweat from my face, then got behind the thing and gave it the most violent push I could manage. It went over the wall, twisting once in the air, and splashed.

I looked down, and instantly wished that I hadn't. It looked exactly like a dark coffin floating off on the sea.

But I stayed there for a minute or so, unable to withdraw my gaze, because of an overwhelming impression that I had done some symbolic act, possessed of a meaning which could not be defined in logical terms, yet heavy, solid—real as that mass of wood drifting away.

I came back slowly, shaking my head, and found myself in the door of the house before I paid attention again to what was before my eyes. Then I stopped dead, one foot on the step which Naomi had cursed for being worn by passing feet. The flame of the yellow lamp was wavering a little in the wind, and it was too high—the smell of its smoke was strong, and the chimney was darkening.

Slowly, as though relishing each single movement, Naomi was unbuttoning the black shirt she wore, looking towards the lamp. She tugged it out of the waist of her pants and slipped it off. The brassiere she wore under it was black, too. I saw she had kicked away her espadrilles.

"Call it an act of defiance," she said in a musing tone—speaking more to herself, I thought, than to me. "I shall put off my mourning clothes." She unzipped her pants and let them fall. Her briefs also were black.

"Now I'm through with mourning. I believe it will be done. It will be done soon enough. Oh yes! Soon enough."

Her slim golden arms reached up behind her back. She dropped the brassiere to the floor, but the last garment she caught up in her hand and hurled at the wall. For a moment she stood still; then seemed to become aware of my presence for the first time and turned slowly towards me.

"Am I beautiful?" she said.

My throat was very dry. I said, "God, yes. You're one of the most beautiful women I've ever seen."

She leaned over the lamp and blew it out. In the instant of falling darkness she said, "Show me."

And, a little later on the rough blanket of the bed, when I had said twice or three times, "Naomi—Naomi!" she spoke again. Her voice was cold and far away.

"I didn't mean to call myself Naomi. What I had in mind was Niobe, but I couldn't remember it."

And very much later, when she had drawn herself so close to me that it seemed she was clinging to comfort, to existence itself, with her arms around me and her legs locked with mine, under the blanket now because the night was chill, I felt her lips move against my ear.

"How long, Derek?"

I was almost lost; I had never before been so drained of myself, as though I had been cork-tossed on a stormy ocean and battered limp by rocks, I could barely open my eyes. I said in a blurred voice, "What?"

"How long?"

I fought a last statement from my wearying mind, neither knowing nor caring what it was. "With luck," I muttered, "it might not take ten years. Naomi, I don't know—" And in a burst of absolute effort, finished, "My God, you do this to me and expect me to be able to think afterwards?"

But that was the extraordinary thing. I had imagined myself about to go down into blackness, into coma to sleep like a corpse. Instead, while my body rested, my mind rose to the pitch beyond consciousness—to a vantage point where it could survey the future. I was aware of the thing I had done. From my crude, experimental machine I knew, would come a second and a third, and the third would be sufficient for the task. I saw and recognized the associated problems, and knew them to be soluble. I conceived names of men I wanted to work on those problems—some who were known to me and who, given the chance I had been given, could create in their various fields, such new techniques as I had created. Meshing like hand-matched cogs, the parts blended into the whole.

A calendar and a clock were in my mind all this while.

Not all of this was a dream; much of it was of the nature of inspiration, with the sole difference that I could feel it happening and that it was right. But towards the very end, I did have a dream—not in visual images but in a kind of emotional aura. I had a completely satisfying sensation, which derived from the fact that I was about to meet for the first time a man who was already my closest friend, whom I knew as minutely as any human being had ever known another.

I was waking. For a little while longer I wanted to bask in that fantastic warmth of emotion; I struggled not to wake while feeling that I was smiling and had been smiling for so long that my cheek muscles were cramped.

Also I had been crying, so that the pillow was damp.

I turned on my side and reached out gently for Naomi, already phrasing the wonderful gift-words I had for her. "Naomi! I know how long it will take now. It needn't take more than three years, perhaps as little as two and a half."

My hand, meeting nothing but the rough cloth, sought further. Then I opened my eyes and sat up with a start.

I was alone. Full daylight was pouring into the room; it was bright and sunny and very warm. Where was she? I must go in search of her and tell her the wonderful news.

My clothes were on the floor by the bed; I pulled them

on, thrust my feet in my sandals, and padded to the door, pausing with one hand on the split jamb to accustom my eyes to the glare.

Just across the narrow street, leaning his elbows on the stone wall, was a man with his back to me. He gave not the slightest hint that he was aware of being watched. It was a man I knew at once, even though I'd met him no more than twice in my life. He called himself Roger Gurney.

I spoke his name, and he didn't turn around. He lifted one arm and made a kind of beckoning motion. I was sure then what had happened, but I walked forward to stand beside him, waiting for him to tell me.

Still he didn't look at me. He merely gestured towards the sharp rocks with which the end of the wall united. He said, "She came out at dawn and went up there. To the top. She was carrying her clothes in her hand. She threw them one by one into the sea. And then—" He turned his hand over, palm down, as though pouring away a little pile of sand.

I tried to say something, but my throat was choked.

"She couldn't swim," Gurney added after a moment. "Of course."

Now I could speak. I said, "But my God! Did you see it happen?"

He nodded.

"Didn't you go after her? Didn't you rescue her?"

"We recovered her body."

"Then—artificial respiration! You must have been able to do something!"

"She lost her race against time," Gurney said after a pause. "She had admitted it."

"I—" I checked myself. It was becoming so clear that I cursed myself for a fool. Slowly I went on, "How much longer would she have been beautiful?"

"Yes." He expressed the word with form. "That was the

thing she was running from. She wanted *him* to return and find her still lovely, and no one in the world would promise her more than another three years. After that, the doctors say, she would have——" He made an empty gesture. "Crumbled."

"She would always have been beautiful," I said. "My God! Even looking her real age, she'd have been beautiful!"

"We think so," Gurney said.

"And so stupid, so futile!" I slammed my fist into my palm. "You too, Gurney—do you realize what you've *done*, you fool?" My voice shook with anger, and for the first time he faced me.

"Why in hell didn't you revive her and send for me? It needn't have taken more than three years! Last night she demanded an answer and I told her ten, but it came clear to me during the night how it could be done in less than three!"

"I thought that was how it must have been." His face was white, but the tips of his ears were—absurdly— brilliant pink. "If you hadn't said that, Cooper; if you hadn't said that."

And then (I was still that wave-tossed cork, up one moment, down the next, up again the next) it came to me what my inspiration of the night really implied. I clapped my hand to my forehead.

"Idiot!" I said. "I don't know what I'm doing yet! Look, you have her body! Get to it—to wherever it is, with the other one, *quick*. What the hell else have I been doing but working to re-create a human being? And now I've seen how it can be done, I can do it—I can re-create her as well as him!" I was in a fever of excitement, having darted forward in my mind to that strange future I had visited in my sleep, and my barely visualized theories were solid fact.

He was regarding me strangely. I thought he hadn't

undertsood, and went on, "What are you standing there for? I can do it, I tell you—I've seen how it can be done. It's going to take men and money, but those can be got."

"No," Gurney said.

"What?" I let my arms fall to my sides, blinking in the sunlight.

"No," he repeated. He stood up, stretching arms cramped by long resting on the rough top of the wall. "You see, it isn't hers any longer. Now she's dead, it belongs to somebody else."

Dazed, I drew back a pace. I said, "Who?"

"How can I tell you? And what would it mean to you if I did? You ought by now to know what kind of people you're dealing with."

I put my hand in my pocket, feeling for my cigarettes. I was trying to make it come clear to myself: now Naomi was dead she no longer controlled the resources which could bring her back. So my dream was—a dream. Oh, God!

I was staring stupidly at the thing which had met my hand; it wasn't my pack of cigarettes but the leather wallet she had given me.

"You can keep that," Gurney said. "I was told you could keep it."

I looked at him. And I *knew*.

Very slowly, I unzipped the wallet. I took out the three cards. They were sealed in plastic. I folded them in half, and the plastic cracked. I tore them across and let them fall to the ground. Then, one by one, I ripped the checks out of the book and let them drift confetti-wise over the wall, down to the sea.

He watched me, the color coming to his face until at last he was flushing red—with guilt, shame, I don't know. When I had finished, he said in a voice that was still level, "You're a fool, Cooper. You could still have bought your dreams with those."

I threw the wallet in his face and turned away. I had gone ten steps, blind with anger and sorrow, when I heard him speak my name and looked back. He was holding the wallet in both hands, and his mouth was working.

He said, "Damn you, Cooper. Oh, damn you to hell! I—I told myself I loved her, and I couldn't have done that. Why do you want to make me feel so *dirty*?"

"Because you are," I said. "And now you know it."

Three men I hadn't seen before came into my house as I was crating the machine. Silent as ghosts, impersonal as robots, they helped me put my belongings in my car. I welcomed their aid simply because I wanted to get to hell out of this mock village as fast as possible. I told them to throw the things I wanted to take with me in the passenger seats and the luggage compartment, without bothering to pack cases. While I was at it, I saw Gurney come to the side of the house and stand by the car as though trying to pluck up courage to speak to me again, but I ignored him, and when I went out he had gone. I didn't find the wallet until I was in Barcelona sorting through the jumbled belongings. It held, this time, thirty-five thousand pesetas in new notes. He had just thrown it on the back seat under a pile of clothes.

Listen. It wasn't a *long* span of time which defeated Naomi. It wasn't three years or ten years or any number of years. I worked it out later—too late. (So time defeated me, too, as it always defeats us.)

I don't know how her man died. But I'm sure I know why she wanted him back. Not because she loved him, as she herself believed. But because he loved her. And without him, she was afraid. It didn't need three years to re-create her. It didn't even need three hours. It needed *three words*.

And Gurney, the bastard, could have spoken them, long before I could—so long before that there was still time. He could have said, "I love you."

These are the totally rich. They inhabit the same planet, breathe the same air. But they are becoming, little by little, a different species, because what was most human in them is—well, this is my opinion—dead.

They keep apart, as I mentioned. And God! God! Aren't you grateful?

Fritz Leiber

America the Beautiful

I am returning to England. I am shorthanding this, July 5, 2000, aboard the Dallas-London rocket as it arches silently out of the diffused violet daylight of the stratosphere into the eternally star-spangled purpling night of the ionosphere.

I have refused the semester instructorship in poetry at UTD, which would have munificently padded my honorarium for delivering the Lanier Lectures and made me for four months second only to the Poet in Residence.

And I am almost certain that I have lost Emily, although we plan to meet in London in a fortnight if she can wangle the stopover on her way to take up her Peace Corps command in Niger.

I am not leaving America because of the threat of a big war. I believe that this new threat, like all the rest, is only another move, even if a long and menacing queen's move, in the game of world politics, while the little wars go endlessly on in Chad, Czechoslovakia, Sumatra, Siam, Baluchistan, and Bolivia as America and the Communist League firm their power boundaries.

And I am certainly not leaving America because of any harassment as a satellitic neutral and possible spy. There may have been surveillance of my actions and lectures, but if so it was as impalpable as the checks they must have made on me in England before granting me visiting clearance. The U.S. intelligence agencies have become almost incredibly deft in handling such things. And I was entertained in America more than royally—I was made to feel at home by a family with a great talent for just that.

Now, I am leaving because of the shadows. The shadows everywhere in America, but which I saw must clearly in Professor Grissim's serene and lovely home. The shadows which would irresistibly have gathered behind my instructor's lectern, precisely as I was learning to dress with an even trimmer and darker reserve while I was a guest at the Grissims' and even to shower more frequently. The shadows which revealed themselves to me deepest of all around Emily Grissim, and which I could do nothing to dispel.

I think that you, or at least I, can see the shadows in America more readily these days because of the very clean air there. Judging only from what I saw with my own eyes in Texas, the Americans have completely licked their smog problem. Their gently curving freeways purr with fast electric cars, like sleek and disciplined silver cats. Almost half the nation's power comes from atomic reactors, while the remaining coal-burning plants loose back

into the air at most a slight shimmer of heat. Even the
streams and rivers run blue and unsmirched again, while
marine life is returning to the eastern Great Lakes. In
brief, America is beautiful, for with the cleanliness, now
greater than that of the Dutch, has come a refinement in
taste, so that all buildings are gracefully shaped and dis-
posed, while advertisements, though molding minds more
surely than ever, are restrained and almost finically inof-
fensive.

The purity of the atmosphere was strikingly brought to
my notice when I debarked at Dallas rocketport and
found the Grissims waiting for me outdoors, downwind
of the landing area. They made a striking group, all of
them tall, as they stood poised yet familiarly together:
the professor with his grizzled hair still close-trimmed in
military fashion, for he had served almost as long as a
line officer and in space service as he had now as a university physicist; his slim, white-haired wife; Emily, like
her mother in the classic high-waisted, long-skirted Di-
rectoire style currently fashionable; and her brother Jack,
in his dress pale grays with sergeant's stripes, on furlough
from Siam.

Their subdued dress and easy attitudes reminded me of a
patrician Roman's toga dropping in precise though seemingly accidental folds. The outworn cliché about America
being Rome to England's Greece came irritatingly to my
mind.

Introductions were made by the professor, who had met
my father at Oxford and later seen much of him during
the occupation of Britain throughout the Three Years'
Alert. I was surprised to find their diction almost the
same as my own. We strolled to their electric station
wagon, the doors of which opened silently at our ap-
proach.

I should have been pleased by the simple beauty of the
Grissims, as by that of the suburban landscape through

which we now sped, especially since my poetry is that of the Romantic Revival, which looks back to Keats and Shelley more even than to Shakespeare. Instead, it rubbed me the wrong way. I became uneasy and within ten minutes found myself beginning to talk bawdy and make nasty little digs at America.

They accepted my rudeness in such an unshocked, urbane fashion, demonstrating that they understood though did not always agree with me, and they went to such trouble to assure me that not all America was like this, there were still many ugly stretches, that I soon felt myself a fool and shut up. It was I who was the crass Roman, I told myself, or even barbarian.

Thereafter Emily and her mother kept the conversation going easily and soon coaxed me back into it, with the effect of smoothing the grumbling and owlish young British poet's ruffled feathers.

The modest one story, shaded by slow-shedding silvery eucalyptus and mutated chaparral, which was all that showed of the Grissim home, opened to receive our fumeless vehicle. I was accompanied to my bedroom-and-study, served refreshments, and left there to polish up my first lecture. The scene in the view window was so faithfully transmitted from the pickup above, the air fresher if possible than that outdoors, that I found it hard to keep in mind I was well underground.

It was at dinner that evening, when my hosts made such a nicely concerted effort to soothe my nervousness over my initial lecture, and largely succeeded, that I first began truly to like and even respect the Grissims.

It was at the same instant, in that pearly dining room, that I first became aware of the shadows around them.

Physical shadows? Hardly, though at times they really seemed that. I recall thinking, my mind still chiefly on my lecture, something like, *These good people are so wedded to the way of war, the perpetual little wars and*

*the threat of the big one, and have been so successful in
masking the signs of its strains in themselves, that they
have almost forgotten that those strains are there. And
they love their home and country, and the security of their
taut way of life, so deeply that they have become un-
aware of the depth of that devotion.*

My lecture went off well that night. The audience was
large, respectful, and seemingly even attentive. The number of African and Mexican faces gave the lie to what I'd
been told about integration being a sham in America. I
should have been pleased, and I temporarily was, at the
long, mutedly drumming applause I was given and at the
many intelligent, flattering comments I received afterward. And I should have stopped seeing the shadows
then, but I didn't.

Next morning Emily toured me around city and coun-
tryside on a long silvery scooter, I riding pillion behind
her. I remember the easy though faintly formal way in
which she drew my arms around her waist and laid her
hand for a moment on one of mine, meanwhile smiling
cryptically over-shoulder. Besides that smile, I remember
a charming Spanish-American graveyard in pastel stucco,
the towering Kennedy shrine, the bubbling, iridescent tubes
of algae farming converging toward the horizon, and
rockets taking off in the distance with their bright, smoke-
less exhausts. Emily was almost as unaffected as a British
girl and infinitely more competent, in a grand style. That
one day the shadows vanished altogether.

They returned at evening when after dinner we gathered in the living room for our first wholly unhurried and
relaxed conversation, my lectures being spaced out in a
leisurely—to Americans, not to me—one day in two
schedule.

We sat in a comfortable arc before the wide fireplace,
where resinous woods burned yellow and orange. Occasionally Jack would put on another log. From time to

time, a light shower of soot dropped back from the precipitron in the chimney, the tiny particles as they fell flaring into brief white points of light, like stars.

A little to my surprise, the Grissims drank as heavily as the English, though they carried their liquor very well. Emily was the exception to this family pattern, contenting herself with a little sherry and three long, slim reefers, which she drew from an elegant foil package covered with gold script and Lissajous curves, and which she inhaled sippingly, her lips rapidly shuddering with a very faint, low, trilling sound.

Professor Grissim set the pattern by deprecating the reasons for America's domestic achievements, which I had led off by admitting were far greater than I'd expected. They weren't due to any peculiar American drive, he said, and certainly not to any superior moral fiber, but simply to technology and computerized civilization given their full head and unstinting support. The powerful sweep of those two almost mathematical forces had automatically solved such problems as overpopulation, by effortless and aesthetic contraception, and stagnant or warped brain potential, by unlimited semiautomated education and psychiatry—just as on a smaller scale the drug problem had largely been resolved by the legalization of marijuana and peyote, following the simple principle of restricting only the sale of quickly addictive chemicals and those provably damaging to nervous tissue—"Control the poisons, but let each person learn to control his intoxicants, especially now that we have metabolic rectifiers for the congenitally alcoholic."

I was also told that American extremism, both of the right and left, which had seemed such a big thing in mid-century, had largely withered away or at least been muted by the great surge of the same forces which were making America ever more beautiful and prosperous. Cities were no longer warrens of discontent. Peace marches and

Minutemen rallies alike, culminating in the late sixties, had thereafter steadily declined.

While impressed, I did not fall into line, but tried to point out some black holes in this glowing picture. Indeed, feeling at home with the Grissims now and having learned that nothing I could say would shock them into anger and confusion, I was able to be myself fully and to reveal frankly my anti-American ideas, though of course more politely and, I hoped, more tellingly than yesterday—it seemed an age ago—driving from the rocketport.

In particular, I argued that many or most Americans were motivated by a subtle, even sophisticated puritanism, which made them feel that the world was not safe unless they were its moral arbiters, and that this puritanism was ultimately based on the same swollen concern about property and money—industry, in its moral sense—that one found in the Swiss and Scottish Presbyterians and most of the early Protestants.

"You're puritans with a great deal of style and restraint and wide vision," I said. "Yet you're puritans just the same, even though your puritanism is light-years away from that of the Massachusetts theocrats and the harsh rule Calvin tried to impose on Geneva. In fact," I added uncautiously, "your puritanism is not so much North European as Roman."

Smiles crinkled briefly at that and I kicked myself for having myself introduced into the conversation that hackneyed comparison.

At this point Emily animatedly yet coolly took up the argument for America, pointing out the nation's growing tolerance and aestheticism, historically distinguishing Puritanism from Calvinism, and also reminding me that the Chinese and Russians were far more puritanical than any other peoples on the globe—and not in a sophisticated or subtle way either.

I fought back, as by citing the different impression I'd

got of the Russians during my visits in the Soviet Union and by relaying the reports of close colleagues who had spent time in China. But on the whole Emily had the best of me. And this was only partly due to the fact that the longer I sparred with her verbally, the less concerned I became to win my argument, and the more to break her calm and elicit some sharp emotional reaction from her, to see that pale skin flush, to make those reefer-serene eyes blaze with anger. But I wasn't successful there either.

At one point Jack came to her aid, mildly demonstrating for American broad-mindedness by describing to us some of the pleasure cities of southern Asia he'd visited on R.&R.

"Bangkok's a dismal place now, of course," he began by admitting, "with the Com-g'rillas raiding up to and even into it, and full of fenced-off bombed and booby-trapped areas. Very much like the old descriptions of Saigon in the sixties. As you walk down the potholed streets, you listen for the insect hum of a wandering anti-personnel missile seeking human heat, or the faint flap-flap of an infiltrator coming down on a whirligig parachute. You brace your thoughts against the psychedelic strike of a mind-bomb. Out of the black alley ahead there may charge a fifty-foot steel centipede, the remote-controlled sort we use for jungle fighting, captured by the enemy and jiggered to renegade.

"But most of old Bangkok's attractive features—and the entrepreneurs and girls and other entertainers that go with them—have been transferred en masse to Kandy and Trincomalee in Ceylon." And he went on to describe the gaily orgiastic lounges and bars, the fresh pastel colors, the spicy foods and subtly potent drinks, the clean little laughing harlots supporting their families well during the ten years of their working life between fifteen and twenty-five, the gilded temples, the slim dancers with movemnts stylized as their black eyebrows, the priests robed in orange and yellow.

I tried to fault him in my mind for being patronizing, but without much success.

"Buddhism's an attractive way of life," he finished, "except that it doesn't know how to wage war. But if you're looking only for nirvana, I guess you don't need to know that." For an instant his tough face grew bleak, as if he could do with a spot of nirvana himself, and the shadows gathered around him and the others more thickly.

During the following off-lecture evenings we kept up our fireplace talks and Emily and I returned more than once to our debate over puritanism, while the rest listened to us with faint, benevolent smiles, that at times seemed almost knowing. She regularly defeated me.

Then on the sixth night she delivered her crowning argument, or celebrated her victory, or perhaps merely followed an impulse. I had just settled myself in bed when the indirect lighting of my "doorbell" flooded the room with brief flashes, coming at three-second intervals, of a rather ghastly white light. Blinking, I fumbled on the bedside table for the remote control of the room's appliances, including tri-V and door, and thumbed the button for the latter.

The door moved aside and there, silhouetted against the faint glow of the hall, was the dark figure of Emily, like a living shadow. She kept her finger, however, on the button long enough for two more silent flashes to illuminate her briefly. She was wearing a narrow kimono—Jack's newest gift, she later told me—and her platinum hair, combed straight down like an unrippling waterfall, almost exactly matched the silvery, pale gray silk. Without quite overdoing it, she had made up her face somewhat like a temple dancer's—pale powder, almost white; narrow slanting brows, almost black; green eye shadow with a pinch of silvery glitter, and the not-quite-jarring sensual note of crimson lips.

She did not come into my room, but after a pause during which I sat up jerkily and she became again a shadow, she beckoned to me.

I snatched up my dressing gown and followed her as she moved noiselessly down the hall. My throat was dry and constricted, my heart was pounding a little, with apprehension as well as excitement. I realized that despite my near week with the Grissims, a part of my mind was still thinking of the professor and his wife as a strait-laced colonel and his lady from a century ago, when so many retired army officers lived in villas around San Antonio, as they do now too around the Dallas-Fort Worth metropolitan area.

Emily's bedroom was not the austere silver cell or self-shrine I had sometimes imagined, especially when she was scoring a point against me, but an almost cluttered museum-workshop of present interests and personal memorabilia. She'd even kept her kindergarten study-machine, her first CO_2 pistol, and a hockey stick, along with mementos from her college days and her Peace Corps tours.

But those I noticed much later. Now pale golden light from a rising full moon, coming through the great view window, brimmed the room. I had just enough of my wits left to recall that the real moon was new, so that this must be a tape of some past night. I never even thought of the Communist and American forts up there, with their bombs earmarked for Earth. Then, standing straight and tall and looking me full in the eyes, like some Amazonian athlete, or Phryne before her judges, Emily let the kimono glide down from her shoulders.

In the act of love she was energetic, but tender. No, the word is courteous, I think. I very happily shed a week of tensions and uncertainties and self-inflicted humiliations.

"You still think I'm a puritan, don't you?" she softly

asked me afterward, smiling at me sideways with the
smeared remains of her crimson mouth, her gray eyes
enigmatic blurs of shadow.

"Yes, I do," I told her forthrightly. "The puritan playing the hetaera, but still the puritan."

She answered lazily, "I think you like to play the Hun
raping the vestal virgin."

That made me talk dirty to her. She listened attentively
—almost famishedly, I thought, for a bit—but her final
comment was "You do that very well, dear," just before
using her lips to stop mine, which would otherwise have
sulphurously cursed her insufferable poise.

Next morning I started to write a poem about her but
got lost in analysis and speculation. Tried too soon, I
thought.

Although they were as gracious and friendly as ever, I
got the impression that the other Grissims had quickly
become aware of the change in Emily's and my relationship. Perhaps it was that they showed a slight extra
fondness toward me. I don't know how they guessed—
Emily was as cool as always in front of them, while I
kept trying to play myself, as before. Perhaps it was that
the argument about puritanism was never resumed.

Two evenings afterward the talk came around to Jack's
and Emily's elder brother Jeff, who had fallen during the
Great Retreat from Jammu and Kashmir to Baluchistan.
It was mentioned that during his last furlough they had
been putting up an exchange instructor from Yugoslavia,
a highly talented young sculptress. I gathered that she and
Jeff had been quite close.

"I'm glad Jeff knew her love," Emily's mother said
calmly, a tear behind her voice, though not on her cheeks.
"I'm very glad he had that." The professor unobtrusively
put his hand on hers.

I fancied that this remark was directed at me and was
her way of giving her blessing to Emily's and my affair.

I was touched and at the same time irritated—and also irritated at myself for feeling irritated. Her remark had brought back the shadows, which darkened further when Jack said a touch grimly and for once with a soldier's callousness, though grinning at me to remove any possible offense, "Remember not to board any more lady artists or professors, Mother, at least when I'm on leave. Bad luck."

By now I was distinctly bothered by my poetry block. The last lectures were going swimmingly and I ought to have been feeling creative, but I wasn't. Or rather, I was feeling creative but I couldn't create. I had also begun to notice the way I was fitting myself to the Grissim family—muting myself, despite all the easiness among us. I couldn't help wondering if there weren't a connection between the two things. I had received the instructorship offer, but was delaying my final answer.

After we made love together that night—under a sinking crescent moon, the real night this time, repeated from above—I told Emily about my first trouble only. She pressed my hand. "Never stop writing poetry, dear," she said. "America needs poetry. This family—"

That broken sentence was as close as we ever got to talking about marriage. Emily immediately recovered herself with an uncharacteristically ribald "Cheer up. I don't even charge a poem for admission."

Instead of responding to that cue, I worried my subject. "I should be able to write poetry here," I said. "America is beautiful, the great golden apple of the Hesperides, hanging in the west like the setting sun. But there's a worm in the core of that apple, a great scaly black dragon."

When Emily didn't ask a question, I went on, "I remember an advertisement. 'Join all your little debts into one big debt.' Of course, they didn't put it so baldly, they made it sound wonderful. But you Americans are like that. You've collected all your angers into one big anger.

You've removed your angers from things at home—where you seem to have solved your problems very well, I must admit—and directed those angers at the Communist League. Or instead of angers, I could say fears. Same thing."

Emily still didn't comment, so I continued, "Take the basic neurotic. He sets up a program of perfection for himself—a thousand obligations, a thousand ambitions. As long as he works his program, fulfilling those obligations and ambitions, he does very well. In fact, he's apt to seem like a genius of achievement to those around him, as America does to me. But there's one big problem he always keeps out of his program and buries deep in his unconscious—the question of who he really is and what he really wants—and in the end it always throws him."

Then at last Emily said, speaking softly at first, "There's something I should tell you, dear. Although I talk a lot of it from the top of my mind, deep down I loathe discussing politics and international relations. As my old colonel used to tell me, 'It doesn't matter much which side you fight on, Emily, so long as you have the courage to stand up and be counted. You pledge your life, your fortune, and your sacred honor, and live up to that pledge!' And now, dear, I want to sleep."

Crouching on the edge of her bed before returning to my room, listening to her breathing regularize itself, I thought, "Yes, you're looking for nirvana too. Like Jack." But I didn't wake her to say it, or any of the other things that were boiling up in my brain.

Yet the things I left unsaid must have stayed and worked in my mind, for at our next fireside talk—four pleasant Americans, one Englishman with only one more lecture to go—I found myself launched into a rather long account of the academic Russian family I stayed with while delivering the Pushkin Lectures in Leningrad, where the smog and the minorities problems have been licked too. I stressed the Rosanovs' gentility, their friendliness, the tolerance and sophistication which had replaced the old rigid insistence on *kulturny* behavior, and also the faint melancholy underlying and somehow vitiating all they said. In short, I did everything I knew to underline their similarity to the Grissims. I ended by saying, "Professor Grissim, the first night we talked, you said America's achievement had been due almost entirely to the sweep of science, technology, and computerized civilization. The people of the Communist League believe that too—in fact, they made their declaration of faith earlier than America."

"It's very strange," he mused, nodding. "So like, yet so unlike. Almost as if the chemical atoms of the East were subtly different from those of the West. The very electrons—"

"Professor, you don't actually think—"

"Of course not. A metaphor only."

But whatever he thought, I don't believe he felt it only as a metaphor.

Emily said sharply to me, "You left out one more similarity, the most important. That they hate the Enemy with all their hearts and will never trust or understand him."

I couldn't find an honest and complete answer to that, though I tried.

The next day I made one more attempt to turn my feelings into poetry, dark poetry, and I failed. I made my refusal of the instructorship final, confirmed my reservation on the Dallas-London rocket for day after tomorrow, and delivered the last of the Lanier Lectures.

The Fourth of July was a quiet day. Emily took me on a repeat of our first scooter jaunt, but although I relished the wind on my face and our conversation was passably jolly and tender, the magic was gone. I could hardly see America's beauty for the shadows my mind projected on it.

Our fireside conversation that night was as brightly banal. Midway we went outside to watch the fireworks. It was a starry night, very clear of course, and the fireworks seemed vastly remote—transitory extra starfields of pink and green and amber. Their faint cracks and booms sounded infinitely distant, and needless to say, there was not a ribbon or whiff of chemical smoke. I was reminded of my last night in Leningrad with the Rosanovs after the Pushkin Lectures. We'd all strolled down the Kirovskiy Prospekt to the Bolshaya Neva, and across its glimmering waters watched the Vladivostok mail rocket take off from the Field of Mars up its ringed electric catapult taller far than the Eiffel Tower. That had been on a May Day.

Later that night I went for the first time by myself to Emily's door and pressed its light-button. I was afraid she wouldn't stop by for me and I needed her. She was in a taut and high-strung mood, unwilling to talk in much more than monosyllables, yet unable to keep still, pacing like a restless feline. She wanted to play in the view window the tape of a real battle in Bolivia with the original sounds too, muted down. I vetoed that and we settled for an authentic forest fire recorded in Alaska.

Sex and catastrophe fit. With the wild red light pulsing and flaring in the bedroom, casting huge wild shadows, and with the fire's muted roar and hurricane crackle and explosions filling our ears, we made love with a fierce and desperate urgency that seemed almost—I am eternally grateful for the memory—as if it would last forever. Sex and a psychedelic trip also have their meeting point.

Afterward I slept like a sated tiger. Emily waited until dawn to wake me and shoo me back to my bedroom.

Next day all the Grissims saw me off. As we strolled from the silver station wagon to the landing area, Emily and I dropped a little behind. She stopped, hooked her arms around me, and kissed me with a devouring ferocity. The others walked on, too well bred ever to look back.

The next moment she was her cool self again, sipping a reefer.

Now the rocketship is arching down. The stars are paling. There is a faint whistling as the air molecules of the stratosphere begin to carom off the titanium skin. We had only one flap, midway of freefall section of the trip, when we briefly accelerated and then decelerated to match, perhaps in order to miss a spy satellite or one of the atomic-headed watchdog rockets eternally circling the globe. The direction comes, "Secure seat harnesses."

I just don't know. Maybe I should have gone to America drunk as Dylan Thomas, but purposefully, bellowing my beliefs like the word or the thunderbolts of God. Maybe then I could have fought the shadows. No. . . .

I hope Emily makes it to London. Perhaps there, against a very different background, with shadows of a different sort . . .

In a few more seconds the great jet will begin to brake, thrusting its hygienic, aseptic exhaust of helium down into the filthy cancerous London smog, and I will be home.

The Annex

During the last hour of the night, the charge nurse looked in at the critical in Room 11, intensive-care section, coronary. She scowled and made an ugly, displeased mouth and hastened to replace the dislodged I.V. needle in the vein inside the elbow of the right arm, immobilized by the straps, the board and the side rail of the bed. She checked the glucose drip, made a small adjustment of the flow valve, checked oxygen supply, listened to the ragged labor of the pulse and went off and found the pretty little special drinking coffee in the treatment room and joking with the red-headed intern.

After chewing her out with a cold expertise that welled tears into the blue eyes, she herded her back to her night watch over the patient.

"I wasn't gone three minutes, honest," she said.

"An hour before dawn they get restless," the charge nurse said. "As if they had someplace to go, some appointment to keep."

When the first gray light of the morning made the shape of the window visible, he dressed quickly and went out. He guessed that they would not be expecting him to leave that room so soon after arriving.

There were shadows of night still remaining in the empty streets, so that even though he knew his way and walked swiftly, the city seemed strange to him. They were changing it so quickly these past few years. The eye becomes accustomed to the shape and bulk of structures, giving them only a marginal attention; yet when, so abruptly, they were gone, one had the feeling of having made a wrong turn somewhere. Then even the unchanged things began to look half strange.

He turned a dark corner and saw the hotel lights in the distance. A taxi came swiftly to the cross-town corner, made a wrenching, shuddering turn and sped up the empty avenue, and he caught a silhouette glimpse of the sailboat hats of nuns in the dark interior, two or three of them.

He had not been in the hotel for years. He saw at once that it was quite changed. That certain quaintness of the lobby that once set off the high style of the moneyed people and the women of the theatre was now merely a shabbiness. He realized that he could have guessed it, because were it not changed, they would not be mixed up in this sort of thing. And his shabby assignment in an unknown room would have occurred in some other place, perhaps even in another city at another time.

There was no one behind the desk. He felt in his pocket

for the identification he would have to present and felt fear and irritation when he did not find it at once. Then, among coins, he fingered the shape of it and took it out and held it in his clasped hand. As he wondered whether to tap the desk bell, he saw movement out of the side of his eye and turned and saw a man walking toward him out of the lobby shadows.

"Mr. Davis?" the small man said; and as he came into the light, his face was elusively familiar. He searched memory and finally recalled the image of the same face, a bellhop uniform in dull red and gray, big brass circle of the master key ring looped around the scrawny neck. And the name came back.

"Do you remember me, Leo? From before?"

"Sure," the man said. He leaned against the desk and yawned. Davis knew the man did not remember him at all.

"You're the manager now?"

"So they keep telling me."

"Come up in the world, eh?"

"I guess so." He yawned again. "You got that thing?"

He felt unaccountably shy about revealing what they had given him. He said, "I keep telling them that they should use ordinary things. But they get fanciful. It just makes everything harder to explain when things go wrong. What kind of a sentimental nut would have a gold miniature of his own dog tag made? A grown man is supposed to get over being in a war."

"Look, I have to see it." Leo's tone was patient and bored, and Davis knew the man had no interest in what he thought and very little interest in why he had come here.

He held his hand out and the little wafer gleamed on his open palm. Leo took it, glanced at it and put it in his own pocket.

"They didn't tell me you'd keep it."

"The room you want is four-two-four-two."

"Are you supposed to keep it? Did they make that clear?"

"Forty-two forty-two. Four thousand, two hundred and forty-two, Mr. Davis. OK?"

"All right. I'll assume you're supposed to keep it, Leo. It's their problem, not mine. But you're supposed to turn over the key, I know *that*."

"I can't, buddy, because the only keys here are the keys to the main house here. You should know that and they should know that. Right? What we're talking about is the annex. Which is being torn down."

"Then there isn't anybody in it?"

"Did I say that, mister? Did anybody say that?"

"There's no reason to get ugly about it, Leo."

"Who's ugly? Listen, they got old foops in there living there since the year one, and lease agreements and all that stuff, so about the only thing they can do is work around them until they get sick of all the noise and mess and get out. There aren't many left now. I think maybe your party is the only one left on that floor, but I don't keep close track. I've got enough to do here without worrying about over there."

"So what do I do about a key? Am I supposed to go knock on the door, for God's sake?"

"Mrs. Dorn is over there. She's got a master key to the whole annex."

"Does she know about me?"

"Why should she? Just con her a little, Mr. Davis. Play it by ear. OK?"

"I don't have much choice, I guess."

"Has anybody lately? Come this way."

Leo led the way back through the lobby and through a huge empty kitchen, where night lights picked up the gleam and shape of stainless steel racks and tables. He

pulled a door open and turned on a weak bulb at the head
of a narrow flight of stairs.

"The regular way over there has been boarded up, so
what you do is just follow the way a red pipe runs along
the ceiling there, and when you come to stairs finally, go
on up and you'll find her around someplace."

Three steps down, he turned to say his thanks in some
massively sarcastic way; but as he turned, the door was
slammed. There were distant lights in the vast reaches of
the basement, just enough for him to make out the red
pipe suspended by straps from the low ceiling overhead.
There was a sweaty dampness in the basement. In some
far corner, a laboring machine was making a slow and
heavy chuffing sound. It made a vibration he could feel
through the soles of his shoes as he walked. He noticed
that the red pipe overhead was of some kind of plastic
material, sufficiently flexible so that there was a perceptible expansion and contraction as the machine made its
thick and rhythmic sound.

He estimated that he had walked more than a city block
before he came to the stairs, where the red pipe disappeared into a wall. These were unxpectedly wide and
elegant stairs, marble streaked with gray and green, as-
cending in a gentle curve. At the top of the stairs, he
pushed a dark door open and found himself in an enormous lobby. It had the silence of a museum. Dropcloths
covered the shapes of furniture. Plaster dust was gritty on
the floor. Some huge beams had fallen and were propped
at an angle, as in pictures of bombings.

"Mrs. Dorn!" he called. "Mrs. Dorn!" The sound did
not seem to carry. It died at once into the silence.

Then he heard a click-tock of high heels and he could
not tell where the sound was coming from. "Yes?" she
said. "You, there! Up here!" Her voice was musical; the
tone, impatient. He looked up and saw her standing at
the broad ornate railing of a mezzanine floor, looking

down at him, in silhouette against a window beyond her.
"Yes? What do you want?"

"Can I speak to you a minute?"

"I'm very busy. Well . . . come on up."

She turned away. He looked around and saw the stairs
and went up. There was a library and writing room at the
top of the stairs. Several doors opened from the room.
He tried them, one by one, and found they opened onto
corridors. Then, close behind him, she chuckled and, as
he turned, startled, she said, "It's really very confusing. I
used to get hopelessly lost when I first came here."

She looked like someone he had known, somewhere,
perhaps a long time ago. She had a soft and pretty face,
dark wings of careless hair, and she looked at him in a
familiar and mocking way of old secrets shared. She wore
a shift of some tweedy gray substance over a young,
sturdy body with a vital heft of hip and weight of breast.

"I wonder, Mrs. Dorn, if you could. . . ."

"Just a moment, please. I missed this room somehow,
and the crews will be arriving any minute, and it would be
just my rotten luck if they started here, wouldn't it?" She
began to walk slowly around the room, pausing from time
to time, pausing to hold at arm's length a piece of soft
yellow chalk in the measuring gesture of the artist. She
nodded to herself from time to time and then would mark
with the chalk a piece of paneling, or a chair, or the frame
of an old painting.

At last she sighed and turned toward him with a smile
of enduring patience.

"Done, I guess. As well as I can do it, anyway. They
don't really give a damn about saving anything. You have
to watch them like hawks. They'll pretend they didn't see
the mark and they'll smash stuff to powder and then look
so *terribly* innocent. They hate old things, I guess. And
hate the loveliest old things worst of all. They just want to
come in and biff, bang, crunch and truck it away and get

it over with and go on to the next job. My, how they resent me, and resent having to save things and handle them so gently and take them to our warehouse. You wouldn't believe it."

The marks she made each time was a D with a cross drawn through it, like a cancellation.

"What did you want?" she asked.

"They told me that you're the one to see. You can lend me the master key."

"Really? And exactly what room do you want to get into? And why?"

"Four-two-four . . . oh, Forty-two forty. It will take only a . . . very few minutes."

"On the forty-second floor. Now isn't that quaint! Isn't that the living end!"

"What's so funny, Mrs. Dorn? I don't think anything is particularly funny."

"I couldn't possibly explain it to you. I'll have to show you."

"You could let me take the key, couldn't you?"

"My dear man, so much has been torn down and thrown away and smashed, you could wander around up there for weeks trying to find a way to the right floor and the right wing. Even if I believed you, I'd have to go with you in any case."

She led the way back down and through the silence of the lobby and to a back corridor, and into a bird-cage elevator no more than five feet square. She reached and clanged the door shut, turned a worn brass handle and they began to creak slowly upward. He stared up through the ceiling of woven metal strips and saw the sway of the moving cables and, far overhead, a pale square of gray sky.

The animation and mocking amusement had gone out of her. She leaned sagging, looking downward, finger tips on the brass lever, and he sensed that he had no part in what she was thinking. He could look at her with that feeling of invasion one has in watching someone sleep. There was a small mole below the corner of her mouth, on the pale concavity below the soft weight of her underlip. Her lashes were long and dark. He saw the lift and fall of her slow breathing and was aware of a warmth and scent of her breath. There were two deep pockets in the gray shift. The master key would have to be in one or the other. So it could be done. There was always a way.

Suddenly he had the feeling he was being trapped in some curious way, was being led from his assignment into a plan devised for some other reason, a plan wherein his role was minor; and looking at the panel above her resting hand, he saw what had probably given him subtle warning. There were brass buttons for the floors, pressed so many hundred thousand times the incised digits were almost worn away; yet when the gray light struck them properly, he could make out the topmost numeral of the vertical row—21.

"So that's it," he said. "That's what's funny." He made his mouth stretch wide in the knowing grin. The girl looked at him, startled and puzzled. "There's no forty-second floor," he said.

Frowning, she turned and looked at the row of buttons and then back at him. "You're serious? Don't you know about the annex at all? You know how the transients are. Top floor. Top floor. It's all they can think about. But the people who stay have to have private lives, don't they? Not all cluttered up with salesmen and people coming to town for the theatre and all that. You've never been in the business, have you? All the city hotels are just the same, you know. The elevators for the transients go only so high, just to such and such a number, and the quiet floors, where people live, are above that, always, and they have their private ways to get up to them."

She was so very patient that he felt ashamed of accusing

her and felt irritated with himself for not having guessed, long ago, what she told him. There had always been enough clues. There were always people going through the hotel lobbies, looking neither to the right nor to the left, walking by the regular elevators to some special place and service awaiting them.

But when the elevator stopped and they got out, she reached back into it, pressed the lowest button, yanked her arm out quickly and slammed the latticework door. It began to creak downward, with a clicking of pulleys and rasp of cables. She looked up at him and wrinkled her nose in mischief and mockery, saying, "Don't look so worried. There'll be other ways down." He remembered that she had not told him the joke, and he was once again annoyed at her.

These were broad corridors, pale gray, with composition floors, lighted by misted glass panels set into the ceiling. He tried to walk beside her, but she kept quickening her pace, and he realized she wanted him to walk behind her, a person guided rather than a companion. Many times they reached an intersection where the corridors stretched for vast distances, and sometimes she would pause to orient herself and then turn confidently right or left.

He noticed that all the numbers had been taken off the doors. He could see the raw holes where they had been screwed through gray paint into the plywood.

She was fifteen feet ahead of him, the dark hair bouncing at the nape of her neck to her swift, buoyant stride. The coarse gray fabric pulled in alternating diagonal tensions against her rear, and somehow he knew that were she quite still and quite bare, were he to place his hands so that his finger tips were hooked around the shelf of hip socket, feeling the warm, smooth slide of membrane over bone, holding her from the rear, his hands placed as a player holds a basketball for the long set shot, then through some delicious coincidence of design, the pads of his thumbs would fit precisely into the two deep dimples spaced below her spine. He shook himself out of the erotic musing, remembering how often they had told him that assignments were mishandled too often for exactly this reason.

At the end of a corridor, she pulled a heavy fire door open and turned to give him a bawdy wink, to run her tonguetip across her lips, as though she had read his mind and his weakness; and he determined not to look at her as she climbed the stairs ahead of him, and looked instead at the steel treads set into the concrete. He lost track of the number of flights they climbed. It winded him; and when he helped her push another fire door open, he tried to conceal his laboring lungs and to seem as fresh as she.

These corridors were a pale yellow, like weak winter sunlight, and at last they came to a small elevator standing open. The fluorescence inside was harsh and there was a sharp minty odor, as though it had recently been scrubbed with some cheap, strong antiseptic. It accelerated upward with silent velocity that hollowed his belly and made his knees bend slightly. It opened automatically on a narrower, dingy, old-fashioned corridor. She reached into the elevator as before; and when the door hissed shut and she turned to speak, he said, "I know. There'll be other ways down."

"That isn't what I was going to say."

"I'm sorry. What were you going to say?"

"I can't say it now. You spoiled it."

Again he followed her. These corridors were set at odd angles. The room doors were shiny dark with old coats of varnish. The room numbers were not removed and they were of tarnished brass, fluted and curly and ornate. All the rooms were in the 4000 series, but they were not in any reasonable order, 4100 and something across from or next door to 4800 and something.

She stopped very abruptly; and as he came upon her, he heard what she had heard—the gritty sound of latch and bolt—and then, twenty feet ahead of them, an old couple, dressed for winter, came out of one of the rooms, complaining at each other, fussing, asking if he or she had forgotten this or that, dropping small packages and picking them up.

Just before the old couple turned and noticed them, Mrs. Dorn hooked her arm around his waist and forced him to a slow walk. He put his arm, interlocked, around her, and she reached up with her free hand, placed it against his cheek, chuckled in a furry way, turned her mouth up to the awkward kiss while walking, so that as they passed the couple, he heard tsk's and clucks of their disapproval. "Darling, darling," she murmured. "Dave, darling."

Behind them he heard the old man's voice, without making out the words. There was a harsh resonance to it and then it cracked into a high quaver and then went deep again.

He smiled inside himself, thinking it sounded exactly like Ricky trying to manage his fourteen-year-old voice as it alternately squeaked and rumbled. The finger tips of the arm that was around her waist touched the top of the pocket on the left side of the gray shift, and with sneaky and daring inspiration, he slid his hand down into the pocket, bending his knees inconspicuously to lower himself just enough, the palm of his hand against round, warm thigh under fabric, and with his finger tips he touched the cylinder of yellow chalk and then the thin edge of metal. With the metal held against the nail of his index finger by the pad of his middle finger, he drew it out of the deep pocket and worked it into the palm of his hand.

She stopped and turned and leaned against the corridor wall and, with her hands resting lightly on his shoulders, looked up at him, still mocking him, saying, "You're just not very bright, Dave, darling."

The old people were gone, around a distant corner of the old hallway. Suddenly, he realized that she had cleverly kept them from seeing his face, so that they would be unable to identify him later. And with a sense of disbelief, he realized she had called him by his name.

"You could have told me how much you knew about this," he said.

"It's better for you to guess, dear. Look at what you took."

He opened his palm and saw the miniature gold tag. Name, rank, serial number, blood type O, meaning zero, meaning blood type nothing. The shock was enormous. He was suddenly afraid he might cry like a child and shame himself in front of her. "How did you . . . How could Leo have. . . ."

"Leo? Don't be silly. I had it all along. There were always two, you know. Don't you remember that, even? No, keep it, dear. If I have to have it back, you can always give it to me. Without any fuss. Promise?"

"Sure, but if you could just tell me. . . ."

"I can show you, Dave. Come along."

She paused at the next turning and bit her lip and, standing beside her, he saw that the floor itself dipped down in a gentle curve and lifted again at another place in the distance, where it turned again. It was swaying slightly, the whole corridor, like the bridges primitive peoples wove across deep swift rivers. She told him to walk carefully and stay close to the corridor wall. She motioned to him to stop and they were, he saw, on either side of a double door. It was room 4242. If she knew the rest of it, she would know the right number. It had been so placed that half of it was on each door, so that each was labelled 42. Even though she knew, he did not want her to watch what had to be done, watch the task assigned to him; but before he could ask her to go away, to give him the key and go away, go back and wait for him around the corner, out of sight, she put a bright red key in the lock and the double doors opened inward.

Inward, but outward. They opened onto the nothing of a dizzy height, making a vent for a cold wind that came husking down the hallway behind him and pushed him a long clumsy stride to stand on the very brink. Far, far, far below, the bug shapes of city cars and trucks moved very slowly, as when seen from an aircraft. He teetered, toes over the edge, and slowly fought back the sickness and the terror, knowing he could not let her see that he suddenly realized how cynically and savagely they had tricked him. He adjusted himself to the slight sway of the corridor and rode it easily, smiling and casual for her benefit, aware of how narrowly she was watching him.

Then came a deep and powerful thud, more vibration than sound. It came welling up from below and it danced the swaying corridor, nearly toppling him out. It came again and again and again. He learned to ride the new motion. The girl whimpered. He looked far down, almost directly down, and said, "It's nothing. Your friends have come to work. They've got some kind of a derrick thing down there and they're swinging one of those big cannon balls against the foundation."

He stepped back with care and reached and took her hand. Her hand was cold and hesitant. He led her past the open and windy space and back to where, once again, the structure was solid underfoot, trembling almost imperceptibly to each subsonic thud. She pulled her hand free and, after walking slowly, looking at the room numbers, chose one, and opened the door, motioning him to come in. The room was in semidarkness, gray light outlining the window. She closed the door and he heard her sigh.

Reaction made him feel weak and sick. He saw the shape of the bed and moved to it and sat on the edge of it.

She came to him and pushed at his shoulder and he lay back, grateful that she understood. He swung his legs on to the bed and she went to the foot and unlaced his shoes and took them off.

"We'd better not make very much noise," she whispered.

"Of course."

"Do you understand about the old people?"

"I know there's something I'm supposed to understand."

"That's enough for now."

She disappeared in the shadows and then he saw her again in silhouette in front of the gray of the window. He heard her sigh and he saw her, with slow and weary motion, tug the shift off over her head, toss it aside, pat her rumpled hair back into order, then bend and slip her shoes off. She stood near the corner of the window, half turned, standing quite still in silhouette, hips in relaxed and wary tilt, and he remembered one of the girls in that Degas print standing off at the side, standing in exactly the same position.

He knew she would turn and come to him but would not understand about what weakness had done to him. He did not want to confess that kind of weakness to her.

He said, "Even when they do very tricky things, that doesn't mean the rules are changed. We have to follow the rules, just as if everything were happening to someone else, to some people they want to keep, instead of to us. You did it their way, and you know there isn't really any other way down from here. This is all we have left."

"So if I knew all along?" she asked, prompting him.

"If you knew how it was going to be, then you had to know you were a part of it, too."

Not turning, still standing at the gray of the window, she said sadly, softly, "See? You keep understanding more and more of it. Sleep for a little while, darling. Then you'll know the rest of it."

At a few minutes past six, Dr. Samuel Barringer opened the door of Room 11 in the intensive-care section. In the shadows of the room, he saw the young nurse standing in silhouette by the gray of the window, looking out, standing there with a look of wistful grace.

At the sound of the latch as he closed the door, she spun with a guilty start, greeted him in her gentle and formal morning voice and handed him the clip-board with the patient's chart and the notation she had made since his visit four hours earlier. He held it under the low light for a moment, handed it back to her, then reached through the orifice in the transparent side of the oxygen tent to gently place the pads of his first two fingers against the arterial throb in the slack throat. He stood in a half bow, his eyes closed, listening and measuring through his finger tips. He was a big blond bear of a man, simultaneously clumsy and deft, as bears can be.

The nurse stood, awaiting instructions. He told her he would be back in a few minutes, and he walked to the far end of the corridor, to the waiting-room beyond the nurses' station. Sylvia sat alone there, at the end of the couch by the lamp table, staring out the big window. The hospital tower was higher than the buildings to the west of it, and she could see the wide, slow river in the morning haze. Daylight muted the yellow glow of the lamp beside her.

She turned and saw him and suddenly her dark eyes looked enormous and her face was more pale. "Sam? Is—"

"They didn't call me back. I just came in and checked him, and I have a couple of others to check, and it's standard procedure, Sylvie. No perceptible change."

He walked past her to the big window and shoved his

fists into his hip pockets and looked out at the new day.

After a little while, she said, "He's been trying to take it easier since that little coronary. He really has. But you know how Dave is. He said he was going to weed his practice down to about eight very rich and nervous old ladies with minor ailments. Sam?"

He turned and looked at her, at the lean, mature vitality of her face. "What, honey?"

"What's the prognosis, Sam?"

He shrugged his bear shoulders. "Too early to tell." He looked out the window and saw a freighter being nudged into the channel by the tugs. He wished he were on it and that everybody on board was sworn never to tell Dr. Barringer where they were going or how long they'd be gone.

"Sam, please! That was a big one. Oh, God, I know that was a big one! Remember me, Sam? Eighteen years we three have known one another. I'm a nurse . . . was a nurse. Remember? You don't have to pat me on the head, Sam."

It was easy to remember the Sylvie Dorn of 18 years ago, that chunky, flirtatious, lively girl, now a whip-slender matron, dark hair with the first touches of gray. Thirty-eight? Mother of Ricky, Susan, Timmy—god-mother to his own pair of demons. And Dave is—was—is forty-two.

"Sam?" she said again.

He turned from the window and went lumbering to the couch, thinking of all the times you make this decision and then decide how to wrap words around it to match the person you tell. But this one was close to the past and all the years, close to the heart.

He sat beside her and took her hands, and swallowed a rising thickness in his throat, blinked, swallowed again and said in a pebbly voice, "I'm sorry, Sylvie. Dave hasn't got enough heart muscle left to run a toy train. And there's not one damned thing we can do about it or for it."

She pulled her hands free and lunged against him, and
he held her in his big arms and patted her as she strained
at the first great hard spasmodic sob and got past it and
in about two or three minutes pulled herself back to a
control and a forlorn stability he knew she would be able
to maintain.

She dabbed her eyes and blew her nose and said,
"Today sometime?"

"Probably."

"Tell them you've given permission for me to stay in
there with him, will you?"

"Of course. I'll be in every once in a while."

"And thank your dear gal for taking over our tribe,
Sam. Sam? Do you think he'll know I'm . . . I'm there
with him?"

First, he thought, you throw the stone and then you
throw the lump of sugar. No point in telling her that death
had occurred, that Dave, as Dave, was long gone and that
the contemporary miracles of medical science were keeping some waning meat alive, in the laboratory sense of the
word.

"From everything we can learn and everything we can
guess, Sylvie, I feel certain that he'll be aware of you
being there, holding his hand."

When the first gray light of the morning made the shape
of the window visible, he dressed quickly and went out.
He guessed that they would not be expecting him to leave
that room so soon after arriving.

There were shadows of night still remaining in the empty
streets, so that even though he knew his way and walked
swiftly, the city seemed strange to him.

The Shoddy Lands

Being, as I believe, of sound mind and in normal health, I am sitting down at 11 p.m. to record, while the memory of it is still fresh, the curious experience I had this morning.

It happened in my rooms in college, where I am now writing, and began in the most ordinary way with a call on the telephone. "This is Durward," the voice said. "I'm speaking from the porter's lodge. I'm in Oxford for a few hours. Can I come across and see you?" I said yes, of course. Durward is a former pupil and a decent enough fellow; I would be glad to see him again. When he turned up at my door a few moments later I was rather annoyed to find that he had a young woman in tow. I loathe either men or women who speak as if they were coming to see you alone and then spring a husband or a wife, a fiancé or a fiancée on you. One ought to be warned.

The girl was neither very pretty nor very plain, and of course she ruined my conversation. We couldn't talk about any of the things Durward and I had in common because that would have meant leaving her out in the cold. And she and Durward couldn't talk about the things they (presumably) had in common because that would have left me out. He introduced her as Peggy and said they were engaged. After that, the three of us just sat and did social patter about the weather and the news.

I tend to stare when I am bored, and I am afraid I must have stared at that girl, without the least interest, a good deal. At any rate I was certainly doing so at the moment when the strange experience began. Quite suddenly, without any faintness or nausea or anything of that sort, I found myself in a wholly different place. The familiar room vanished; Durward and Peggy vanished. I was alone. And I was standing up.

My first idea was that something had gone wrong with my eyes. I was not in darkness, nor even in twilight, but everything seemed curiously blurred. There was a sort of daylight, but when I looked up I didn't see anything that I could very confidently call a sky. It might, just possibly, be the sky of a very featureless, dull, grey day, but it lacked any suggestion of distance. "Nondescript" was the word I would have used to describe it. Lower down and closer to me, there were upright shapes, vaguely green in colour, but of a very dingy green. I peered at them for quite a long time before it occurred to me that they might be trees. I went nearer and examined them; and the impression they made on me is not easy to put into words. "Trees of a sort," or, "Well, trees, if you call *that* a tree," or, "An attempt at trees," would come near it. They were the crudest, shabbiest apology for trees you could imagine. They had no real anatomy, even no real branches; they were more like lamp-posts with great, shapeless blobs of green stuck on top of them. Most children could draw better trees from memory.

It was while I was inspecting them that I first noticed the light: a steady, silvery gleam some distance away in the Shoddy Wood. I turned my steps towards it at once, and then first noticed what I was walking on. It was comfortable stuff, soft and cool and springy to the feet; but when you looked down it was horribly disappointing to the eye. It was, in a very rough way, the colour of grass; the colour grass has on a very dull day when you look at it while thinking pretty hard about something else. But there were no separate blades in it. I stooped down and tried to find them; the closer one looked, the vaguer it seemed to become. It had in fact just the same smudged, unfinished quality as the trees: shoddy.

The full astonishment of my adventure was now beginning to descend on me. With it came fear, but, even more, a sort of disgust. I doubt if it can be fully conveyed to anyone who has not had a similar experience. I felt as if I had suddenly been banished from the real, bright, concrete, and prodigally complex world into some sort of second-rate universe that had all been put together on the cheap; by an imitator. But I kept on walking towards the silvery light.

Here and there in the shoddy grass there were patches of what looked, from a distance, like flowers. But each patch, when you came close to it, was as bad as the trees and the grass. You couldn't make out what species they were supposed to be. And they had no real stems or petals; they were mere blobs. As for the colours, I could do better myself with a shilling paintbox.

I should have liked very much to believe that I was

dreaming, but somehow I knew I wasn't. My real conviction was that I had died. I wished—with a fervour that no other wish of mine has ever achieved—that I had lived a better life.

A disquieting hypothesis, as you see, was forming in my mind. But next moment it was gloriously blown to bits. Amidst all that shoddiness I came suddenly upon daffodils. Real daffodils, trim and cool and perfect. I bent down and touched them; I straightened my back again and gorged my eyes on their beauty. And not only their beauty but—what mattered to me even more at that moment— their, so to speak, honesty; real, honest, finished daffodils, live things that would bear examination.

But where, then, could I be? "Let's get on to that light. Perhaps everything will be made clear there. Perhaps it is at the centre of this queer place."

I reached the light sooner than I expected, but when I reached it I had something else to think about. For now I met the Walking Things. I have to call them that, for "people" is just what they weren't. They were of human size and they walked on two legs; but they were, for the most part, no more like true men than the Shoddy Trees had been like trees. They were indistinct. Though they were certainly not naked, you couldn't make out what sort of clothes they were wearing, and though there was a pale blob at the top of each, you couldn't say they had faces. At least that was my first impression. Then I began to notice curious exceptions. Every now and then one of them became partially distinct; a face, a hat, or a dress would stand out in full detail. The odd thing was that the distinct clothes were always women's clothes, but the distinct faces were always those of men. Both facts made the crowd—at least, to a man of my type—about as uninteresting as it could possibly be. The male faces were not the sort I cared about; a flashy-looking crew—gigolos, fripoons. But they seemed pleased enough with themselves. Indeed they all wore the same look of fatuous admiration.

I now saw where the light was coming from. I was in a sort of street. At least, behind the crowd of Walking Things on each side, there appeared to be shop-windows, and from these the light came. I thrust my way through the crowd on my left—but my thrusting seemed to yield no physical contacts—and had a look at one of the shops.

Here I had a new surprise. It was a jeweller's, and after the vagueness and general rottenness of most things in that queer place, the sight fairly took my breath away. Everything in that window was perfect; every facet on every diamond distinct, every brooch and tiara finished down to the last perfection of intricate detail. It was good stuff too, as even I could see; there must have been hundreds of thousands of pounds' worth of it. "Thank Heaven!" I gasped. "But will it keep on?" Hastily I looked at the next shop. It *was* keeping on. This window contained women's frocks. I'm no judge, so I can't say how good they were. The great thing was that they were real, clear, palpable. The shop beyond this one sold women's shoes. And it was still keeping on. They were real shoes; the toe-pinching and very high-heeled sort which, to my mind, ruins even the prettiest foot, but at any rate real.

I was just thinking to myself that some people would not find this place half as dull as I did, when the queerness of the whole thing came over me afresh. "Where the Hell," I began, but immediately changed it to "Where on earth"—for the other word seemed, in all the circumstances, singularly unfortunate—"Where on earth have I got to? Trees no good; grass no good; sky no good; flowers no good, except the daffodils; people no good; shops, first class. What can that possibly mean?"

The shops, by the way, were all women's shops, so I soon lost interest in them. I walked the whole length of that street, and then, a little way ahead, I saw sunlight.

Not that it was proper sunlight, of course. There was no break in the dull sky to account for it, no beam slanting down. All that, like so many other things in that world, had not been attended to. There was simply a patch of sunlight on the ground, unexplained, impossible (except that it was there), and therefore not at all cheering; hideous, rather, and disquieting. But I had little time to think about it; for something in the centre of that lighted patch—something I had taken for a small building —suddenly moved, and with a sickening shock I realized that I was looking at a gigantic human shape. It turned round. The eyes looked straight into mine.

It was not only gigantic, but it was the only complete human shape I had seen since I entered that world. It was female. It was lying on sunlit sand, on a beach apparently, though there was no trace of any sea. It was very nearly naked, but it had a wisp of some brightly coloured stuff round its hips and another round its breasts; like what a modern girl wears on a real beach. The general effect was repulsive, but I saw in a moment or two that this was due to the appalling size. Considered abstractly, the giantess had a good figure; almost a perfect figure, if you like the modern type. The face—but as soon as I had really taken in the face, I shouted out.

"Oh, I say! There you are. Where's Durward? And where's this? What's happened to us?"

But the eyes went on looking straight at me and through me. I was obviously invisible and inaudible to her. But there was no doubt who she was. She was Peggy. That is, she was recognizable; but she was Peggy changed. I don't mean only the size. As regards the figure, it was Peggy improved. I don't think anyone could have denied that. As to the face, opinions might differ. I would hardly have called the change an improvement myself. There was no more—I doubt if there was as much—sense or kindness or honesty in this face than in the original Peggy's. But it was certainly more regular. The teeth in particular, which I had noticed as a weak point in the old Peggy, were perfect, as in a good denture. The lips were fuller. The complexion was so perfect that it suggested a very expensive doll. The expression I can best describe by saying that Peggy now looked exactly like the girl in all the advertisements.

If I had to marry either I should prefer the old, unimproved Peggy. But even in Hell I hoped it wouldn't come to that.

And, as I watched, the background—the absurd little bit of sea-beach—began to change. The giantess stood up. She was on a carpet. Walls and windows and furniture grew up around her. She was in a bedroom. Even I could tell it was a very expensive bedroom though not at all my idea of good taste. There were plenty of flowers, mostly orchids and roses, and these were even better finished than the daffodils had been. One great bouquet (with a card attached to it) was as good as any I have ever seen. A door which stood open behind her gave me a view into a bathroom which I should rather like to own, a bathroom with a sunk bath. In it there was a French maid fussing about with towels and bath salts and things. The maid was not nearly so finished as the roses, or even the towels, but what face she had looked more French than any real Frenchwoman's face could.

The gigantic Peggy now removed her beach equipment and stood up naked in front of a full-length mirror. Apparently she enjoyed what she saw there; I can hardly express how much I didn't. Partly the size (it's only fair to remember that) but, still more, something that came as a terrible shock to me, though I suppose modern lovers and husbands must be hardened to it. Her body was (of course) brown, like the bodies in the sunbathing advertisements. But round her hips, and again round her breasts, where the coverings had been, there were two bands of dead white which looked, by contrast, like leprosy. It made me for the moment almost physically sick. What staggered me was that she could stand and admire it. Had she no idea how it would affect ordinary male eyes? A very disagreeable conviction grew in me that this was a subject of no interest to her; that all her clothes and bath salts and two-piece swimsuits, and indeed the voluptuousness of her every look and gesture, had not, and never had had, the meaning which every man would read, and was intended to read, into them. They were a huge overture to an opera in which she had no interest at all; a coronation procession with no Queen at the centre of it; gestures about nothing.

And now I became aware that two noises had been going for a long time; the only noises I ever heard in that world. But they were coming from outside, from somewhere beyond that low, grey covering which served the Shoddy Lands instead of a sky. Both the noises were knockings; patient knockings, infinitely remote, as if two outsiders, two excluded people, were knocking on the walls of that world. The one was faint, but hard; and with it came a voice saying, "Peggy, Peggy, let me in." Durward's voice, I thought. But how shall I describe the other knocking? It was, in some curious way, soft; "soft as wool and sharp as death," soft but unendurably heavy, as if at each blow some enormous hand fell on the outside of the Shoddy Sky and covered it completely. And with that knocking came a voice at whose sound my bones turned to water: "Child, child, child, let me in before the night comes."

Before the night comes—instantly common daylight rushed back upon me. I was in my own rooms again and my two visitors were before me. They did not appear to notice that anything unusual had happened to me, though, for the rest of that conversation, they might well have supposed I was drunk. I was so happy. Indeed, in a way

I was drunk; drunk with the sheer delight of being back in the real world, free, outside the horrible little prison of that land. There were birds singing close to a window; there was real sunlight falling on a panel. That panel needed repainting; but I could have gone down on my knees and kissed its very shabbiness—the precious real, solid thing it was. I noticed a tiny cut on Durward's cheek where he must have cut himself shaving that morning; and I felt the same about it. Indeed anything was enough to make me happy; I mean, any Thing, as long as it really was a Thing.

Well, those are the facts; everyone may make what he pleases of them. My own hypothesis is the obvious one which will have occurred to most readers. It may be too obvious; I am quite ready to consider rival theories. My view is that by the operation of some unknown psychological—or pathological—law, I was, for a second or so, let into Peggy's mind; at least to the extent of seeing her world, the world as it exists for her. At the centre of that world is a swollen image of herself, remodelled to be as like the girls in the advertisements as possible. Round this are grouped clear and distinct images of the things she really cares about. Beyond that, the whole earth and sky are a vague blur. The daffodils and roses are especially instructive. Flowers only exist for her if they are the sort that can be cut and put in vases or sent as bouquets; flowers in themselves, flowers as you see them in the woods, are negligible.

As I say, this is probably not the only hypothesis which will fit the facts. But it has been a most disquieting experience. Not only because I am sorry for poor Durward. Suppose this sort of thing were to become common? And how if, some other time, I were not the explorer but the explored?

Walter M. Miller

Crucifixus Etiam

Manue Nanti joined the project to make some dough. Five dollars an hour was good pay, even in A.D. 2134 and there was no way to spend it while on the job. Everything would be furnished: housing, chow, clothing, toiletries, medicine, cigarettes, even a daily ration of one hundred eighty proof beverage alcohol, locally distilled from fermented Martian mosses as fuel for the project's vehicles. He figured that if he avoided crap games, he could finish his five-year contract with fifty thousand dollars in the bank, return to Earth, and retire at the age of twenty-four. Manue wanted to travel, to see the far corners of the world, the strange cultures, the simple people, the small towns, deserts, mountains, jungles—for until he came to Mars, he had never been farther than a hundred miles from Cerro de Pasco, his birthplace in Peru.

A great wistfulness came over him in the cold Martian night when the frost haze broke, revealing the black, gleam-stung sky, and the blue-green Earth-star of his birth. *El mundo de mi carne, de mi alma*, he thought—yet, he had seen so little of it that many of its places would be more alien to him than the homogenously ugly vistas of Mars. These he longed to see: the volcanoes of the South Pacific, the monstrous mountains of Tibet, the concrete cyclops of New York, the radioactive craters of Russia, the artificial islands in the China Sea, the Black Forest, the Ganges, the Grand Canyon—but most of all, the works of human art: the pyramids, the Gothic cathedrals of Europe, *Notre Dame du Chartres*, Saint Peter's, the tile-work wonders of Anacapri. But the dream was still a long labour from realization.

Manue was a big youth, heavy-boned and built for labour, clever in a simple mechanical way, and with a wistful good humour that helped him take a lot of guff from whisky-breathed foremen and sharp-eyed engineers who made ten dollars an hour and figured ways for making more, legitimately or otherwise.

He had been on Mars only a month, and it hurt. Each time he swung the heavy pick into the red-brown sod, his face winced with pain. The plastic aerator valves, surgically stitched in his chest, pulled and twisted and seemed to tear with each lurch of his body. The mechanical oxygenator served as a lung, sucking blood through an artificially grafted network of veins and plastic tubing, frothing it with air from a chemical generator, and returning it to his circulatory system. Breathing was unnecessary, except to provide wind for talking, but Manue breathed in desperate gulps of the 4.0 psi Martian air; for he had seen the wasted, atrophied chests of the men who had served four or five years, and he knew that when they returned to Earth—if ever—they would still need the auxiliary oxygenator equipment.

"If you don't stop breathing," the surgeon told him, "you'll be all right. When you go to bed at night, turn the oxy down low—so you feel like panting. There's a critical point that's just right for sleeping. If you get it too low, you'll wake up screaming, and you'll get claustrophobia. If you get it too high, your reflex mechanisms will go to pot and you won't breathe; your lungs'll dry up after a time. Watch it."

Manue watched it carefully, although the oldsters laughed at him—in their dry wheezing chuckles. Some of them could scarcely speak more than two or three words at a shallow breath.

"Breathe deep, boy," they told him. "Enjoy it while you can. You'll forget how pretty soon. Unless you're an engineer."

The engineers had it soft, he learned. They slept in a pressurized barracks where the air was ten psi and twenty-five per cent oxygen, where they turned their oxies off and slept in peace. Even their oxies were self-regulating, controlling the output according to the carbon dioxide content of the input blood. But the Commission could afford no such luxuries for the labour gangs. The payload of a cargo rocket from Earth was only about two per cent of the ship's total mass, and nothing superfluous could be carried. The ships brought the bare essentials, basic industrial equipment, big reactors, generators, engines, heavy tools.

Small tools, building materials, foods, non-nuclear fuels —these things had to be made on Mars. There was an open pit mine in the belly of Syrtis Major where a "lake" of nearly pure iron-rust was scooped into smelter, and processed into various grades of steel for building purposes, tools, and machinery. A quarry in the Flathead Mountains dug up large quantities of cement rock, burned it and crushed it to make concrete.

It was rumoured that Mars was even preparing to grow her own labour force. An old-timer told him that the Commission had brought five hundred married couples to a new underground city in the Mare Erythraeum, supposedly as personnel for a local commission headquarters, but according to the old-timer, they were to be paid a bonus of three thousand dollars for every child born on the red planet. But Manue knew that the old "troffies" had a way of inventing such stories, and he reserved a certain amount of scepticism.

As for his own share in the Project, he knew—and needed to know—very little. The encampment was at the north end of the Mare Cimmerium, surrounded by the bleak brown and green landscape of rock and giant lichens, stretching towards sharply defined horizons except for one mountain range in the distance, and hung over by a blue sky so dark that the Earth-star occasionally became dimly visible during the dim daytime. The encampment consisted of a dozen double-walled stone huts, windowless, and roofed with flat slabs of rock covered over by a tarry resin boiled out of the cactuslike spineplants. The camp was ugly, lonely, and dominated by the gaunt skeleton of a drill rig set up in its midst.

Manue joined the excavating crew in the job of digging a yard-wide, six-feet-deep foundation trench in a hundred-yard square around the drill rig, which day and night was biting deeper through the crust of Mars in a dry cut that necessitated frequent stoppages for changing rotary bits. He learned that the geologists had predicted a subterranean pocket of tritium oxide ice at sixteen thousand feet, and that it was for this that they were drilling. The foundation he was helping to dig would be for a control station of some sort.

He worked too hard to be very curious. Mars was a nightmare, a grim, womanless, frigid, disinterestedly evil world. His digging partner was a sloe-eyed Tibetan nicknamed "Gee" who spoke the Omnalingua clumsily at best. He followed two paces behind Manue with a shovel, scooping up the broken ground, and humming a monotonous chant in his own tongue. Manue seldom heard his own language, and missed it; one of the engineers, a haughty Chilean, spoke the modern Spanish, but not to such as Manue Nanti. Most of the other labourers used either Basic English or the Omnalingua. He spoke both, but longed to hear the tongue of his people. Even when he tried to talk to Gee, the cultural gulf was so wide that satisfying communication was nearly impossible. Peruvian jokes were unfunny to Tibetan ears, although Gee bent double with gales of laughter when Manue nearly crushed his own foot with a clumsy stroke of the pick.

He found no close companions. His foreman was a narrow-eyed, orange-browed Low German named Vögeli, usually half-drunk, and intent upon keeping his lungpower by bellowing at his crew. A meaty, florid man, he stalked slowly along the lip of the excavation, pausing to stare coldly down at each pair of labourers who, if they dared to look up, caught a guttural tonguelashing for the moment's pause. When he had words for a digger, he called a halt by kicking a small avalanche of dirt back into the trench about the man's feet.

Manue learned about Vögeli's disposition before the end of his first month. The aerator tubes had become nearly unbearable; the skin, in trying to grow fast to the plastic, was beginning to form a tight little neck where the tubes entered his flesh, and the skin stretched and burned and stung with each movement of his trunk. Sud-

denly he felt sick. He staggered dizzily against the side of
the trench, dropped the pick, and swayed heavily, bracing
himself against collapse. Shock and nausea rocked him,
while Gee stared at him and giggled foolishly.

"Hoy!" Vögeli bellowed from across the pit. "Get back
on that pick! Hoy, there! Get with it—"

Manue moved dizzily to recover the tool, saw patches of
black swimming before him, sank weakly back to pant in
shallow gasps. The nagging sting of the valves was a portable hell that he carried with him always. He fought an
impulse to jerk them out of his flesh; if a valve came
loose, he would bleed to death in a few minutes.

Vögeli came stamping along the heap of fresh earth
and lumbered up to stand over the sagging Manue in the
trench. He glared down at him for a moment, then
nudged the back of his neck with a heavy boot. "Get to
work!"

Manue looked up and moved his lips silently. His forehead glinted with moisture in the faint sun, although the
temperature was far below freezing.

"Grab that pick and get started."

"Can't," Manue gasped. "Hoses—hurt."

Vögeli grumbled a curse and vaulted down into the
trench beside him. "Unzip that jacket," he ordered.

Weakly, Manue fumbled to obey, but the foreman
knocked his hand aside and jerked the zipper down.
Roughly he unbuttoned the Peruvian's shirt, laying open
the bare brown chest to the icy cold.

"No!—not the hoses, *please!"*

Vögeli took one of the thin tubes in his blunt fingers
and leaned close to peer at the puffy, calloused nodule of
irritated skin that formed around it where it entered the
flesh. He touched the nodule lightly, causing the digger
to whimper.

"No, please!"

"Stop snivelling!"

Vögeli laid his thumbs against the nodule and exerted a sudden pressure. There was slight popping sound as the skin slid back a fraction of an inch along the tube. Manue yelped and closed his eyes.

"Shut up! I know what I'm doing." He repeated the process with the other tube. Then he seized both tubes in his hands and wiggled them slightly in and out, as if to ensure a proper resetting of the skin. The digger cried weakly and slumped in a dead faint.

When he awoke, he was in bed in the barracks, and a medic was painting the sore spots with a bright yellow solution that chilled his skin.

"Woke up, huh?" the medic grunted cheerfully. "How do you feel?"

"Malo!" he hissed.

"Stay in bed for the day, son. Keep your oxy up high. Make you feel better."

The medic went away, but Vögeli lingered, smiling at him grimly from the doorway. "Don't try goofing off tomorrow too."

Manue hated the closed door with silent eyes, and listened until Vögeli's footsteps left the building. Then, following the medic's instructions, he turned his oxy to maximum, even though the faster flow of blood made the chest-valves ache. The sickness fled, to be replaced with a weary afterglow. Drowsiness came over him, and he slept.

Sleep was a dread black-robed phantom on Mars. Mars pressed the same incubus upon all newcomers to her soil: a nightmare of falling, falling, falling into bottomless space. It was the faint gravity, they said, that caused it. The body felt buoyed up, and the subconscious mind recalled down-going elevators, and diving aeroplanes, and a fall from a high cliff. It suggested these things in dreams, or if the dreamer's oxy were set too low, it conjured up a nightmare of sinking slowly deeper, and deeper in cold, black water that filled the victim's throat. Newcomers were segregated in a separate barracks so that their nightly screams would not disturb the old-timers who had finally adjusted to Martian conditions.

But now, for the first time since his arrival, Manue slept soundly, airily, and felt borne up by beams of bright light.

When he awoke again, he lay clammy in the horrifying knowledge that he had not been breathing! It was so comfortable not to breathe. His chest stopped hurting because of the stillness of his rib-cage. He felt refreshed and alive. Peaceful sleep.

Suddenly he was breathing again in harsh gasps, and cursing himself for the lapse, and praying amid quiet tears as he visualized the wasted chest of a troffie.

"Heh heh!" wheezed an oldster who had come in to readjust the furnace in the rookie barracks. "You'll get to be a Martian pretty soon, boy. I been here seven years. Look at *me*."

Manue heard the gasping voice and shuddered; there was no need to look.

"You just as well not fight it. It'll get you. Give in, make it easy on yourself. Go crazy if you don't."

"Stop it! Let me alone!"

"Sure. Just one thing. You wanna go home, you think. I went home. Came back. You will, too. They all do, 'cept engineers. Know why?"

"Shut up!" Manue pulled himself erect on the cot and hissed anger at the old-timer, who was neither old nor young, but only withered by Mars. His head suggested that he might be around thirty-five, but his body was weak and old.

The veteran grinned. "Sorry," he wheezed. "I'll keep my mouth shut." He hesitated, then extended his hand. "I'm Sam Donnell, mech-repairs."

Manue still glowered at him. Donnell shrugged and dropped his hand.

"Just trying to be friends," he muttered and walked away.

The digger started to call after him but only closed his mouth again, tightly. Friends? He needed friends, but not a troffie. He couldn't even bear to look at them, for fear he might be looking into the mirror of his own future.

Manue climbed out of his bunk and donned his fleece-skins. Night had fallen, and the temperature was already twenty below. A soft sift of icedust obscured the stars. He stared about in the darkness. The mess hall was closed, but a light burned in the canteen and another in the foremen's club, where the men were playing cards and drinking. He went to get his alcohol ration, gulped it mixed with a little water, and trudged back to the barracks alone.

The Tibetan was in bed, staring blankly at the ceiling. Manue sat down and gazed at his flat, empty face.

"Why did you come here, Gee?"

"Come where?"

"To Mars."

Gee grinned, revealing large black-streaked teeth. "Make money. Good money on Mars."

"Everybody make money, huh?"

"Sure."

"Where's the money come from?"

Gee rolled his face toward the Peruvian and frowned. "You crazy? Money come from Earth, where all money come from."

"And what does Earth get back from Mars?"

Gee looked puzzled for a moment, then gathered anger because he found no answer. He grunted a monosyllable in his native tongue, then rolled over and went to sleep.

Manue was not normally given to worrying about such things, but now he found himself asking, "What am I doing here?"—and then, "What is *anybody* doing here?"

The Mars Project had started eighty or ninety years ago, and its end goal was to make Mars habitable for colonists without Earth support, without oxies and insulated suits and the various gadgets a man now had to use to keep himself alive on the fourth planet. But thus far, Earth had planted without reaping. The sky was a bottomless well into which Earth poured her tools, dollars, manpower, and engineering skill. And there appeared to be no hope for the near future.

Manue felt suddenly trapped. He could not return to Earth before the end of his contract. He was trading five years of virtual enslavement for a sum of money which would buy a limited amount of freedom. But what if he lost his lungs, became a servant of the small aerator for the rest of his days? Worst of all: whose ends was he serving? The contractors were getting rich—on government contracts. Some of the engineers and foremen were getting rich—by various forms of embezzlement of government funds. But what were the people back on Earth getting for their money?

Nothing.

He lay awake for a long time, thinking about it. Then he resolved to ask someone tomorrow, someone smarter than himself.

But he found the question brushed aside. He summoned enough nerve to ask Vögeli, but the foreman told him harshly to keep working and quit wondering. He asked the structural engineer who supervised the building, but the man only laughed, and said: "What do you care? You're making good money."

They were running concrete now, laying the long strips of Martian steel in the bottom of the trench and dumping in great slobbering wheelbarrowfuls of grey-green mix. The drillers were continuing their tedious dry cut deep into the red world's crust. Twice a day they brought up a yard-long cylindrical sample of the rock and gave it to a

geologist who weighed it, roasted it, weighed it again, and
tested a sample of the condensed steam—if any—for
tritium content. Daily, he chalked up the results on a
blackboard in front of the engineering hut, and the technical staff crowded around for a look. Manue always
glanced at the figures, but failed to understand.

Life became an endless routine of pain, fear, hard
work, anger. There were few diversions. Sometimes a
crew of entertainers came out from the Mare Erythraeum,
but the labour gang could not all crowd in the pressurized
staff-barracks where the shows were presented, and when
Manue managed to catch a glimpse of one of the girls
walking across the clearing, she was bundled in fleece-
skins and hooded by a parka.

Itinerant rabbis, clergymen, and priests of the world's
major faiths came occasionally to the camp: Buddhist,
Moslem, and the Christian sects. Padre Antonio Selni
made monthly visits to hear confessions and offer Mass.
Most of the gang attended all services as a diversion from
routine, as an escape from nostalgia. Somehow it gave
Manue a strange feeling in the pit of his stomach to see
the Sacrifice of the Mass, two thousand years old, being
offered in the same ritual under the strange dark sky of
Mars—with a section of the new foundation serving as an
altar upon which the priest set crucifix, candles, relic-
stone, missal, chalice, paten, ciborium, cruets, et cetera.
In filling the wine-cruet before the service, Manue saw
him spill a little of the red-clear fluid upon the brown soil
—wine, Earth-wine from sunny Sicilian vineyards, tram-
pled from the grapes by the bare stamping feet of children.
Wine, the rich red blood of Earth, soaking slowly into the
crust of another planet.

Bowing low at the consecration, the unhappy Peruvian
thought of the prayer a rabbi had sung the week before:
"Blessed be the Lord our God, King of the Universe, Who

makest bread to spring forth out of the Earth."

Earth chalice, Earth blood, Earth God, Earth wor-shippers—with plastic tubes in their chests and a great sickness in their hearts.

He went away saddened. There was no faith here Faith needed familiar surroundings, the props of culture Here there were only swinging picks and rumbling machinery and sloshing concrete and the clatter of tools and the wheezing of troffies. Why? For five dollars an hour and keep?

Manue, raised in a back-country society that was almost a folk-culture, felt deep thirst for a goal. His father had been a stonemason, and he had laboured lovingly to help build the new cathedral, to build houses and mansions and commercial buildings, and his blood was mingled in their mortar. He had built for the love of his community and the love of the people and their customs, and their gods. He knew his own ends, and the ends of those around him. But what sense was there in this endless scratching at the face of Mars? Did they think they could make it into a second Earth, with pine forests and lakes and snow-capped mountains and small country villages? Man was not that strong. No, if he were labouring for any cause at all, it was to build a world so unearthlike that he could not love it.

The foundation was finished. There was very little more to be done until the drillers struck pay. Manue sat around the camp and worked at breathing. It was becoming a conscious effort now and if he stopped thinking about it for a few minutes, he found himself inspiring shallow, meaningless little sips of air that scarcely moved his diaphragm. He kept the aerator as low as possible, to make himself breathe great gasps that hurt his chest, but it made him dizzy, and he had to increase the oxygenation lest he faint.

Sam Donnell, the troffie mech-repairman, caught him about to slump dizzily from his perch atop a heap of rocks, pushed him erect, and turned his oxy back to normal. It was late afternoon, and the drillers were about to change shifts. Manue sat shaking his head for a moment, then gazed at Donnell gratefully.

"That's dangerous, kid," the troffie wheezed. "Guys can go psycho doing that. Which you rather have: sick lungs or sick mind?"

"Neither."

"I know, but—"

"I don't want to talk about it."

Donnell stared at him with a faint smile. Then he shrugged and sat down on the rock heap to watch the drilling.

"Oughta be hitting the tritium ice in a couple of days," he said pleasantly. "Then we'll see a big blow."

Manue moistened his lips nervously. The troffies always made him feel uneasy. He stared aside.

"Big blow?"

"Lotta pressure down there, they say. Something about the way Mars got formed. Dust cloud hypothesis."

Manue shook his head. "I don't understand."

"I don't either. But I've heard them talk. Couple of billion years ago, Mars was supposed to be a moon of Jupiter. Picked up a lot of ice crystals over a rocky core. Then it broke loose and picked up a rocky crust—from another belt of the dust cloud. The pockets of tritium ice catch a few neutrons from uranium ore—down under. Some of the tritium goes into helium. Frees oxygen. Gases form pressure. Big blow."

"What are they going to do with the ice?"

The troffie shrugged. "The engineers might know."

Manue snorted and spat. "They know how to make money."

"Heh! Sure, everybody's gettin' rich."

The Peruvian stared at him speculatively for a moment. "Señor Donnell, I—"

"Sam'll do."

"I wonder if anybody knows why . . . well . . . why we're really here."

Donnell glanced up to grin, then waggled his head. He fell thoughtful for a moment, and leaned forward to write in the earth. When he finished, he read it aloud.

"A plough plus a horse plus land equals the necessities of life." He glanced up at Manue. "Fifteen hundred A.D."

The Peruvian frowned his bewilderment. Donnell rubbed out what he had written and wrote again.

"A factory plus steam turbines plus raw materials equals necessities plus luxuries. Nineteen hundred A.D."

He rubbed it out and repeated the scribbling. "All those things plus nuclear power and computer controls equal a surplus of everything. Twenty-one hundred A.D."

"So?"

"So, it's either cut production or find an outlet. Mars is an outlet for surplus energies, manpower, money. Mars Project keeps money turning over, keeps everything turning over. Economist told me that. Said if the Project folded, surplus would pile up—big depression on Earth."

The Peruvian shook his head and sighed. It didn't sound right somehow. It sounded like an explanation somebody figured out after the whole thing started. It wasn't the kind of goal he wanted.

Two days later, the drill hit ice, and the "big blow" was only a fizzle. There was talk around the camp that the whole operation had been a waste of time. The hole spewed a frosty breath for several hours, and the drill crews crowded around to stick their faces in it and breathe great gulps of the helium-oxygen mixture. But then the blow subsided, and the hole leaked only a wisp of steam.

Technicians came, and lowered sonar "cameras" down

to the ice. They spent a week taking internal soundings
and plotting the extent of the ice-dome on their charts.
They brought up samples of ice and tested them. The
engineers worked late into the Martian nights.

Then it was finished. The engineers came out of their
huddles and called to the foremen of the labour gangs.
They led the foremen around the site, pointing here,
pointing there, sketching with chalk on the foundation,
explaining in solemn voices. Soon the foremen were
bellowing at their crews.

"Let's get the derrick down!"

"Start that mixer going!"

"Get that steel over here!"

"Unroll that dip-wire!"

"Get a move on! Shovel that fill!"

Muscles tightened and strained, machinery clamoured
and rang. Voices grumbled and shouted. The operation
was starting again. Without knowing why, Manue shov-
elled fill and stretched dip-wire and poured concrete for
a big slab to be run across the entire hundred-yard square,
broken only by the big pipe-casing that stuck up out of
the ground in the centre and leaked a thin trail of steam.

The drill crew moved their rig half a mile across the
plain to a point specified by the geologists and began
sinking another hole. A groan went up from structural
boys: "Not *another* one of these things!"

But the supervisory staff said, "No, don't worry about
it."

There was much speculation about the purpose of the
whole operation, and the men resented the quiet secrecy
connected with the project. There could be no excuse for
secrecy, they felt, in time of peace. There was a certain
arbitrariness about it, a hint that the Commission thought
of its employees as children, or enemies, or servants. But
the supervisory staff shrugged off all questions with: "You
know there's tritium ice down there. You know it's what

we've been looking for. Why? Well—what's the difference? There are lots of uses for it. Maybe we'll use it for one thing, maybe for something else. Who knows?"

Such a reply might have been satisfactory for an iron mine or an oil well or a stone quarry, but tritium suggested hydrogen-fusion. And no transportation facilities were being installed to haul the stuff away—no pipelines nor railroad tracks nor glider ports.

Manue quit thinking about it. Slowly he came to adopt a grim cynicism towards the tediousness, the back-breaking labour of his daily work; he lived from day to day like an animal, dreaming only of a return to Earth when his contract was up. But the dream was painful because it was distant, as contrasted with the immediacies of Mars: the threat of atrophy, coupled with the discomforts of continued breathing, the nightmares, the barrenness of the landscape, the intense cold, the harshness of men's tempers, the hardship of labour, and the lack of a cause.

A warm, sunny Earth was still over four years distant, and tomorrow would be another back-breaking, throat-parching, heart-tormenting, chest-hurting day. Where was there even a little pleasure in it? It was so easy, at least, to leave the oxy turned up at night, and get a pleasant restful sleep. Sleep was the only recourse from harshness, and fear robbed sleep of its quiet sensuality—unless a man just surrendered and quit worrying about his lungs.

Manue decided that it would be safe to give himself two completely restful nights a week.

Concrete was run over the great square and trowelled to a rough finish. A glider train from Mare Erythraeum brought in several huge crates of machinery, cut-stone masonry for building a wall, a shipful of new personnel, and a real rarity: lumber, cut from the first Earth-trees to be grown on Mars.

A building began going up with the concrete square for foundation and floor. Structures could be flimsier on

Mars; because of the light gravity, compression-stresses were smaller. Hence, the work progressed rapidly, and as the flat-roofed structure was completed, the technicians began uncrating new machinery and moving it into the building. Manue noticed that several of the units were computers. There was also a small steam-turbine generator driven by an atomic-fired boiler.

Months passed. The building grew into an integrated mass of power and control systems. Instead of using the well for pumping, the technicians were apparently going to lower something into it. A bomb-shaped cylinder was slung vertically over the hole. The men guided it into the mouth of the pipe casing, then let it down slowly from a massive cable. The cylinder's butt was a multi-contact socket like the female receptacle for a hundred-pin electron tube. Hours passed while the cylinder slipped slowly down beneath the hide of Mars. When it was done, the men hauled out the cable and began lowering stiff sections of pre-wired conduit, fitted with a receptacle at one end and a male plug at the other, so that as the sections fell into place, a continuous bundle of control cables was built up from "bomb" to surface.

Several weeks were spent in connecting circuits, setting up the computers, and making careful tests. The drillers had finished the second well hole, half a mile from the first, and Manue noticed that while the testing was going on, the engineers sometimes stood atop the building and stared anxiously towards the steel skeleton in the distance. Once while the tests were being conducted, the second hole began squirting a jet of steam high in the thin air, and a frantic voice bellowed from the roof top.

"Cut it! Shut it off! Sound the danger whistle!"

The jet of steam began to shriek a low-pitched whine across the Martian desert. It blended with the rising and falling *OOOOawwww* of the danger siren. But gradually it subsided as the men in the control station shut down the machinery. All hands came up cursing from their hiding places, and the engineers stalked out to the new hole carrying Geiger counters. They came back wearing pleased grins.

The work was nearly finished. The men began crating up the excavating machinery and the drill rig and the tools. The control-building devices were entirely automatic, and the camp would be deserted when the station began operation. The men were disgruntled. They had spent a year of hard labour on what they had thought to be a tritium well, but now that it was done, there were no facilities for pumping the stuff or hauling it away. In fact, they had pumped various solutions *into* the ground through the second hole, and the control station shaft was fitted with pipes that led from lead-lined tanks down into the earth.

Manue had stopped trying to keep his oxy properly adjusted at night. Turned up to a comfortable level, it was like a drug, ensuring comfortable sleep—and like addict or alcoholic, he could no longer endure living without it. Sleep was too precious, his only comfort. Every morning he awoke with a still, motionless chest, felt frightening remorse, sat up gasping, choking, sucking at the thin air with whining rattling lungs that had been idle too long. Sometimes he coughed violently, and bled a little. And then for a night or two he would correctly adjust the oxy, only to wake up screaming and suffocating. He felt hope sliding grimly away.

He sought out Sam Donnell, explained the situation, and begged the troffie for helpful advice. But the mech-repairman neither helped nor consoled nor joked about it. He only bit his lip, muttered something non-committal, and found an excuse to hurry away. It was then that Manue knew his hope was gone. Tissue was withering, tubercules forming, tubes growing closed. He knelt abjectly beside his cot, hung his face in his hands, and cursed softly, for there was no other way to pray an unanswerable prayer.

A glider train came in from the north to haul away the disassembled tools. The men lounged around the barracks or wandered across the Martian desert, gathering strange bits of rock and fossils, searching idly for a glint of metal or crystal in the wan sunshine of early fall. The lichens were growing brown and yellow, and the landscape took on the hues of Earth's autumn if not the forms.

There was a sense of expectancy around the camp. It could be felt in the nervous laughter, and the easy voices, talking suddenly of Earth and old friends and the smell of food in a farm kitchen, and old half-forgotten tastes for which men hungered: ham searing in the skillet, a cup of frothing cider from a fermenting crock, iced melon with honey and bits of lemon, onion gravy on homemade bread. But someone always remarked, "What's the matter with you guys? We ain't going home. Not by a long shot. We're going to another place just like this."

And the group would break up and wander away, eyes tired, eyes haunted with nostalgia.

"What're we waiting for?" men shouted at the supervisory staff. "Get some transportation in here. Let's get rolling."

Men watched the skies for glider trains or jet transports, but the skies remained empty, and the staff remained close-mouthed. Then a dust column appeared on the horizon to the north, and a day later a convoy of tractor-trucks pulled into camp.

"Start loading aboard, men!" was the crisp command.

Surly voices: "You mean we don't go by air? We gotta ride those kidney bouncers? It'll take a week to get to Mare Ery! Our contract says—"

"Load aboard! We're not going to Mare Ery yet!"

Grumbling, they loaded their baggage and their weary

bodies into the trucks, and the trucks thundered and clattered across the desert, rolling towards the mountains.

The convoy rolled for three days towards the mountains, stopping at night to make camp, and driving on at sunrise. When they reached the first slopes of the foothills, the convoy stopped again. The deserted encampment lay a hundred and fifty miles behind. The going had been slow over the roadless desert.

"Everybody out!" barked the messenger from the lead truck. "Bail out! Assemble at the foot of the hill."

Voices were growling among themselves as the men moved in small groups from the trucks and collected in a milling tide in a shallow basin, overlooked by a low cliff and a hill. Manue saw the staff climb out of a cab and slowly work their way up the cliff. They carried a portable public address system.

"Gonna get a preaching," somebody snarled.

"Sit down, please!" barked the loud-speaker. "You men sit down there! Quiet—quiet, please!"

The gathering fell into a sulky silence. Will Kinley stood looking out over them, his eyes nervous, his hand holding the mike close to his mouth so that they could hear his weak troffie voice.

"If you men have questions," he said, "I'll answer them now. Do you want to know what you've been doing during the past year?"

An affirmative rumble arose from the group.

"You've been helping to give Mars a breathable atmosphere." He glanced briefly at his watch, then looked back at his audience. "In fifty minutes, a controlled chain reaction will start in the tritium ice. The computers will time it and try to control it. Helium and oxygen will come blasting up out of the second hole."

A rumble of disbelief arose from his audience. Someone shouted: "How can you get air to blanket a planet from one hole?"

"You can't," Kinley replied crisply. "A dozen others are going in, just like that one. We plan three hundred, and we've already located the ice pockets. Three hundred wells, working for eight centuries, can get the job done."

"Eight centuries! What good—"

"Wait!" Kinley barked. "In the meantime, we'll build pressurized cities close to the wells. If everything pans out, we'll get a lot of colonists here, and gradually condition them to live in a seven or eight psi atmosphere—which is about the best we can hope to get. Colonists from the Andes and the Himalayas—they wouldn't need much conditioning."

"What about us?"

There was a long plaintive silence. Kinley's eyes scanned the group sadly, and wandered towards the Martian horizon, gold and brown in the late afternoon. "Nothing—about us," he muttered quietly.

"Why did we come out here?"

"Because there's danger of the reaction getting out of hand. We can't tell anyone about it, or we'd start a panic." He looked at the group sadly. "I'm telling you now, because there's nothing you could do. In thirty minutes—"

There were angry murmurs in the crowd. "You mean there may be an explosion?"

"There *will* be a limited explosion. And there's very little danger of anything more. The worst danger is in having ugly rumours start in the cities. Some fool with a slip-stick would hear about it, and calculate what would happen to Mars if five cubic miles of tritium ice detonated in one split second. It would probably start a riot. That's why we've kept it a secret."

The buzz of voices was like a disturbed beehive. Manue Nanti sat in the midst of it, saying nothing, wearing a dazed and weary face, thoughts jumbled, soul drained of feeling.

Why should men lose their lungs that after eight centuries of tomorrows, other men might breathe the air of Mars as the air of Earth?

Other men around him echoed his thoughts in jealous mutterings. They had been helping to make a world in which they would never live.

An enraged scream arose near where Manue sat. "They're going to blow us up! They're going to blow up Mars."

"Don't be a fool!" Kinley snapped.

"Fools they call us! We *are* fools! For ever coming here! We got sucked in! Look at *me*!" A pale dark-haired man came wildly to his feet and tapped his chest. "Look! I'm losing my lungs! We're all losing our lungs! Now they take a chance on killing everybody."

"Including ourselves," Kinley called coldly.

"We oughta take him apart. We oughta kill everyone who knew about it—and Kinley's a good place to start!"

The rumble of voices rose higher, calling both agreement and dissent. Some of Kinley's staff were looking nervously towards the trucks. They were unarmed.

"You men sit down!" Kinley barked.

Rebellious eyes glared at the supervisor. Several men who had come to their feet dropped to their hunches again. Kinley glowered at the pale upriser who called for his scalp.

"Sit down, Handell!"

Handell turned his back on the supervisor and called out to the others. "Don't be a bunch of cowards! Don't let him bully you!"

"You men sitting around Handell. Pull him down."

There was no response. The men, including Manue, stared up at the wild-eyed Handell gloomily, but made no move to quiet him. A pair of burly foremen started through the gathering from its outskirts.

"Stop!" Kinley ordered. "Turpin, Schultz—get back. Let the men handle this themselves."

Half a dozen others had joined the rebellious Handell. They were speaking in low tense tones among themselves.

"For the last time, men! Sit down!"

The group turned and started grimly towards the cliff. Without reasoning why, Manue slid to his feet quietly as Handell came near him. "Come on, fellow, let's get him," the leader muttered.

The Peruvian's fist chopped a short stroke to Handell's jaw, and the dull *thuk* echoed across the clearing. The man crumpled, and Manue crouched over him like a hissing panther. "Get back!" he snapped at the others. "Or I'll jerk his hoses out."

One of the others cursed him.

"Want to fight, fellow?" the Peruvian wheezed. "I can jerk several hoses out before you drop me!"

They shuffled nervously for a moment.

"The guy's crazy!" one complained in a high voice.

"Get back or he'll kill Handell!"

They sidled away, moved aimlessly in the crowd, then sat down to escape attention. Manue sat beside the fallen man and gazed at the thinly smiling Kinley.

"Thank you, son. There's a fool in every crowd." He looked at his watch again. "Just a few minutes, men. Then you'll feel the earth-tremor, and the explosion, and the wind. You can be proud of that wind, men. It's new air for Mars, and you made it."

"But we can't breathe it!" hissed a troffie.

Kinley was silent for a long time, as if listening to the distance. "What man ever made his own salvation?" he murmured.

They packed up the public address amplifier and came down the hill to sit in the cab of a truck, waiting.

It came as an orange glow in the south, and the glow was quickly shrouded by an expanding white cloud. Then, minutes later the ground pulsed beneath them, quivered and shook. The quake subsided, but remained as a hint of vibration. Then after a long time, they heard the dull-throated thundering across the Martian desert. The roar continued steadily, grumbling and growling as it would do for several hundred years.

There was only a hushed murmur of awed voices from the crowd. When the wind came, some of them stood up and moved quietly back to the trucks, for now they could go back to a city for reassignment. There were other tasks to accomplish before their contracts were done.

But Manue Nanti still sat on the ground, his head sunk low, desperately trying to gasp a little of the wind he had made, the wind out of the ground, the wind of the future. But his lungs were clogged, and he could not drink of the racing wind. His big calloused hand clutched slowly at the ground, and he choked a brief sound like a sob.

A shadow fell over him. It was Kinley, come to offer his thanks for the quelling of Handell. But he said nothing for a moment as he watched Manue's desperate Gethsemane.

"Some sow, others reap," he said.

"Why?" the Peruvian choked.

The supervisor shrugged. "What's the difference? But if you can't be both, which would you rather be?"

Nanti looked up into the wind. He imagined a city to the south, a city built on tear-soaked ground, filled with people who had no ends beyond their culture, no goal but within their own society. It was a good sensible question: which would he rather be—sower or reaper?

Pride brought him slowly to his feet, and he eyed Kinley questioningly. The supervisor touched his shoulder.

"Go on to the trucks."

Nanti nodded and shuffled away. He had wanted some-

thing to work for, hadn't he? Something more than the
reasons Donnell had given. Well, he could smell a reason,
even if he couldn't breathe it.

Eight hundred years was a long time, but then—long
time, big reason. The air smelled good, even with its
clouds of boiling dust.

He knew now what Mars was—not a ten-thousand-a-
year job, not a garbage can for surplus production. But an
eight-century passion of human faith in the destiny of the
race of Man. He paused short of the truck. He had wanted
to travel, to see the sights of Earth, the handiwork of
Nature and of history, the glorious places of his planet.

He stooped, and scooped up a handful of the red-brown
soil, letting it sift slowly between his fingers. Here was
Mars—his planet now. No more of Earth, not for Manue
Nanti. He adjusted his aerator more comfortably and
climbed into the waiting truck.

Frederik Pohl

Three Portraits and a Prayer

Howard Chandler Christy:

The Lovely Young Girl

When Dr. Rhine Cooperstock was put under my care I was enlarged with pride. Dr. Cooperstock was a hero to me. I don't mean a George Washington, all virtue and no fire, I mean he was a dragon killer. He had carried human knowledge far into the tiny spaces of an atomic nucleus. He was a very great man. And I was his doctor and he was dying.

Dr. Cooperstock was dying in the finest suite in the

Morgan Pavilion and with all the best doctors. (I am not modest.) We couldn't keep him alive for more than a matter of months, and we couldn't cure him at all. But we could make him comfortable. If round-the-clock nurses and color television constitute comfort.

I don't ask you to understand technical medical terms. He was an old man, his blood vessels deteriorating, and clots formed, impeding the circulation. One day a clot would form in heart, brain or lungs and he would die. If it was in the lung it would be painful and slow. In the heart, painful and fast. In the brain most painful of all, but so fast it would be a mercy.

Meanwhile we fed him heparin and sometimes coumarol and attempted by massages and heat and diet to stave off the end. Although, in fact, he was all but dead anyway, so little freedom of movement we allowed him.

"Martin, the leg hurts. You'd better leave a pill," he would say to me once or twice a week, and I would hesitate. "I don't know if I can make it to the bathroom tonight, Martin," he would say, his tone cheerfully resigned. Then he would call for the bedpan while I was there, or mention casually that some invisible wrinkle in the sheet caused him pain and stand by bravely while the bed was remade, and say at last, self-deprecating, "I think I will need that pill, Martin." So I would allow myself to be persuaded and let him have a red-and-white capsule and in the morning it would be gone. I never told him that they contained only aspirin and he never admitted to me that he did not take the pills at all but was laboriously building up a hoard against the day when the pain would be really serious and he would take them all at once.

Dr. Cooperstock knew the lethal dose as well as I did. As he knew the names of all his veins and arteries and the chemistry of his disease. A man like Rhine Cooperstock, even at seventy, can learn enough medicine for that in a week.

He acquired eleven of the little capsules in one month at the Pavilion; I know, because I counted them after he left. That would have been enough for suicide, if they had not been aspirin. I suppose he would have stopped there, perhaps beginning to take a few, now and then, both to keep me from getting suspicious and for the relief of the real pain he must have felt. But he did leave. Nan Halloran came and got him.

She invaded the Pavilion like a queen. Expensive, celebrated hospital, we were used to the famous; but this was Nan Halloran, blue-eyed, black-haired, a face like a lovely child and a voice like the sway of hips. She was a most remarkable woman. I called her a queen, but she was not that, she was a goddess, virgin and fertile. I speak subjectively, of course, for in medical fact she was surely not one and may not have been either. She breezed into the room, wrinkling her nose. "Coopie," she said, "what is that awful smell? Will you do me a favor, dear? I need it very much."

You would not think that a man like Dr. Cooperstock would have much to do with a television star; but he knew her; years before, when he was still teaching sometimes, she had somehow wandered into his class. "Hello, Nan," he said, looking quite astonished and pleased. "I'll do anything I can for you, of course. That smell," he apologized, touching the leg with its bright spots of color and degenerated tissues, "is me."

"Poor Coopie." She looked around at me and smiled. Although I am fat and not attractive and know in my heart that, whatever long-term wonders I may work with the brilliance of my mind and the cleverness of my speech, no woman will ever lust for me on sight, I tingled. I looked away. She said sweetly, "It's about that fusion power thing, Coopie. You know Wayne Donner, of course? He and I are good friends. He has these utility company interests, and he wants to convert them to fusion power, and I told him you were the only man who could help him."

Dr. Cooperstock began to laugh, and laughed until he was choking and gagging. I laughed too, although I think that in all the world Dr. Cooperstock and I must be two of the very few men who would laugh at the name of Wayne Donner. "Nan," he said when he could, "you're amazing. It's utterly impossible, I'm afraid."

She sat on the edge of his bed with a rustle of petticoats. She had lovely legs. "Oh, did that hurt you? But I didn't even touch your leg, dear. Would you please get up and come now, because the driver's waiting?"

"Nan!" he cried. "Security regulations. Death. Lack of proper engineering! Did you ever think of any of those things? And they're only a beginning."

"If you're going to make objections we'll be here all day, darling. As far as security is concerned," she said, "this is for the peaceful use of atomic power, isn't it? I promise you that Wayne has enough friends in the Senate that there will be no problem. And the engineering's all right, because Wayne has all those people already, of course. This isn't any little Manhattan Project, honey. Wayne spends *money*."

Dr. Cooperstock shook his head and, although he was smiling, he was interested, too. "What about death, Nan?" he said gently.

"Oh, I know, Coopie. It's terrible. But you can't lick this thing. So won't you do it for me? Wayne only needs you for a few weeks and he already talked to some doctors. They said it would be all right."

"Miss Halloran," I said. I admit I was furious. "Dr. Cooperstock is my patient. As long as that is so, I will decide what is or is not all right."

She looked at me again, sweetly and attentively.

I have now and had then no doubt at all; I was absolutely right in my position. Yet I felt as though I had committed the act of a clumsy fool. She was clean and lovely, her neck so slim that the dress she wore seemed too large for her, like an adorable child's. She was no child; I knew that she had had a hundred lovers because everyone knows that, even doctors who are fat and a little ugly and take it all out in intelligence. Yet she possessed an innocence I could not withstand. I wanted to take her sweetly by the hand and shelter her, and walk with her beside a brook and then that night crush her and caress her again and again with such violence and snorting passion that she would Awaken and then, with growing abandon, Respond. I did know it was all foolishness. I did. But when she mentioned the names of five or six doctors on Donner's payroll who would care for Dr. Cooperstock and suggested like a child that with them in charge it would really be all right, I agreed. I even apologized. Truth to tell, they were excellent men, those doctors. But if she had named six chiropractors and an unfrocked abortionist I still would have shrugged and shuffled and stammered, "Oh, well, I suppose, Miss Halloran, yes, it will be all right."

So we called the nurses in and very carefully dressed the old man and wheeled him out into the hall. I said something else that was foolish in the elevator. I said, because I had assumed that it was so, that she probably had a cab waiting and a cab would not do to transport a man as sick as Dr. Cooperstock. But she had been more sure of herself than that. The driver who was waiting was at the wheel of a private ambulance.

> *A TIME cover,*
> *attributed to Artzybasheff,*
> *with mosaic of dollar signs.*

I did not again hear of Dr. Cooperstock for five weeks. Then I was telephoned to come and get him, for he was ready to return to the Pavilion to die. It was Wayne Donner himself who called me.

I agreed to come to one of Donner's New York offices to meet him, for in truth I was curious. I knew all about him, of course—rather, I knew as much as he wished anyone to know. I have seen enough of the world's household names in the Pavilion to know what their public relations men can do. The facts that were on record about Wayne Donner were that he was very rich. He had gone from a lucky strike in oil and the twenty-seven and a half per cent depletion allowance to aluminum. And thence to electric power. He was almost the wealthiest man in the world, and I know his secret.

He could afford anything, anything at all, because he had schooled himself to purchase only bargains. For example, I knew that he was Nan Halloran's lover and, although I do not know her price, I know that it was what he was willing to pay. Otherwise he would have given her that thin, bright smile that meant the parley was over, there would be no contract signed that day, and gone on to another incredible beauty more modest in her bargaining. Donner allowed himself to want only what he could get. I think he was the only terrible man I have ever seen. And he had nearly been President of the United States! Except that Governor Hewlett of Ohio spoke so honestly and so truthfully about him in the primaries that not all of Donner's newspapers could get him the vote; what was terrible was not that he then destroyed Hewlett, but that Hewlett was not destroyed for revenge. Donner hated too deeply to be satisfied with revenge, I think; he was too contemptuous of his enemies to trouble to crush them. He would not give them that satisfaction. Hewlett was blotted out only incidentally. Because Donner's papers had built the campaign against him to such a pitch that it was actually selling papers, and thus it was profitable to go on to ruin the man. When I saw Donner he had Hewlett's picture framed in gilt in his waiting room. I wondered how many of his visitors understood the message. For that matter I wondered how many needed it.

When I was admitted, Dr. Cooperstock was on a relaxing couch. "Hello, Martin," he said over the little drone of its motor. "This is Wayne Donner. Dr. Finneman. Dr. Grace."

I shook hands with the doctors first, pettishly enough but I felt obliged to show where I stood, and then with Donner. He was very courteous. He had discovered what bargains could be bought with that coin too. He said, "Dr. Finneman here has a good deal of respect for you, Doctor. I'm sure you're well placed at the Pavilion. But if you ever consider leaving I'd like to talk to you."

I thanked him and refused. I was flattered, though. I thought of how his fusion-power nonsense might have killed Dr. Cooperstock before he was ready to die, and I thought of him with Nan Halloran, sweat on that perfect face. And I am not impressed by money.

Yet I was flattered that he would take the trouble and time, and God knows how much an hour of his time was worth, to himself offer me a job. I was flattered even though I knew that the courtesy was for his benefit, not mine. He wanted the best he chose to afford—in the way of a doctor, in my case, but the best of everything else too. If he hired a gardener he would want the man to be a very good gardener. Aware as he was of the dignities assumed by a professional man, he had budgeted the time to give me a personal invitation instead of letting his housekeeper or general manager attend to it. It was only another installment of expense he chose to afford and yet I was glad to get out of there. I was almost afraid I would consider and say yes, and I hated that man very much.

When we got Dr. Cooperstock back and bedded and
checked over I examined the records Dr. Finneman had
sent. He had furnished complete tests and a politely
guarded prognosis, and of course he was right; Cooperstock was sinking, but not fast; he was good for another
month or two with luck. I told him as much, snappishly.
"Don't be angry with me, Martin," he said, "you'd have
done the same thing for Nan if she asked you."

"Probably, but I'm not dying."

"Don't be vulgar, Martin."

"I'm not a nuclear physicist, either."

"It's only to make a few dollars for the man, Martin.
Heavens. What difference can another billion or two make
to Donner? Besides," he said strongly, "you know I've
always opposed this fetish of security. Think of Oppen-
heimer, not allowed to read his own papers! Think of the
waste, the same work done in a dozen different places,
because in Irkutsk they aren't allowed to know what's
going on in Denver and in Omaha somebody forgot to
tell them."

"Think of Wayne Donner with all the power in the
world," I said.

He said, "I guess Nan hit you harder than I thought to
make you so mad."

Although I watched the papers I did not see anything
about converting Donner's power stations to fusion energy.
In fact, I didn't see much of Donner's name at all, which
caused me to wonder. Normally he would have been
spotted in the Stork or cruising off Bimini or in some other
way photographed and written about a couple of times
a week. His publicity men must have been laboring extra
hard.

Nan Halloran came to see Dr. Cooperstock but I did
not join them. I spent my time with him when there was
no one else, after my evening rounds. Sometimes we

played cards but more often I listened to him talk. The physics of the atomic nucleus was poetry when he talked of it. He told me about Gamow's primordial atom from which all the stars and dust clouds had exploded. He explained Fred Hoyle to me, and Heisenberg. But he was tiring early now.

Behind the drawer of his night table, in a used cigarette package thumbtacked to the wood, his store of red-and-white capsules was growing again. They were still aspirin. But I think I would not have denied him the real thing if he had known the deception and asked. We took off two toes in March and it was only a miracle that we saved the leg.

> *By Gilbert Stuart.*
> *His late period.*
> *Size 9' x 5'; heroic.*

In the beginning of May newspaper stories again began to appear about Donner, but I could not understand them. The stories were datelined Washington. Donner was reported in top-level conferences, deeply classified. There were no leaks, no one knew what the talks were about. But the presidential press secretary was irritable with the reporters who asked questions, and the cabinet members were either visibly worried or visibly under orders to keep their mouths shut. *And* worried. I showed one or two of the stories to Dr. Cooperstock, but he was too tired to guess at implications.

He was hanging on, but it would not be for long. Any night I expected the call from his nurses, and we would not be able to save him again.

Then I was called to my office. I was lecturing to fourth-year men when the annunciator spoke my name; and when I got to my office Governor Hewlett was there.

"I need to see Dr. Cooperstock," he said. "I'm afraid

it may excite him. The resident thought you should be present."

I said, "I suppose you know that any shock may kill him. I hope it's important."

"It is important. Yes." The Governor limped ahead of me to the elevator, his bald head gleaming, smiling at the nurses with his bad teeth and his wonderful eyes. Dr. Cooperstock was a hero to me. Governor Hewlett was something less, perhaps a saint or a martyr. He was what St. George would have been if in the battle he had been killed as well as the dragon; Hewlett had spent himself against Donner in the campaign and now he lingered on to serve out his punishment for his daring, the weasels always chipping away at him, a constant witness before commissions and committees with slanders thick in the air, a subject for jokes and political cartoons. A few senators and others of his own party still listened to him, but they could not save him from the committees.

The Governor did not waste words. "Dr. Cooperstock, what have you done? What is Wayne Donner up to?"

Cooperstock had been dozing. Elaborately he sat up. "I don't see, sir, that it is—"

"Will you answer me, please? I'm afraid this is quite serious. The Secretary of Defense, who was with me in the House fifteen years ago, told me something I did not suspect. Do you know that he may be asked to resign and that Wayne Donner may get his job?"

Dr. Cooperstock said angrily, "That's nonsense. Donner's just a businessman. Anyway, what conceivable difference can—"

"It makes a difference, Dr. Cooperstock, because the rest of the cabinet is to be changed around at the same time. Every post of importance is to go to a man of Donner's. You recall that he wanted to be President. Perhaps this time he does not want to bother with a vote. What weapon have you given him to make him so strong, Dr. Cooperstock?"

"Weapon? Weapon?" Cooperstock stopped and began to gasp, lying back on his pillow, but he thrust me away when I came to him. "I didn't give him any weapon," he said thoughtfully, after staring at the Governor's face for a moment, forcing his lungs to work more easily. "At least, I don't think I did. It was only a commercial matter. You see, Governor, I have never believed in over-classification. Knowledge should be free. The basic theory—"

"Donner doesn't intend to make it free, Dr. Cooperstock, he plans to keep it for himself. Please tell me what you know."

"Well, it's fusion power," Cooperstock said.

"The hydrogen bomb?"

"Oh, for God's sake, Governor! It is fusion of hydrogen, yes, but not in any sense a bomb. The self-supporting reaction takes place in a magnetic bottle. It will not explode, even if the bottle fails; you would have to coax it to make it blow up. Only heat comes out, with which Donner is going to drive steam generators, perfectly normal. I assure you there is no danger of an accident."

"I was not thinking of an accident," said the Governor after a moment.

"Well—in that event—I mean, it is true," said Cooperstock with some difficulty, "that, yes, as the reactor is set up, it would be possible to remove the safeguards. This is only the pilot model. The thing *could* be done."

"By remote control, as I understand," said Hewlett wearily. "And in that event each of Donner's power stations would become a hydrogen bomb. Did you know that he has twenty-four of them under construction, all over the nation?"

Cooperstock said indignantly, "He could not possibly have twenty-four installations completed in this time. I

can hardly believe he has even one! In the New York
plant on the river we designed only the fusion chamber
itself. The hardware involved in generating power will
take months."

"But I don't think he bothered with the hardware for
generating power, you see," said the Governor.

Dr. Cooperstock began to gasp again. The Governor
sat watching him for a moment, his face sagging with a
painful fatigue, and then roused himself and said at last,
"Well, you shouldn't have done this, Dr. Cooperstock, but
God bless you, you're a great man. We all owe you a
debt. Only we'll have to do something about this now."

In my office the Governor took me aside. "I am sorry
to have disturbed your patient. But it was important, as
you see."

"Donner is a terrible man."

"Yes, I think that describes him. Well. It's all up to us
now," said the Governor, looking very gray. "I confess
I don't know what we can do."

"Surely the government can handle—"

"Doctor," he said, "I apologize for troubling you with
my reflections, I've not much chance to talk them out
with anyone, but I assure you I have thought of everything
the government can do. Donner has eight oil senators in
his pocket, you know. They would be delighted to filibus-
ter any legislation. For more direct action, I'm afraid we
can't get what we need without a greater risk than I can
lightly contemplate. Donner has threatened to blow up
every city of over eight hundred thousand, you see. I now
find that this threat is not empty. Thank you, Doctor," he
said, getting up. "I hope I haven't distressed your patient
as much as he has distressed me."

He limped to the door, shook hands and was gone.

Half an hour later it was time for my rounds. I had
spent the time sitting, doing nothing, almost not even
thinking.

But I managed to go around, and then Dr. Cooperstock's nurse signaled me. He had asked her to phone Nan Halloran for him, and should she do it? There was a message: "I have something else for Wayne."

I found that puzzling but, as you will understand, I was in an emotionally numb state; it was difficult to guess at what it meant. I told the nurse she could transmit the message. But when Nan Halloran arrived, an hour or two later, I waited in the hall outside Dr. Cooperstock's room until she came out.

"Why, Doctor," she said, looking very lovely.

I took her by the arm. It was the first time I had touched that flesh, we had not even shaken hands before; I took her to my office. She seemed eager to go along with me. She asked no questions.

In the office, the door closed, I was extremely conscious of being alone in the room with her. She knew that, of course. She took a cigarette out of her purse, sat down and crossed her legs. Gallant, I stumbled to my desk and found a match to light her cigarette.

"You've been worrying Coopie," she said reproachfully. "You and that Hewlett. Can't he stay out of a simple business matter?"

She surprised me; it was such a foolish thing to say and she was not foolish. I told her very briefly what Hewlett had said. No one had told me to be silent. She touched my hand, laughing. "Would it make so very much difference . . . Martin? (May I?) Donner's not a monster."

"I don't know that."

She said impishly, "I do. He's a man like other men, Martin. And really he's not so young, even with all the treatments. What would you give him, with all his treatments? Twenty more years, tops?"

"A dictatorship even for twenty minutes is an evil thing, Miss Halloran," I said, wondering if I had always sounded so completely pompous.

"Oh, but bad words don't make bad things. Sakes! Think what they could call *me*, dear! Donner's only throwing his weight around, and doesn't everyone? As much weight as he has?"

"Treason—" I began, but she hardly let me get even the one word out.

"No bad words, Martin. You'd be astonished if you knew what wonderful things Wayne wants to do. It takes a man like him to take care of some problems. He'll get rid of slums, juvenile delinquents, gangsters . . ."

"Some problems are better not solved. Hitler solved the Jewish question in Europe."

She said sweetly, "I respect you, Martin. So does Wayne. You have no idea how much he and Dr. Cooperstock think of you, and so do I, so please don't do anything impulsive."

She walked out the room and left it very empty.

I felt turgid, drained and a little bit stupid. I had never wanted anything as much as I had wanted her.

It was several minutes before I began to wonder why she had taken the trouble to entice me in a pointless conversation. I knew that Nan Halloran was her own bank account, spent as thriftily as Donner's billions. I wondered what it was that I had had that she was willing to purchase with the small change of a few words and a glimpse of her knees and the scent of her perfume.

Before I had quite come to puzzle the question through, while I was still regretting I had had no higher-priced commodity for her, my phone rang. It was Dr. Cooperstock's nurse, hysterical.

Nan Halloran's conversation had not been pointless. While we were talking two ambulance attendants had come to assist Dr. Cooperstock into a wheelchair, and he was gone.

To Whom

all things concern

On the fourth day of May Dr. Cooperstock defected and in the morning of the fifth Governor Hewlett telephoned me. "He's not back?" he said, and I said he wasn't, and Hewlett, pausing only a second, said, "Well. We can't wait any longer. The Army is moving in."

I went from my office to the operating room and I was shaking as I scrubbed in.

It was a splenectomy, but the woman was grossly fat, with a mild myocarditis that required external circulation. It took all of my attention, for which I was grateful. We were five hours in the room, but it was successful and it was not until I was smoking a cigarette in the little O.R. lounge that I began to shake.

Twenty-four nuclear bombs in twenty-four cities. And of course one of them, the one that we knew was ready to go off, was in the city I was in. I remembered the power plant, off in the Hudson River under the bridge, yellow brick and green glass. It was not more than a mile away.

And yet I was alive. The city was not destroyed. There had been no awful blast of heat and concussion.

I walked into the recovery room to look at the splenectomy. She was all right, but the nurse stared at me, so I went back to my office, realizing that I was crying.

And Nan Halloran was there waiting for me, looking like a drunken doll.

She pulled herself together as I came in. Her lipstick was smeared, and she shook. "You win, Martin," she said, with a little laugh. "Who would have thought old Coopie was such a lion? He gave me something for you."

I poured her a drink. "What happened?"

"Oh," said she. She drank the whiskey, politely enough, but showing she needed it. "Coopie came to Wayne and made a deal. Politics, he said, is out of my line, but you owe me something. I've helped you, I'll help you more, only you must promise that research will be free and well endowed. He had it very carefully worked out, the man is a genius." She giggled and held out her glass. "Funny. Of course he's a genius. So Wayne took the hook and said it was a deal, what was Coopie going to do for him next? And Coopie offered to show him how to convert the power plant to a different kind of bomb. Neutrons, he said." So Dr. Cooperstock had taken the billionaire down into the guarded room and, explaining how it was possible to change the type of nuclear reaction from a simple hot explosion to a cold, killing flood of rays that would leave the city unharmed, if dead, he had diverted the hydrogen fuel supply, starved the reaction and shut off the magnetic field that contained it.

And then he had told Donner all deals were off.

There was nothing hard about rebuilding the field and restarting the reaction, of course. It took only a few days; but Donner no longer had days. "I told Wayne," said Nan Halloran gravely, draining her glass, "I told him he should wait until he had all the bombs ready, but he's—he was— he's still, but I think not for long, hard-headed. I have to go now, my plump friend, and I do thank you for the drink. I believe they're going to arrest me." She got up and picked up her white gloves, and at the door she paused and said "Did I tell you? I've got so many things on my mind Coopie's dead. He wouldn't let Wayne's doctors touch him."

They did arrest her, of course. But by and by, everything calming down, they let her go again. She's even starring in the movies again, you can see her whenever you like I've never gone.

The letter in the envelope was from Dr. Cooperstock and it said:

I've pulled their fuses, Martin, for you and the Governor, and if it kills me, as you should know it must, please don't think that I mind dying. Or that I am afraid to live, either. This is not suicide. Though I confess that I cannot choose between the fear of living in this world and the fear of what may lie beyond it.

The leg is very bad. You would not even let me wear elastic socks, and for the past hour I have been crawling around the inside of Donner's stainless-steel plumbing. It was really a job for a younger man, but I couldn't find one in time.

So I suppose these are my last words, and I wish I could make them meaningful. I expect there is a meaning to this. Science, as one of my predecessors once said—Teller, was it?—has become simpler and more beautiful. And surely it has become more wonderful and strange. If gravity itself grows old and thin, so that the staggering galaxies themselves weaken as they clutch each other, it seems somehow a much lesser thing that we too should grow feeble. Yet I do hate it. I am able to bear it at all, indeed, only through a Hope which I never dared confess even to you, Martin, before this.

When I was young I went to church and dreaded dying for the fear of hellfire. When I was older I dreaded nothing; and when I was older still I began to dread again. The hours, my friends, in which I held imaginary conversations with the God I denied—proving to Him, Martin, that He did not exist—were endless. God, harsher, more awful and more remote. I could not pray to Him, Creator of the Big Bang, He Who Came Before the Monobloc. But I could fear Him.

Now I am not afraid of Him. A galaxy twenty billion years old has given me courage. If there was no monobloc there can have been no God Who made it. I live in the hope of the glorious steady state!

It was weak and wicked of me to give Donner a gun to point at the world, therefore, and I expect it is fair if I die taking it back; but it is not to save the world that I do it but to save my own soul in the galaxies yet to be born. For if the steady state is true there is no end to time. And infinity is not bounded, in any way. Everything must happen in infinity. Everything must happen . . . an infinity of times.

So Martin, in those times to come, when these atoms that compose us come together again, under what cis-Andromedan star I cannot imagine, we will meet—if there is infinity it is sure—and I can hope. In that day may we be put together more cleanly, Martin. And may we meet again, all of us, in shapes of pleasing strength and health, members of a race that is, I pray, a little wiser and more kind.

That was the letter from Dr. Rhine Cooperstock. I folded it away. I called my secretary on the intercom to tell her that his suite would now be free for another patient; and I went out into the spring day, to the great black headlines with Donner's name over all the papers and to the life that Cooperstock had given back to us all.